COUSIN PAUL.

BY

JESSIE GLENN.

"Be not conformed to this world: but be ye transformed by the renewing of your mind, that ye may prove what is that good, and acceptable and perfect will of God."

NEW YORK:
G. W. CARLETON & CO., PUBLISHERS.
LONDON: S. LOW, SON & CO.
MDCCCLXVIII.

TO

Mrs. CHARLES NEFF,

THE DEAR FRIEND

WHOSE UNFAILING SYMPATHY AND ENCOURAGEMENT

HAS CHEERED MANY A DESPONDING HOUR, AND INSPIRED ME WITH CONFIDENCE
TO INTRODUCE

"COUSIN PAUL"

TO THE PUBLIC, THIS BOOK IS LOVINGLY DEDICATED, BY

THE AUTHOR.

PREFACE.

THE object of this story is to show forth many of the evils of the present day in fashionable society, chiefly among the highest classes; and prominent among all, are the flirtations indulged in, by both married and single. The writer hopes that the errors so faithfully portrayed in the early life of Paul and Rebecca, may prove a warning to those readers who now see no harm in what the world calls "a harmless flirtation."

If the sincere repentance of both these characters may be imitated by even one person who is alike guilty, that *one* may rest assured that a prayer of thankfulness will arise from the heart of her, whose only object in thus depicting the follies of the present age, has been to do good.

THE AUTHORESS.

CONTENTS.

COUSIN PAUL

CHAPTER I.

THE SNOW-STORM

"Out of the bosom of the Air,
Out of the cloud-folds of her garment shaken,
Over the woodlands brown and bare,
Over the harvest-fields forsaken,
Silent, and oft, and slow,
Descends the snow."

THE storm increased rapidly, now.

All the morning, dark, grey, murky clouds had loomed up from the west.

At noon the snow-flakes began to fall.

One by one, one by one, softly, lightly, with weird-like stillness, came the beautiful white snow.

Golden-haired Bessie Brown was watching its noiseless descent, as she stood behind the crimson folds of the curtains, in her father's handsome library.

She had viewed, with dreamy wonderment, the piles of dark shadows clouding the heavens; she had marked the first feathery flake as it hung suspended in the air on its journey earthward; had seen another and another follow, until now, the whole atmosphere was full of them, and the earth was fast folding, in a mantle of spotless whiteness.

The wind was rising, too.

She heard its rushing, whistling voice, as it swept around the sides of the large old mansion, and she knew that it was having a grand frolic, in those winding garden walks, in front of the residence. She smiled as she saw the snow whirl hither and thither, seeking to alight, yet before it touched a resting-place, the arch rogue would seize it in his embrace, and send it with a whistling laugh high up over the trees, where it circled around a while, then alighted softly among the branches of the evergreens that stood each side the porch, or dropped slily upon the once green hedge, that surrounded the garden.

It was a purely beautiful sight.

Faster and faster fell the snow, whiter and whiter grew the ground, until it became one vast, smooth sheet of spotless purity and beauty. The branches of every tree were quite loaded with fantastic, yet snowy garments; each tiny shrub was bending beneath an unexpected burden. The hill in the distance had also its white robe, and the brook that wound at its foot, was almost hidden by the smooth, white covering.

Bessie Brown stood motionless at the window, her fair face pressed close against the panes, her blue eyes feasting on the scene without. She was weaving strange romances of beauty and gracefulness, drawn from the dancing, fairy-like movements of those tiny flakes, and the cunning of their merry friend, Master Wintry Wind, as he frisked so gaily among them.

How rapidly the snow kept falling! Myriads and myriads of little crystal shapes were flying all around, and Bessie's eyes sparkled, as she saw their whirling movements. Long she mused over the scene, almost forgetful of the expected arrival of Minnie Morton, an old schoolmate and dear friend residing in New York, who was to visit her on the morrow, if this snow did not prevent. It was her anxiety about the gathering storm that had brought her to the window, but it was the wild beauty of the scene that had chained her there so long.

It was indeed a charming picture! that cheerful room within, with its bright fire, its handsome appointments, its warmth and coziness; that young girl, with her lithe figure leaning against the casement, her blue eyes filled with reverie as she gazed on the scene without. Then there was that outward winter landscape! The beautiful snow, so white, so pure, shrouding the garden and the hillside, the tall tree, the graceful shrub, and the music of the wind as it rushed onward, playing with its feathery friends such strange, fantastic tricks, all combined to make the charm complete.

So Bessie dreamed on! So the snow-flakes gathered on! then darkness came, and drove her from the window, to a seat beside her father, a handsome man of forty-five, who had just entered.

"Well, pet, what have you been doing this afternoon?" asked he, as he laid his hand caressingly upon her golden hair.

"Building airy castles, and watching the snow-flakes," returned she, demurely.

"A truly romantic occupation, well suited to a girl of seventeen! The castles were connected with Minnie's arrival, I presume."

"Partly, papa! Do you think the storm will detain her?"

"I hope not, for your sake, my daughter; you seem to anticipate so much pleasure in seeing her. Darling, it seems strange that one so gay and worldly, so very different from my domestic and Christian girl, should be her fondly loved friend!"

"I know, dear father, that Minnie is full of life and gaiety now, but she is good-hearted and affectionate, and you know I loved her long before I found my Heavenly Friend. May it not be, that I may induce her to think of better things than parties, or pleasure-seeking, to place her affections on things above, instead of the frivolities of earthly fashions? Oh! I long, dear father, to lead my friend to Jesus."

"That were a blessing indeed; for you know, my child, "That he which converteth the sinner from the error of his way, shall save a soul from death, and shall hide a multitude of sins." At least, Bessie, you can pray for her you love, remembering,

> "That praying breath,
> Is never spent in vain,"

I also will bring her case to the throne of grace. But there comes Sister Charity, as I must always call your sewing-basket; and her arrival I consider a signal for my newspaper to come forth. But who now is suffering, and to be clothed by Bessie Brown's charitable industry?"

"Mary Gaffney's children are very destitute, I found on Saturday, on a visit to them. I have been quite busy all the week, sewing for their benefit. See, I have nearly finished the last garment! Won't the little creatures be delighted!"

"They may well be, those dresses are so warm and comfortable. I suppose you realize now the Bible truth your mother often whispered to you, 'It is more blessed to give, than to receive?'"

"Indeed I do, papa; I enjoy the children's glee so much! Their dancing eyes and merry laughter when the new clothes are displayed, amply repay all the trouble of selecting, fitting, and making."

So Bessie Brown plied the needle busily, until the clock struck ten, when she carefully folded the completed work, and carrying "Sister Charity" away, she placed the family Bible on the centre-table beside her parent, then summoned Mrs. Sanger, the housekeeper, and the Protestant cook, to their evening devotions. A portion of God's holy word was then solemnly read, and an earnest prayer was offered, full of faith and devotion, in which the expected friend was fervently remembered.

Softly pressing a good-night kiss upon the fresh young lips of his only child, Mr. Brown sought his apartment, while Bessie gave another glance from the window to the snow-clad earth without, then closing the blinds for the night, and seeing that all other portions of the house were properly fastened, she ascended the stairs, singing a verse of the beautiful hymn—

"Sweet hour of prayer! sweet hour of prayer!
Thy wings shall my petitions bear,
To him whose truth and faithfulness
Engage the waiting soul to bless;
And since he bids me seek his face,
Believe his word, and trust his grace,
I'll cast on him my every care,
And wait for thee, sweet hour of prayer."

A short time passed, and then her blue eyes were closed in sleep, and all was quiet in the loving home-nest at Cedar Lawn.

Mr. Brown, the owner of this country residence to which we have introduced our readers, had amassed a comfortable fortune in the flour and grain business, at Rochester, and in retiring, had purchased a lovely, quiet spot, near a flourishing village in New York State, on the Erie Railroad, and with his wife and only child, the gentle Bessie, then about fifteen, he thought to spend the rest of his days amid rural pleasures, and in the enjoyment of the purest home affections. One year of sweet repose followed, and then suddenly his fondly loved companion was summoned to the rest that awaits the people of God. It was a sorrowful stroke to the lonely husband and only daughter, but they knew that God chasteneth whom he loveth, and with tearful eyes, yet holy resignation, they said Thy will, not mine, be done.

Bessie was very young to be deprived of a pious mother's counsels, just at entering womanhood; yet she had given her heart to Jesus some months before her mother's death, and now she became her father's solace and companion. A competent housekeeper took charge of the more arduous duties of the establishment, but Bessie's fair fingers gave the tasteful air to each apartment, her refined taste imparted a charm to the already handsome residence.

Bessie was not beautiful, but there was something peculiarly attractive in the winning smile that played around her sweet young mouth, and an intelligent look in those bright blue eyes, that could not but please. So the young girl was a general favorite, loved alike by rich and poor; by the rich, admired for her amiability and artlessness; by the poor, loved for the many bounties she bestowed, for her benevolence, and indefatigableness in answering and discovering their many necessities.

So sweet Bessie Brown slept peacefully, and serenely, under her father's roof this stormy night, for loving hearts were around her, and many lips breathed blessings upon her young and devoted pathway.

CHAPTER II.

SLEIGHING.

"The snow, the snow, the fleecy snow,
And the bells so full of glee!
Bring out the bay, and the dapple grey,
And a sleighing go with me.
Then jingle, jingle, jing, let the sleigh-bells ring,
As swiftly we glide along,
Our hearts keep time to the merry chime
While our voices swell the song."

THE morning sun ushered in a scene of rare beauty.

The storm of the previous evening had ended in a gentle rain, which, in freezing, had given an icy crust to the surface of snow, and had frozen upon the housetops, and trees, in sparkling icicles, long and slender, yet unrivalled in brilliancy, as the sun shone on them, making every branch and bough a treasury of crystal gems. Bessie uttered an exclamation of delight, as she drew up the shades of her chamber window, at an early hour, and gathered in, at a glance, the exquisiteness of the scene. Like so many diamonds did the varied colors reflected in those icy jewels shine, while the whole earth seemed to be braided with gems.

"How beautiful! how glorious!" murmured she. "Can it be possible that any person could look upon a scene like this, and not see the tracings of the finger of Omnipotence? Could any one bo so dead to the beauties of creation, as not to adore the matchless power of the Creator? not feel thankful to that love that has sprinkled such choice beauties around the pathway of his erring children?"

Sweet child! she little knew the blinding grasp with which Satan often clutches the hearts of his victims! How should she realize the growing rapidity with which unbelief was creeping over our country? She, whose heart was all alive to the goodness and majesty of the Almighty?

Eight o'clock came and the ice-gems still flashed upon the tree boughs, and glittered in brilliant forms, from the shrubs and fences.

Then Lightfoot and Fly drew the large family sleigh, with its handsome soft robes, to the east door, and Bessie was soon half hidden in their ample folds, and after being warmly tucked in by the side of her father, went gliding down the carriage path, to the open road without.

How the snow crisped under the flying feet of the swift steeds, as they dashed away, the sleigh-bells jingling merrily, and the gay laugh of its young occupant floating out upon the morning air.

They were going to the depot for Minnie Morton.

The cars were in, and had just moved on again, snuffing, and snorting, as they dashed away, speeding round a curve, and disappearing, in a breath, from sight and hearing.

Standing on the platform was a tall, yet graceful young girl, her dark eyes sparkling with pleasure, as they met the blue ones that peeped from the rich coverings to greet her.

Mr. Brown drove close to the platform, and bounding out, shook hands warmly with his young friend, then lifting Bessie to his side, the two girls joyfully embraced.

"Bessie, I am so glad to see you! It is so long since I have looked upon your dear face!" exclaimed the new comer.

"Oh, Minnie, I have thought so much of your visit! It is indeed delightful to meet again."

So they chatted on, until the horses had been turned faces homeward; then they were soon smilingly stowed beneath the wrappings, the whip gave a warning crack, the sleigh-bells jingled, and away went the glad party, over the smooth crisping snow.

"Oh! oh! how beautiful! how like an enchanted dream of fairy-land!" exclaimed Minnie, her eyes dancing with delight, as, leaving the depot, they sped into an open road through a thick grove of evergreens, frosted on every branch and twig with icy coatings, and long, pendent, glittering jewels.

"Yes! it is the very Spirit of the Beautiful, passing over earth. It should lead our thoughts to a scene of heavenly splendor above, to which *this* is a mere shadow!" returned Mr. Brown.

"I had no idea that the country was so beautiful in winter," again spoke Minnie, her eyes never leaving the frost ornaments, around.

"You see very different diamonds from these in New York, Minnie," whispered Bessie; "these are God's brilliants! see how they sparkle in the sunlight."

"Charming!" exclaimed Minnie; "I hope this snow will last the whole week that I stay. Sleigh-riding is so invigorating, and I am quite worn out with parties, and such dissipations."

"It will last quite a while I think. At all events we will improve it, while it is here; so prepare for another ride this afternoon, but do not look for frost jewels; they are beginning to melt already."

They were home almost too soon, but jumping lightly from the sleigh, Minnie was shown directly to Bessie's lovely room, which she fondly hoped her friend would share with her.

"There is another like it, across the hall, Minnie, you can have, if you prefer being alone; but I would so much rather have you here," said Bessie.

"Then here it shall be, dear; do you think I could bear to be from you one unnecessary moment during my stay? Besides, I am quite in love with this room; it is sunshine itself, just like my petite companion. How tasty it all looks," continued she; "what a beautiful carpet, with this delicate ground-work, and rose-bud pattern; then those graceful lambrequins over the white shades, just the tint of the rose-buds, and the dotted muslin gathered so prettily behind the washstand to protect the paper, with its bows of ribbon, color to correspond, I think peculiarly adapted to this lovely bed-room furniture. But really every picture, of the many on the walls, are Scripture engravings! I see, from that, that you are the same sweet little saint you used to be."

These words were uttered while she removed her many wrappings, revealing more perfectly to view the queenly figure of the beautiful speaker. She was a lovely girl, of the same age as Bessie. Her dark hair was gathered back into a waterfall, from which a few soft curls drooped on one side; her dark gipsy eyes were full of fire and witchery, while the handsome brunette complexion added a wonderful charm to the regular features.

Minnie Morton was a beauty and a belle in New York.

She had come to Cedar Lawn, drawn by a true affection for her school friend, as well as for a week of rest from city gaieties—the last reason strongly urged by her mother, who regretted to see her bright eyes dimmed, or her fair spirits jaded, by too much dissipation. While she loved the society of Bessie, she rather dreaded the Methodistical notions of the family, as she lightly termed the true piety of Mr. Brown and his daughter.

"I shall laugh at all religious thrusts, the moment they are commenced," resolved she; "I do wish sweet Bessie was not so ridiculously puritanical! She must return home with me and see something of gay life, and she will be sure to forget those set ways."

The interval between dinner-time and the next ride, the two girls passed together, talking of school-days, and planning rides and amusements, to be accomplished during Minnie's short stay. They had such a store of things to communicate to each other, such an overflow of remembrances, and such a bright future to paint, that their tongues never tired, but flew from one subject to another, with wonderful rapidity.

Then came dinner, and afterward another charming ride.

This time they went to the lake, to see the villagers on the ice.

How swiftly the skaters glided over the smooth, transparent surface! Old and young seemed alike fascinated with the gleeful recreation. Mr. Brown halted a few moments on the shore road, to allow his companions a good view of the merry picture.

"Now, papa, please drive to the edge of yonder wood, where you see that little brown house! Mary Gaffney lives there, and as I have some clothes with me for her children, I will leave them, if you have no objections."

"Very well, pet; they will be welcome, I am sure, this cold day," replied her father.

Mr. Brown drew up before the spot, as he spoke, and the active girl sprang out, and taking a good sized parcel from the sleigh, she disappeared within the small doorway of the poverty-stricken abode.

She tarried quite a while, Minnie thought, as she sat

with Mr. Brown out in the cold, waiting for her, and wondered what it could be that detained her. At last she appeared with a happy smile playing around her lips.

"Why, little Dork, how pleased you look! What occurred in that wretched place?" asked her friend.

"Oh, if you could have seen those children's delight, Minnie, poor, ragged, and half naked as they were, you could easily understand what pleased me! It was delightful to see them warm and comfortable, and to hear their thanks. But what in the world did you call me?"

"Only the very appropriate name of Little Dork! Have you any more charitable calls to make?"

"Yes, one! I made old Goody Smith some warm flannel undergarments, yesterday, to keep off the rheumatism. Papa, will you drive me there?"

"Certainly, my daughter. I am glad you remember old Goody."

"Little Dork seems to be the grand overseer of the poor!" exclaimed Minnie. "How much salary does she receive for her services?"

"Oh, Minnie dear, do not ridicule me for doing what my conscience tells me is only my duty. Our Saviour left the poor with us, you know, charging us to watch over and help them, for he saith, 'As ye do it unto the least of these, ye do it unto me.' But Minnie, I do not like that name."

"Not like the good old Bible name of Dorcas, which I for brevity call Dork! Why, Bessie Brown. I thought you were a walking Old and New Testament, and yet you object to being called a namesake of good old Dorcas!" exclaimed the thoughtless girl, rolling her dark eyes as she spoke with affected sorrow. For shame, Little Dork, for shame!"

There was the least little bit of a pout on Bessie's sweet

lips, as she looked reproachfully at the teasing girl, but it passed away quickly, as she thought how little Minnie realized the importance of the subject of which she now spoke so lightly.

So this is the way it came about, that Minnie Morton always called her friend, Little Dork.

CHAPTER III.

COUSIN PAUL.

"Where'er thou art,
Blessings be shed upon thine inmost heart,
Joy from kind looks, blue skies, and flowery sod,
For that pure voice of thoughtful wisdom sent
Forth from thy cell, in sweetness eloquent,
Of love to men, and quenchless love to God!"

HEMANS.

HE parlor at Cedar Lawn looked very warm and cheerful, with its bright fire in the grate, and elegant comfortableness, that cold winter evening.

Minnie stood by the piano, turning over the sheets of music, that were piled thickly by its side, while Bessie sat in a small rocking-chair, busily gazing at the brilliant fire-light.

"Come, Little Dork, play for me," exclaimed Minnie, "I must hear this march; it looks as if it might be splendid."

"It is splendid, Minnie, but I had rather not murder it. Let me play a waltz, instead!"

"Play the waltz by all means, but then please let me hear the march."

"If you insist, Minnie, I will; but could you hear it once given by Cousin Paul, you would never wish another to attempt those strains," answered Bessie.

"Why, dear, that is truly magnificent. Whose composition is it?" asked Minnie, as the last notes of the plaintively exquisite piece died away.

"It was Cousin Paul's own composition, and never given to the public," returned Bessie, musingly.

"Cousin Paul again! He must be a true genius, Little Dork, to breathe such soul-stirring melody! Tell me of him," returned her companion.

"Paul Russell, Minnie, is a dear friend of papa's, and is one of God's noblest creatures; as I have great reason to be much attached to him, I always call him Cousin Paul, although he is not a relative. He is one of the most lovely characters I ever met; noble in sentiment, brilliant in intellect, and last, though not least, of late years a devoted Christian. Dear Mr. Russell! he is far from his native land now, although I can scarcely tell in what part of England. He has visited our house annually ever since I can remember, when in this country. He has travelled much, and I can assure you, he is a most polished gentleman, and a rare conversationalist. How often I remember with delight, his visits during my early childhood, for some of its happiest moments were passed upon his knee, listening to the charming stories he used to weave for my benefit, for he was very fond of children, and possessed the rare art of instructing, as well as pleasing, his little friends. One story in particular, which he called "A Sigh from a Bed of Moss," left a great impression on my mind, and in fact, I can never forget it."

The girls had left the piano by this time, and having drawn a small tête-à-tête sofa before the sparkling fire, now sat side by side, with hand clasped fondly in hand.

"Tell me that story, darling, please, before you proceed, for I have never recovered from a penchant for nursery-tales yet, even with seventeen years on my brow."

"Cousin Paul's stories were different from those usually told to children, and were purely original. I will tell it in nearly his own words, for I distinctly remember them;

but I cannot convey his tender charm of manner, nor can I imitate his beautiful and melodious voice, for in speaking he was remarkable for his sweetly modulated tones."

PAUL'S STORY.

There was a noble, high mountain, that was covered with weeping willows and trembling aspens, while bright yellow buttercups and white and red clover were nodding in the tall grass. From the side of the mountain gushed a merry little rivulet, that went singing along, singing along, over the white pebbles to a broad river some miles below, while on the banks of this stream lay a beautiful bed of dark green Moss, nestling away in the shade from the sunbeams, and a little way beyond it might be seen a graceful Eglantine, whose red petals were full of beauty, while every breath she drew was so laden with delicious perfume that the air around seemed bathed in roses, and as the wing of the Summer Wind came softly down the mountain to fan the flowers and leaves, and to play with the airy ripples of the Rivulet, it used to stop kindly on its way to scatter some of this delightfully rose-scented air over to the bed of Moss, because it knew that the flower of the Moss was not beautiful, and had no such delicate fragrance. The Moss did not appreciate this kindness of Summer Wind, for when she perceived how delicious and beautiful was her sister, a feeling of jealousy and discontent stole into her bosom, and so, day after day, she would sigh and look very sad and unhappy.

"Sister," said Eglantine, one day, when, as Summer Wind was returning to her side, after bearing an unusual quantity of rose-perfume to her ungrateful neighbor, she unconsciously brought back, under her wing, a sad sigh, fresh from the bosom of the Moss; "Sister, your sigh hath floated into my heart. Why was it breathed, and why was it so very sad?"

There was no answer for some time, and then the low, mournful voice of the Moss replied, complainingly:

"Do you not think that you would sigh also, sweet Eglantine, were you compelled to change places with me, and, laying aside your rose-colored robes, that win so much admiration, and your perfumed breath, that makes the air so delicious, and that supplies the little humming birds and the busy bees that are passing, with nectar—do you not think you would be sad were you obliged to become an ugly piece of Moss, that no one admires, and that does not the least good in the world?" The voice died away, and then another sigh, more mournful than the first, floated into the heart of Eglantine, which pained her so severely, that her petals began to droop with sorrow, and large tears came swelling from her bosom.

Now Summer Wind loved sweet Eglantine, and he could not see her weep, so he folded his wings and fluttered down broken-heartedly into the arms of the Rivulet; and when the Ripples saw him in such despair, they all gathered around to ask the cause of his grief; and when he had told them how the discontented sigh of the Moss had entered the heart of poor Eglantine, and made her weep, low, sorrowful murmurings went around from one Ripple to another, and then all began to moan and sob piteously.

Now it happened that a bright golden Sunbeam, which had left the blue sky to dance around this lovely spot a little while before, had heard the sigh of the Moss, and the question of Eglantine, and so had softly stepped upon one of the leaves of a tall old tree near by, to see what was going on, and thus had become an unobserved listener to the conversation and its effects; and as the commotion grew greater and greater she advanced to the edge of the leaf, and shaking her golden dress until a thousand rays fell upon the mountain, the stream, and even the flowers, she spoke, and every sound ceased at her word.

"I have heard the complainings of our young friend, and the sigh that has so nearly broken the heart of our beautiful Eglantine; and I also have marked the sorrow of her lover, the kind Summer Wind, and his friends, and I now come forward to tell you I have comfort for all; but first let me bind up the wound of our suffering companion;" and dancing down from the leaf to the side of the drooping flower, she threw a beautiful beam into its cup, and in a moment the lovely lady of the rose kingdom ceased weeping, and became as beautiful and fragrant as ever. Then the Sunbeam glided back to her place on the leaf, and turning her eyes to the bed of Moss, she spoke in a low, sweet voice, these words of advice and encouragement.

"Sister Moss, you said a few moments since, that you were never admired, and had no way in which to be useful; and as you are laboring under a sad mistake, I think it becomes my duty to show you your error, and to tell you that a time is coming when it will be your turn to be admired, as well as to inform you how you can be of great service to things around you. Soon the lovely Eglantine, now so beautiful, will be no more, for the children of her race, as she knows full well, are short-lived, and after a little time they all wither and die; then, one by one, each of these graceful green leaves will change and fall, and only the beautiful Moss will be found to tell of the scenes of to-day; then, when there is but little to delight the eye, every one will gaze with rapture at your bright green dress, peering out of the white snow. Then will you be admired in your turn, if you will only be patient until that turn comes. But you can be useful too, Sister Moss, if you will; you can keep the little seeds of other plants warm during the cold winter, protecting them until the snow melts away, and the bright spring-time returns. But that is not all. You can nourish the little insects that sometimes lie on your bosom. You can be a soft pillow for the head of a weary traveller if one chances to pass by; and you can help to line the nests of the wild-wood songsters, and thus keep their little ones warm. So you see, you can be of great service, and be loved and admired, too, Sister Moss."

The Sunbeam ceased speaking then, and the Moss thanked her for her kind words, and after acknowledging her error, and begging to be forgiven, she looked bright and happy again, and showed her repentance was sincere, by going immediately to offer the protection of her soft arms to a poor little insect who was pursued by a fly; and that very day she gave a choice tuft from her robe to a beautiful Oriole, and the grateful bird thanked her in a burst of music, as she placed it in a tree-top near by.

Then the Sunbeam was filled with pleasure when she saw the Moss contented and happy, and marked how Summer Wind daily scattered the rose perfume over her green bed, as of old, for she knew it was her work; and so day after day she gathered together her bright rays, and stealing softly to the same leaf on the tree, she threw them far and near over the spot; but we always noticed that the brightest and softest, were sure to fall on the now beautiful bed of Moss.

"Charming! charming! It is one of the most exquisite morsels for a child I ever heard!" exclaimed Minnie, her dark eyes dancing with pleasure. "But I am so delighted with Cousin Paul, you must certainly tell me more of his history."

CHAPTER IV.

COUSIN PAUL, (CONTINUED.)

"This earth has lost its power to drag me downward,
Its spell is gone ;
My course is now right upward and right onward
To yonder throne."

"SO you ask for more information of my friend, Minnie; I feared I had wearied you in my praises of him," remarked Bessie, in reply to Minnie's earnest desire for her to proceed, as stated in our last chapter.

"Not at all, Little Dork! I am deeply interested. I need hardly ask, after listening to that thrilling March, if he is fond of music?"

"I had nearly replied that he is *all* music! One never tires when he touches the piano, organ, or guitar, for he is master of these as well as of the flute. Sometimes, when I have listened to his impromptu pieces, my full soul could only relieve itself by tears, they were so touchingly sad, and beautiful. Poor Cousin Paul!"

"Why call him poor?" asked Minnie, with deep attention.

"I scarcely can tell why, Minnie, but we always pitied him! There ever seemed a peculiar sadness about Mr. Russell, that whispered of some deep trouble—some heart secret that was full of sorrow; yet while this strange melancholy hung around him, he was the most fascinating of companions."

"Little Dork, pardon me for the question I am about to put, but is not Mr. Russell something dearer to you than a mere friend?" asked Minnie, quizzingly.

"Why, Minnie Morton, what a ridiculous thought!" replied Bessie, drawing up her little figure to its full height, and opening wide her blue eyes, in amazement. "Cousin Paul is old enough to be my father; why, child, he is full thirty-five! Besides, papa and my dear mamma always supposed there was some early love affair, that has blighted his whole life, and thus prevented his marrying."

"Have you any clue to that heart-history, dear?" asked Minnie, again becoming serious.

"We know but little. He was, I have been told, a very wild and gay young man; not dissipated, but thoughtless, and a sad flirt. Still, he was a general favorite. About seven years since, however, he came to visit papa, and seemed, during his entire stay, to be almost entirely beside himself with deep despair, wherefore we could never learn; then suddenly he bade us farewell and sailed for Europe, seemingly crushed and heart-broken. About a year after, he returned, telling my father he had come to know what was to be his future fate, and whether he remained, or went abroad again, would be decided by the nature of a letter he shortly expected. I was only eleven years old when that letter came, but I can never forget the scene that followed.

"Cousin Paul was sitting by the fire in the front parlor; (we lived in Rochester then;) he had been nervous and excited for several days, but particularly so this day. Mamma had sent a messenger to the Post-office, and receiving a neat letter, addressed in a female hand, to Paul Russell, she entered and handed it to him. A deadly pallor stole over his face as he glanced at the writing, then turning away from us, he opened and read it; a moment after, we saw him fall to the floor with the fatal letter clutched in his lifeless hand. Mamma, seeing that he had fainted, sprang to his side, and dispatching me in haste after my father, sat supporting him when we entered. With papa's assistance he soon recovered his consciousness, but he afterwards went into a long fever, and lay ill many weeks. Some of the time, when his fever was very high, he would cry in his delirium, 'Oh! my lost love! Oh! my lost love!' Mamma was his devoted nurse through all that period of suspense and trial, while papa labored to cheer and comfort the afflicted one. Oh! how they both prayed that he might cast all his care on Jesus, and obtain from Him 'that peace which the world cannot give.' He seemed very thoughtful. As soon as he was sufficiently recovered, he again left his native land, to remain, he said, perhaps forever. He wrote often, and about three years after he left us, came the joyful news that he had found his Saviour, and was now happy in the love of Christ. Then came most beautiful and touching letters to me, appeals that a heart of stone could not resist, to come to Jesus.

"'Dear little Bessie,' he wrote, 'will you not think of these things *now*, in your early youth, when all is bright and beautiful before you—before sin rusts and corrodes your soul? Do not wait, my child, until sorrow forces you to throw yourself before the Cross; do not wait to be goaded thither, by trials and bitter chastenings, but come while the roses of youth blossom, while special promises cheer you on.'

"'Come, while the morning of thy life is glowing—
Ere the dim phantom, thou art chasing die—
Ere the gay spell, which earth is round thee throwing,
Fades like the crimson from a sunset sky.
Life is but shadow, save a promise given,
That lights the future with a fadeless ray,

Come, touch the sceptre, win a hope in Heaven
Come, turn thy spirit from this world away.

'Then will the shadows of this brief existence,
Seem airy nothings to thine ardent soul;
And shining brightly in the forward distance
Will, of the patient race, appear the goal—
Home of the weary, where, in peace reposing,
The spirit lingers in unclouded bliss,
Though o'er the dust the curtained grave is closing,
Who would not early choose a lot like this?'

Will you not seek this joy, sweet Bessie? Will you not early come to the Saviour?'

"Such were the pleading letters I constantly received from my faithful friend, until I could not stifle the still small voice within, that kept urging the same dear cause. As day after day passed, and those earnest appeals kept presenting themselves, my soul became fully aroused to its need of pardon through a Saviour's atoning blood. I felt my deep sinfulness by nature, my inability to relieve the horrors of my situation by good works, and I wrote to Cousin Paul a true statement of my feelings and desires. I told him that I longed to be a Christian, yet knew not what I must do to be saved. Never shall I forget his devoted labor in pointing me to the Cross as the refuge for my sin-sick soul—to the dying 'Lamb of God, who taketh away the sins of the world,' as my only ark of safety.

"At last the hour came, when I could claim my precious Saviour as *my own* Redeemer, and friend. A light seemed to beam into my darkened spirit, a sweet peace pervaded my whole heart, and laying my burden of sin at the foot of the Cross, I cried, 'Lord, I believe; help thou mine unbelief.'

"So you see, Minnie, I have every reason to reverence

and love the one who first spoke to me of eternal things, dear Cousin Paul."

A deep sigh was the only reply Bessie received, as she concluded her story; and turning quickly to her companion, she was surprised to find that her cheeks were wet with tears; but before she could speak, Minnie roae hastily, and approaching the piano, ran her fingers abstractedly over the keys.

The heart of the gay Minnie Morton had been deeply touched at the truthful story of Paul Russell, and the conversion of one most fondly loved.

A prayer floated from Bessie's loving heart, and fluttered to the Mercy Seat, as she saw those tears, and the burden of the petition was,

"God save my friend."

CHAPTER V.

THE COUNTRY CHURCH.

I love thy courts, O God!
My pastor's voice falls sweetly on mine ear;
Those aisles so often trod
Remind my spirit that the Lord is near.

IT was the holy Sabbath day, and the church bells were ringing to call worshippers to the house of God.

The air was keen and cold, as Mr. Brown's sleigh glided along, and the cheeks of its young occupants were quite rosy with the frosted air.

The Church which they were approaching, was a neat, white edifice, standing quite back from the main street, and surrounded by a large enclosure, beautifully green in summer, but at this time covered with snow, with the exception of a well shovelled pathway to the building. As they drove up, Minnie noticed that the porch was filled with loungers viewing each fresh arrival and waiting for the services to commence before passing hastily, but I cannot say *noiselessly*, to their respective places. There was a platform at the end of this church-yard, where Mr. Brown stopped to allow the ladies to alight, and after handing them out, he drove to a long row of sheds where stalls were provided to shelter the horses, and driving in, he securely fastened the noble animals, then covering them with blankets, and throwing some food before them, he left them comfortable, while he proceeded to join his family.

Minnie's eyes had noticed all these movements. She also had marked the groups that pressed around the stoves, crowding there, whispering and laughing, with such a want of reverence for the time and place, that although thoughtless and gay, it quite shocked her ideas of propriety.

She had never before been in a country church!

Soon a white-haired clergyman entered, and ascended the pulpit stairs, when, as if this were a signal, a melodeon was touched by, it must be confessed, not very scientific fingers, and Minnie, who had a correct ear, and cultivated taste for music, sent a roguish glance towards Bessie, but was surprised to see the subdued and quiet look upon her peaceful features, and the holy light that lingered in her deep blue eyes.

Old Mr. Barnard's sermon was a good gospel discourse from the text—

"Believe on the Lord Jesus Christ, and ye shall be saved."

He gave a true explanation of these words. There was no attempt at display, no flowery style, nor fashionable delivery; it was merely a plain sermon, well calculated to feed the hearts of those before him.

To Bessie every word was very precious, and she felt, while those aged lips pleaded so earnestly the cause of her dear Redeemer, that the message must surely be blest, to the salvation of many souls, and the thought kept creeping into her heart—

"Will not Minnie listen now? Can she resist so important a truth?"

What was her surprise, then, when, upon once more

entering their chamber, she encountered her friend's unrestrained ridicule of the whole scene, from the people to the choir, from the choir to the pulpit!

"Now do tell me, Little Dork, what instrument is used in your grand cathedral?" she asked, mockingly.

"Why, Minnie, a melodeon, of course, and Harry Smith plays it very well, I think, for a person possessed of sos few advantages."

"You astonish me. I thought it was a hurdy-gurdy," replied the saucy girl, with mock solemnity. "Then the singing was really amazing! Allow me to imitate it, in order to remind you of those mellow cadences." Then Minnie sang in the most ridiculous manner a verse of the hymn that had formed part of the services that morning. The take-off was complete, and in spite of her utmost endeavors Bessie could not repress her smiles as she listened to the well imitated nasal twang, and dragging notes.

"Oh, you did not tell me how long it has been since your chorister commenced taking snuff?" again exclaimed Minnie, with a solemn face.

"Snuff? Why, Minnie, you are entirely mistaken; Mr. Carlton never took a pinch in his life!"

"You do surprise me again! I imagined all the morning that I smelt the fragrant Macaboy; and when his voice sounded so melodiously on my ear, I was certain that it owed its peculiar sweetness to some mysterious snuff-box; and say, Bessie, did you notice that old woman behind us, offer me some meetin seed?"

"Oh, Minnie, how ridiculous! But surely you liked old Mr. Barnard?" remarked Bessie, seeking to change the subject.

"Mr. Barnard, did you call for him? Little Dork, he

stands before you!" replied the gay girl, opening hastily a drawer near by, from which she took a large old-fashioned pair of spectacles, and placing them upon her nose, she stood peering through them with her bright black eyes, then bowing demurely, she opened a Bible and commenced reading, in well mimicked tones, the twenty-third Psalm.

Bessie was really grieved, for she loved her good old pastor, and with tears in her eyes, she begged her friend to cease.

"Now, Little Dork, do not be angry, and I will be just as good as it is possible for such a madcap to be. One thing, however, I am determined upon; which is, that you are going home with me. I must show you what true worship is, and our city pastor's eloquence I know would delight you. Aunt Rebecca, one of the most godly people you ever met, hangs with rapture on his words."

"Aunt Rebecca, who is that, darling? I never heard of her before," returned Bessie.

"If I have not spoken of her, it is not for lack of affection. She is my father's youngest sister; a most charming woman, only thirty-two years of age, and a widow. Little Dork, you must return with me, if only to become acquainted with this darling aunt of mine; you would love each other immediately, for you are both so good and pious."

"Does she live with you?"

"Yes; but she spends her time mostly in her own room. She is very wealthy, very benevolent, very religious, and remarkably beautiful; yet, strange to say, she lives in perfect seclusion, never mingling in the least society, and while gifted with rare accomplishments, she reserves them for the sole benefit of our household.

Truly, Bessie, you will wonder at the peacefulness and purity in her every word and look, while her very presence brings an air of religious consecration."

"I would love to meet her," said Bessie. "How long has she been a widow?"

"It is just seven years since Mr. Douglass died. She still wears the deepest mourning, and her eyes fill with tears, at but a casual mention of his name. You would be surprised to see her splendid beauty, her queenly form, and dignified appearance, for it always excites attention. I acknowledge that Aunt Rebecca, in her seclusion, is a perfect enigma to me. I go to her with all my troubles, for hers is ever a ready sympathy. I prize her advice in all my every-day affairs, for she is ever impartial and kind; but her calm eye always checks my levity, and her mild reproof never fails to stop all love for mischievous censoriousness in her presence. I think, had she been here a little while since, when I so unkindly ridiculed your good old pastor, she would have given one look from her splendid eyes that would have made me heartily ashamed; and to tell the truth, Little Dork, the tears I spied in your blue eyes, have done that already, so you will forgive and forget, won't you, darling?" added the affectionate girl.

"Yes, indeed, Minnie, I knew you were jesting; but cannot you drop that name you have given me?"

"Drop that appropriate, Scriptural appellation? You dear, charming, unreasonable Little Dork—no, never!'

CHAPTER VI.

LITTLE LIZA.

> Sad is my home, sweet one!
> Lonely and mournful seems each once loved room;
> Without my babe, they scarcely seem like home.
> Without my child, each wears a look of gloom!
> There is no corner near, no spot I see,
> But whispers sadly, silently, to me
> Of one caressed, now gone.

THE dining-room at Cedar Lawn was large and unusually cheerful.

It looked especially bright the next morning, when Minnie entered, and seated herself at the breakfast table; the morning sun crept in so cheerily, and the well piled coals upon the grate, threw out such a vivid and sparkling glow. Then the table fairly groaned with its good cheer! Such fragrant coffee, such luscious buckwheats, and such fresh, sweet ham, were truly inviting, while the omelette could not be surpassed. No blue Mondayism was visible in the loving group that surrounded that table, for every one beamed with wit and humor. Minnie looked brilliant and beautiful in a rich crimson morning robe, with a simple white linen collar, pinned at the throat, with a small brooch, composed of a single ruby, surrounded by pearls. Her dark eyes assumed a thoughtful expression, as she seemed studying the merits of the pure Java she was sipping, after a round of sallies and repartee had kept them in a merry mood for some time, then turning wistfully to Mr. Brown, she asked:

"Would you object to parting with Bessie for a couple of weeks, Mr. Brown?"

"That depends entirely upon the circumstances of the case, my dear. If I thought the sacrifice of her company would conduce to her pleasure and profit, I think I could allow her leave of absence."

"Oh, how delighted I am to hear you say so, dear Mr. Brown, for I can soon show you that a few weeks spent in New York, would give her great pleasure, and surely seeing a little of the world, must profit. Can I then obtain your permission to have her accompany me home?"

"What says my daughter?" asked Mr. Brown, glancing inquiringly at the eager countenance of his child."

"Oh! dear, kind papa, if I only might go!" exclaimed she, with earnest animation.

"Well, take her with you, Minnie; but you must not keep her too long, as the time will hang heavily, with no Bessie to greet me."

"Papa! I had forgotten your loneliness! It would be selfish to leave you," returned the daughter, half sadly.

"Not at all, my darling. Rather say it would be selfish for me to deprive you of so much pleasure. Besides, I can invite some friend to visit me, and thus a couple of weeks would soon roll away. Go, by all means, if you wish to, my daughter."

So it was decided that Bessie should return with her friend.

"Little Dork," exclaimed Minnie, about three hours later, as she stood beside the parlor window, "you are about receiving company. A very stylish lady and gentleman have driven to the door." As she spoke, the two left the light pleasure sleigh, while a colored servant took charge of the establishment, as they ascended the steps.

"It is Mrs. Landon and her brother, Charles Percy, exclaimed Bessie, catching a glimpse of the new comer before the door opened.

Minnie enjoyed the visit of Bessie's friends exceedingly for she found them pleasant and highly cultivated. Mrs Landon was the wife of a gentleman, who, being th possessor of a large fortune, had found a home, about tw years before, in the neighboring village. She was a intelligent, warm-hearted and interesting woman, and wa one of Bessie's firmest friends. Her brother resided in New York, being a partner in a wealthy and energetic firm. In person he was tall, and finely moulded, yet he could not be called handsome. However, his laughing blue eyes were full of power in their kindly glances, and his white teeth, fair complexion, and soft, wavy, brown hair, formed many good looks, if not absolute beauty.

Minnie being a stranger, and from the same city, caused a mutual fund of conversation, and while Mrs. Landon was occupied giving Bessie a long account of a fair, in which she had been very active and interested, the young man had quite won Minnie's admiration by his polite endeavors to entertain and amuse her.

Thus an hour passed pleasantly, when Mrs. Landon arose to leave, and in bidding them adieu, she urgently invited them to pass the following Wednesday with her. The invitation being cordially accepted and their company promised for an early hour, the visitors again entered their sleigh and departed.

"How did you like my friends, Minnie?" asked Bessie, as they re-entered.

"Mrs. Landon was charming; and as for the brother, I had no idea that Spotsdale could produce so elegant and polished a gentleman!"

"Nor has it! Mr. Percy merely visits our village occasionally, and never was a resident. Then you are pleased with him?"

"Yes, exceedingly! How long have you been acquainted?"

"About two years. We all hail his coming with real pleasure, as he is a general favorite. You will enjoy a day at Mrs. Landon's, I know, as she is agreeable in her own home, and makes her friends feel so at ease. Charles Percy will also do all in his power to interest and entertain."

"I do not doubt it, dear. I am half in love with him already!"

The next Wednesday found Bessie and her friend at Mrs. Landon's hospitable mansion, and that lady enacting the agreeable hostess to the full extent of the word. After having spent an hour with their needlework, amid merry jests and brilliant flashes of anecdote and gay badinage, Charles Percy declared "needlework a nuisance," and "sitting still, an intolerable bore;" so unmercifully seizing all implements of needle warfare, and placing them under lock and key, he proposed showing Minnie some fine paintings Mr. Landon had brought with him from Italy, while there some years before.

Following to a room across the hall, which was devoted expressly to paintings and statuary, our young friends were soon engaged in an examination of the beauties spread so lavishly around. Passing with delight from one to another, they were exceedingly pleased with the descriptions Mrs. Landon gave of scenes with which she was perfectly familiar, her own childhood having been passed in some of the spots so beautifully portrayed by the artist's pencil.

After lingering with enthusiasm around a charming

picture of a pure Italian sunset scene, Bessie uttered an exclamation of delight as, upon turning a little to her left, she saw, for the first time, the most exquisite painting of a little girl about three years of age, whose large brown eyes seemed gazing into hers with a blending of childlike beauty and simplicity unsurpassed by anything she ever saw upon canvas. There seemed to be living pulsation in the life-like flesh, almost the power of speech in the rosy velvet lips just parted in a loving smile, while the sunny hair, of a light brown, curled in tiny rings from a forehead of purest smoothness and beauty.

Both Bessie and Minnie were enraptured with the picture, supposing, of course, that it was a fancy piece, as it seemed far too beautiful to have ever had an original.

While expatiating upon the exquisite beauty of the face, Minnie was struck by the silence of Mrs. Landon and her brother, while raising her eyes inquiringly to Mr. Percy, she saw him motion to them to come away; at the same time he turned a warning look towards his sister.

Both girls saw the motion, and glancing at Mrs. Landon, could not account for the change in her speaking countenance.

She stood with one hand grasping the back of a chair for support, the other pressed close against her heart.

Her lips, pale as ashes, were wreathed with a woe that could not be described, while her dark eyes were riveted upon the little face, with a yearning, yet unutterable agony.

"Did you observe, Miss Bessie, this Highland Scene? it is well worth your examination," exclaimed young Percy, endeavoring to draw the party from the unfortunate picture, and to arouse the attention of his sister.

Bessie and Minnie turned to the Scottish Scene, but

Mrs. Landon did not notice the movement, as she still gazed with that speechless woe upon the gloriously beautiful child.

"Sister," said the young man, approaching her gently, and passing his arm around her as he spoke, "Sister, will you come to the parlor, now? you are weary and can rest there."

"Rest! did you speak of rest for my poor heart? No! Charles, no! Oh, Liza, Liza! my lily bud, my darling!"

Her eyes never moved from the infantile face as she spoke, but large drops of agonized perspiration gathered upon her brow, while her frame trembled with her great agitation.

Seeing no other way to divert her gaze from the picture, Percy seized a green covering, that lay unperceived upon the floor, and throwing it over the frame, thus hiding it from sight, he turned again to his sister, and taking one hand in his, he passed his arm around her, and thus gently drew her towards the door.

"Oh, Charles, Charles! so have they hidden my darling!" half shrieked the poor woman in tones of agony, as they left the room, while her head sank to his shoulder, and a burst of tears came to her relief.

"Yes, Beatrice, sister, I know! but for my sake try and be calm. Lie down a little while, now dear, and then you will feel better."

They disappeared from sight, as he thus spoke, leaving the two girls in intense amazement at the unexpected scene.

"How singular that such a beautiful face should affect her thus!" said Minnie. "Can there be a story connected with her life, of which you are ignorant?"

"There must be, I think!" returned Bessie, "but I never

heard of any mystery. I have known her a long time, have often been in this room, but I never noticed that picture before, as it has always been covered as Mr. Percy has arranged it now. The curtain must have fallen accidentally, I think. But hush, here comes Mr. Percy."

As Bessie ceased speaking, the young man entered the room. He was extremely pale, while his fine expressive eyes were full of sorrowful emotions.

"You will excuse my sister for a while, I hope," remarked he; "it is very necessary that she is perfectly quiet until she regains her composure, after this unfortunate occurrence. It is strange how that covering could have dropped from its place," added he; "I must secure it more perfectly, to prevent a repetition of this sad scene, as it always affects my poor sister thus, at suddenly seeing that precious little face." Thus speaking, Percy advanced to the picture, and tenderly raising the cover, before fastening it more securely, he again allowed the young girls another gaze into the speaking eyes, and upon the beautiful face beneath.

"Would it be intruding upon private emotions to ask why so perfect a face should agitate her thus?" asked Minnie, timidly.

"Not at all. That dear little creature is my sister's only child, snatched from her under peculiarly distressing circumstances. Allow me to arrange the covering properly, and I will then relate to you the sorrowful story that has darkened her life forever."

The picture was effectually concealed; the door of the gallery was closed, and the girls again entered the parlor, and became attentive listeners to the following tale:

"My sister Beatrice and myself, were children of an English father and an Italian mother. We were both born in London, where we resided until my sister was sixteen, and I fourteen, when my father's business compelled him to remove to New York. There I was further educated, and there we have since resided. About two years after our settlement in this country, Beatrice married Mr. Robert Landon, a gentleman with whom she had become acquainted during a few months spent at the Clarendon Hotel, New York, and for the two succeeding years no happier woman could be found.

"When little Liza was born, her whole spirit seemed imbued with delight. I never saw so fond a mother, nor did I ever see so beautiful a child; from its very birth it seemed to be the one joy of my sister's life. Her love for her treasure amounted almost to a passion, and the little one seemed only in perfect content when in her mother's presence.

"It seemed as if a foreboding of the sad future had even then reached the spirit of both parent and child.

"The confinement of such unwearied maternal watchings was very prostrating to the delicate frame of Beatrice, for her health suddenly failed. To such a state was she reduced, that the only hope of her recovery lay in a voyage, and more genial climate. Having relatives in Italy that my mother longed to see, she accompanied my sister with her husband and child to that distant spot.

"At the time they sailed, the little girl was three years old, and her beauty was the theme of every person that beheld her.

"Poor little Liza!

"Arrived at Florence, they repaired to the extensive villa of Signor Bertram Pompelli, my mother's youngest brother. After several months of visiting from this charming place, Mr. Landon bade his family farewell, leaving them for a business tour under the safe protection of my uncle and his wife. Poor fellow! he little thought that one at least of his beloved ones, would never more gladden his yearning heart.

"Beatrice had quite recovered her wonted health and energy, while little Liza was fast developing, not only in beauty, but in intelligence and genius. At that early age, a rare gift and passion for music was discovered, and she would catch the air of really difficult pieces, and warble them in baby accents around the house.

"'Sing papa a pretty song before he goes,' said Mr. Landon, catching his beautiful 'Lily-bud'—a pet name Beatrice often called her—in his arms, and tossing her gaily in the air.

"The little one glided softly down, and standing by his side, her white hands folded on her breast, her brown eyes fastened upon his in loving glances, she sang a beautiful Italian song she had lately learned—sang it, too, sweetly in that language, but in lisping baby tone.

"Poor Landon will never forget his baby or her song.

"One morning, about a week after the father left, Belle, the nurse, who accompanied them from New York, and was supposed to be perfectly trusty, asked permission to take Liza for a short walk, to be gone, as she said, a very little while. Beatrice was suffering with a sick headache, and had just fallen asleep; therefore, without awaking her, the grandmother gave the desired assent, and in a few moments they were out of sight; while, with the child's loving kiss still upon her lip, my mother returned to her sewing and watch by the side of my sister, who suffered exceeding in those attacks.

"So an hour flew by.

"'Where is Liza?' asked Beatrice, opening her eyes suddenly, as she awoke with a start.

"'Horrible! what a dream I have had; I am so glad it is but a dream!'

"'She will be here presently!' replied my mother. 'The morning was so inviting, Belle took her a short walk. It is time they return now.'

"'I am sorry she went. I saw her in my sleep in such fearful danger. Oh, if any evil should come to my darling! Look out, mother dear, and see if they are returning.'

"My mother examined the street from each window, but no nurse and child could be seen.

"So another hour went by.

"The time for dinner came, and still no Liza!

"Four o'clock. Five o'clock. Six o'clock! Oh God, how can I tell of the agonized suspense of my poor mother and sister, as their bursting hearts cried still, 'No Liza.'

"Miss Minnie, that same horror *still* remains upon the heart of my dear sister, for from that hour to this, the same call is upon her lips in vain: 'Liza! Liza! my Lily-bud, my darling.' Dear little Liza was never heard from more."

"Horrible!" exclaimed both the young girls, as the tears of sympathy rolled down their cheeks. "What could have become of her? Did you never hear from the nurse either?"

"All the clue that could be obtained as to the fate of the poor nurse girl was this: It was known that Belle had an Italian lover, a desperate-looking fellow, while little was know of his character, or place of residence. That day it was ascertained that a young man and woman, with a child answering to the description of our lost darling, were seen in a small boat sailing on the Arno. It was supposed that she met the man while out, and was invited by him to sail, as the day was fine. They never returned with the boat, and after a long search the body of the poor girl was found in the river, but cruelly, shamefully murdered, as three dreadful stabs bore witness. But though diligent efforts were made, and large rewards offered, the child was never heard from, nor could any clue be found as to the whereabouts of the man. There is little doubt, however, that the little one was murdered also, although Beatrice still declares she is alive, suffering, and tormented. My sister for one year was entirely bereft of reason after this dreadful stroke. She paced the floor night and day, shrieking for her child. She tore her hair, and bit her lips in her frenzy. She could neither eat nor sleep, and her wailing cries for 'Liza, Liza,' were harrowing to hear. We had every reason to fear that she was hopelessly insane for life. But after every search had been made, and all that could be done for her recovery had been attended to, Mr. Landon left the scene of his dreadful loss, and brought his stricken wife home. She finally recovered, and now, as four years have flown by since that sad day, she seems well, although even yet a casual reference to her darling, a sudden lifting of the screen from the child's portrait, produces those fearful excitements, and for days after, we fear a return of her former disease. For this reason Mr. Landon has not allowed the disappearance of his child to be known in this place, to which he removed two years since, that he might have perfect quiet and peace for Beatrice. Please, then, do not mention the circumstance of to-day to any of the gossip-loving inhabitants of Spotsdale."

"We surely will not," exclaimed both girls at once.

"Dear Mrs. Landon, no wonder she grieves! The uncertainty of her fate is even more terrible than her actual death would have been!" added Minnie, tears filling her eyes again as she spoke.

"Much more!" returned the young man with a grateful look, for the deep sympathy expressed by the lovely girl.

"But I have saddened you both by my story, and I must plan something to banish those tears. Shall we have a skate after dinner? there is an excellent skating pond near by, and the ice is in fine condition."

The invitation was accepted, and as soon as dinner should be dispatched they proposed to set forth.

Mrs. Landon did not reappear until a few moments before dinner, and then the grief upon her countenance caused the poor girl to shudder. She appeared so different from herself, so absent minded, and so full of nervous fears, that all saw that she was exerting every nerve, to seem at all composed.

The skating arrangement was certainly all for the best, as it allowed the stricken woman relief from their further entertainment, and both girls were delighted that it had been proposed for her sake.

Their skates had been sent for while they were at dinner, and in a short time they were upon the ice.

They had a splendid time there, and after a long afternoon of the gay sport, Percy escorted them home; but not until the arrangement had been made, that they should have his protection to New York, as he thought of leaving, on the following Friday, the day Minnie had promised her parents should find her "homeward bound."

CHAPTER VII.

THE NEW FRIENDS.

"The way is dark, my Father! Cloud on cloud
Is gathering thickly o'er my head, and loud,
The thunders roar above me. See, I stand
Like one bewildered! Father, take my hand,
And from the night
Lead up to light
Thy child."

TOM, bring me the black pony at six; I must go to —— and back to-night."

So spake an American gentleman, standing on the steps of a French hotel, to a colored boy in attendance.

"Surely, Mr. Russell, you will not ride over that unfrequented and dangerous road so late? The sun sank some time since, and it will soon be dark," exclaimed an elderly gentleman near.

"I care not for danger, as I fear none; and for the darkness, it may as well be without as within!" was the gloomy response.

"I am sorry if your mind is in such a dismal condition, my friend, but certainly, it will not improve it to have a collision with the banditti that infest that region, waylaying travellers, and committing deeds of guilt and rapine every chance that offers. Surely you have heard of the occurrences that have transpired so often on that highway; then why go there, unless urgent business calls?" again remarked the second speaker.

"I must ride, Mr. Colwell. I have passed a wretched day, and now need recreation of some kind. Nothing restores tranquillity to a harassed spirit, like a gallop over hill and dale, a fearless race on a noble steed. I must go, but if danger lurks around I will be prepared; I will take my revolver and thus face the foe." So saying, the young man re-entered the hotel, reappearing, as the groom led a splendid coal-black horse to the door. Vaulting gracefully into the saddle, and nodding a grave adieu to his friend, Paul Russell dashed away, and as he rode along, now swift, now slow, now up a gentle hill, now over a level plain, we will pause a few moments to describe him, as, being the hero of our tale, he needs more than a casual glance, and then we will proceed to explain the period in which we again introduce him. He has slackened his first half reckless speed, and as the graceful animal falls into a nimble trot, we have a good view of the fine form of the rider. He was quite tall, while the fully developed chest, the gracefully moulded frame, were unsurpassed in nobility and elegance. His hair was a jet black, slightly inclined to curl, while a splendid full beard of the same shade, to which a razor was rarely applied, with a finely shaped moustache, added much to his manly and attractive appearance. But the chief charm of his face lay in the expressive midnight eyes, fringed with long, dark lashes, that seemed to penetrate your every thought, although a sadness lingered in each look, that whispered of sorrow and of care. His teeth were even, and pearly white, his lips red, and shaped with much beauty and gentleness; around whose graceful curves a smile rarely fluttered, although the beholder would be instantly captivated by its peculiar sweetness, when one did by chance appear.

We have taken a writer's privilege of going backward

in our story several years, and as we introduce Cousin Paul now, it is nearly three years after his last return to Europe, and before the reception of the letter of which Bessie Brown gave an account to her friend. The reader will recollect that Bessie spoke of the despair that seemed to fill his bosom, as he left his native shores *forever*, as he said in parting.

Thus, then, Bessie spoke of his troubled spirit, and it is with that same burdened heart, we find him.

The evening shadows had gathered thickly as the young man rode onward, while the stillness was broken only by the mournful song of the nightingale, or the disconsolate notes of the whippoorwill, whose tones still rang through the wood that stood each side the road over which he was now slowly advancing. The moon did not rise until quite late, but still, as the night was clear, and star after star made its appearance in the broad expanse above, he could see quite well, and therefore he rode on, while his thoughts went back over the blue Atlantic, to friends and scenes now closed to him forever. A deep sigh ever and anon burst from his lips, while a still more suffering look appeared upon his brow, as his meditations deepened. Once his lips parted, and these words—"Oh, my darling, can this last forever?" gushed forth, breaking the stillness, and causing Paul to start at the very sound of his own voice.

Suddenly he stopped his horse and listened intently.

"Surely I heard a cry for help! Hark! there it goes again farther on! Some one is being attacked by those robbers Colwell spoke of. I must go to the rescue."

Pulling from his breast pocket his trusty revolver, he spoke softly to the pony and dashed onward.

As he drew near the spot from which he judged the cry had proceeded, he distinctly saw a carriage standing, while figures were moving around it. Shouting as if to a band of followers, "Come on, boys, we'll have them now," he bore down to the group. As he did so, two men darted towards the wood, but not before Russell had time to point his weapon and fire.

A groan told that one at least was injured, but the other must have assisted his flight, as both quickly disappeared, while Russell lost no time in again sending a fiery message to the spot, then dashed on to the assistance of the unfortunate travellers.

On reaching the carriage, he found that the coachman had been knocked from his seat, with a blow that rendered him senseless, but he soon recovered, as Paul lifted him from the ground, and on rising found that he was not materially injured. The gentleman who was inside had escaped molestation by Paul's opportune arrival, but being in wretched health, the fright had overcome him to such a degree, that as Paul opened the door, he found him lying pale and exhausted, with the blood gushing from his trembling lips. A hemorrhage of the lungs had been occasioned by his deep excitement.

The coachman, who was again quite himself, informed Paul that the gentleman's name was Ernest Moreland, that he was an Englishman, travelling for his health, and having been delayed in his journey, and a stranger in that region, he was taking him to the hotel at ——, being the nearest to their present location, when the robbers suddenly appeared, demanding their money and watches, and only Paul's providential appearance had put them to flight.

Russell, observing the faint condition of the poor young man, instantly ordered the coachman to fasten his pony securely to the rear of the carriage, and drive rapidly on, while he supported the invalid stranger. In a few moments, they were passing at full speed over the road towards the hotel our friend had left a few hours since.

They reached the place in safety about ten o'clock, and Mr. Moreland was placed in a well ventilated, and airy room, upon a clean bed, and a physician was immediately summoned, who at length succeeded in stopping the hemorrhage, but prescribed perfect quiet, and kind watching; while the pitying look he gave the sick man, assured Russell that he considered him not long for this world.

All night Russell sat by the sufferer's bedside, watching every movement and anticipating every want.

He was a tender nurse, and with a woman's softness, he smoothed his pillow, and wiped his pallid brow, never allowing him to speak, as the physician had strictly forbidden it; but the blue eyes of the patient often expressed their mute gratitude, while a slight pressure of his hand spoke a world of thanks.

How often a *look* can convey to another the feelings of a full heart in the absence of words, a still, soft touch, assure us that the soul is mightily moved, even when the lips are closed, and the voice is still.

So Paul knew full well the language of that eye and hand, and his sympathizing heart yearned with unutterable tenderness, to yet more soothe the pale and suffering one before him.

"Is there anything more I can do for you, Mr. Moreland?" he said, leaning gently over him, about two in the morning, for he saw that he did not sleep, and that his eyes turned restlessly from himself to a table near at hand, while a longing look seemed to linger in the gaze.

"Do not speak but one word, and I will understand and gladly serve you."

Bending low, he caught the whisper, "Read," and following his eyes to the small stand before mentioned, among some articles that had been taken from his portemanteau, to administer to his comfort, he noticed a small pocket Bible.

A smile of peace and tranquillity glided to the lips of Moreland, as Paul opened the book, and seating himself nearer the light, in tones of striking sweetness and melody, commenced reading some of the beautiful, soul-stirring Psalms of David.

Shall I pause a moment to tell the secret aversion of Paul Russell's heart to this occupation, notwithstanding his seeming cheerful acquiescence? Shall I whisper the sad truth that it had been months, nay years, since his fingers had touched that holy book, or his eyes rested on those precious truths?

Reader! Russell was a man of the world, wild, thoughtless, yet now sad and troubled, but like a host of others battling through his checkered life, "having no hope, and without God in the world."

As he read, a feeling of awe stole to his spirit, and a trembling could be observed in his tones, that told of an awakened interest in those long neglected words. He had finished the twenty-third Psalm, and glancing toward the bed, had noted the upraised hand and eye of his listener, had caught the full glory of the smile that played over his features.

"Surely," he thought, "those words were written expressly for him, if I can at all interpret such speaking glances."

Still he read on, through the twenty-fourth and into the twenty-fifth psalm. A start followed the reading of the seventh verse.

"Remember not the sins of my youth, nor my transgressions; according to thy mercy remember thou me for thy goodness sake, O Lord."

Then again in the sixteenth, seventeenth, and eighteenth verses, "Turn thee unto me and have mercy upon me, for I am desolate and afflicted." "The troubles of my heart are enlarged: O bring thou me out of my distresses."

"Look upon mine affliction and my pain, and forgive all my sins."

A deep sigh burst from his lips as he read, while the spirit uttered the voiceless words, "now truly that prayer is not for him who lies there with that holy smile; but for a wretched outcast like myself." He could read no more until the strange mist that had gathered over his eyes had cleared away.

What could that mist be? Tears, surely not tears?

Throwing the book upon the table, he started to his feet and began pacing the floor with hurried strides.

He forgot the silent form upon the bed, whose blue eyes were watching him with questioning interest; he saw not the thin white hand that the sick man stretched toward him, as he passed now backward, now forward, over that room in that solemn still night hour; no, his thoughts had passed far back from that chamber into the unforgotten past, and were busy with the scenes and sins of former days.

"The sins of my youth! those fearful sins! strange how they press upon my heavy heart! would that they could be remembered no more!" at length he exclaimed, as, in turning in his nervous walk, he for the first time noticed the still outstretched hand of the sick man, and passing to his side, he laid his own, all trembling, in that eager clasp.

He felt the sympathy of the touch; he understood the

wish that the poor fellow had to comfort him, although his life depended upon his silence, and beseeching him not to speak, he brought the Bible to which he pointed, and placing it in his hand, he read the words upon which the finger of Moreland rested. They were these :

"Blessed is he whose transgression is forgiven, whose sin is covered."

Paul's eyes remained fastened upon these words full a moment before he spoke again, but then it was with a look of utter wretchedness that he exclaimed—

"But *I* am not the blessed one referred to, for alas my transgressions are not forgiven, my sins are not covered."

Again the feeble hands of Ernest Moreland turned over the pages of the holy word of God, and again Paul followed the tracing of his finger.

"But if we walk in the light, as he is in the light, we have fellowship one with another, and the blood of Jesus Christ his son cleanseth us from all sin."

"I thank you for the words, my dear friend," exclaimed Russell, after he had fully examined the passage; "I see there is comfort there; try to sleep now for my sake, that you may soon be able to converse; then show me what it is to be a Christian, that I may be blessed by having my sins covered. Sleep now, and I will watch faithfully beside you as you rest."

CHAPTER VIII.

SEEKING LIGHT.

"The cross is heavy, Father! I have borne
It long, and still do bear it. Let my worn
And fainting spirit rise to that blest land
Where crowns are given. Father, take my hand,
And reaching down,
Lead to the crown
Thy child."

TWO weeks had passed away, and still Ernest Moreland was confined to his room, feeble and languid, yet calm and tranquil. Paul Russell had scarcely left his side during the days of his illness. He had watched him by night, and by day, tenderly ministering to his wants, and alleviating his trials by his presence and sympathizing carefulness.

He had become strangely and deeply attached to his invalid companion. It was so long since he had possessed an object to love, that he yearned over this stranger friend with a brother's tenderness, yet as day by day the affection strengthened between them, he sighed with inward anguish over the saddening, yet sure prospect that they were soon to be parted forever, and while his friend would be happy in the presence of his Saviour, he would be wretchedly alone.

Alone! what a perfect desolation is embodied in the very word. Alone! Two little syllables, yet a world of saddest meaning hidden in their bosom: Alone!

Poor Paul for many years had felt the full force of that word. Far from his native land, far from all he loved on earth, a wanderer, dejected, desolate, he had found one friend at last to love in that foreign land, one heart that returned his pure affection, but the shadow of death was folding around him, another and a better land beckoning him onward, and he saw that very soon he would wander on spiritless, friendless, alone! Sadly alone!

Yet Ernest was better to all appearance, as we again see him. He could walk around his room, could converse on different topics, could express his thanks to his devoted friend, who, although so recently a stranger, had nursed and cared for him as a brother. Yet still, notwithstanding his apparent increase of strength, the insidious disease worked on, eating his vitals, secretly working sure decay, and an early death.

As we see them this afternoon, Ernest is lying back in a large easy-chair, his handsome wrapper drawn around him, while his thoughtful eyes are intently fixed upon his friend.

Paul sat near, beside a window; his fingers had been thrust carelessly through his jet black curls, throwing them back from his open brow, revealing the deep sadness in his large dark eyes, and the mournfulness hovering around his pale features.

He had been disclosing his life-history to his friend; he had been speaking of an early sin that had shed a blight upon his whole life, and darkened his prospect of peace forever; had told of his coming to this distant land, seeking forgetfulness, rest, quiet, something to quench the gnawings of remorse, that was ever filling his bosom; he then referred to that silent night scene, that Holy Bible, from which he had read for the first time in so many years, and added that those words were continually haunting him, and now he begged that he would tell him what he should do to obtain the blessing of having his transgressions forgiven, and his sins covered.

"I have listened with deep attention to your history, my friend, nay, almost brother," returned Ernest; "it interests me, mainly, because of the evidence it furnishes of the natural shortsightedness of men. You declare your convictions of wrong-doing, but evidently your trouble arises entirely from what men may think of you, and from consequences to which you are liable from the enactments of men. This is clear from the fact that you adopted the plan of flying from the scene of your transgressions, seeking peace on a foreign shore. You have failed. Though away from those scenes, and beyond the reach of early associates, yet the peace you seek, comes not. Do you not see that this is because you offended in that wrong-doing, One, whose presence you cannot flee, and whose justice reaches to every land and every clime? Nay, do you not see that your continued trouble is the effect of the quickening of your conscience, which results from the working therein of that Spirit, who can communicate with man's heart, any and everywhere, and who can present all things in their true light? Now, let me say, you have erred in supposing that you can flee from the consciousness of wrong when you have been guilty of it, and in framing to yourself a refuge, in the matter of new scenes and new employments. Guilt is not to be cancelled in this way. Conscience is not to be trifled with in this way. Truth is not to be blindfolded in this way. There is but one way to peace of mind, and that is by the way of honest and reverential dealing with truth.

"I had begun to feel that there is no refuge for me," said Paul, in reply, "but that I am doomed to suffer these pangs without hope of relief. Pray tell me what you mean?"

"If you have read the Bible, you will remember a singular statement, made by our Lord and Saviour. He says, 'I am the way, and the truth, and the life;' now do you not perceive here, that in order to reach life, we are to go by a 'way' in which deceit, fraud, attempt to hide, stands out chief element?"

"I see a contrast: but what do you mean by paying deference to truth?"

"Why nothing less than looking at your deeds in their true light, as *sins*, not merely *wrongs*—that is, as offences against God, and not merely against man; and then acknowledging, repenting, and craving pardon of them," returned Moreland.

"Acknowledge I do; repent surely I can; but I never thought of pardon! I have expected punishment only," said Paul, sadly.

"That comes of thinking only of the relations of your deeds to the enactments of men. They know of nothing but punishment, because they know of no method of satisfying law beside. But, happily for you, the Great God is not only a Lawgiver and a Judge, but in the person of the Son, a Redeemer."

"A Redeemer! your words are strange as they are welcome. Please explain!" said Paul, anxiously.

"Happy am I to do so. Listen for your good. The great fact exists that all men are sinners, transgressors of God's law, and consequently condemned to eternal death, the penalty of such trangression. God is a God that hath no pleasure in the death of the sinner, but that he turn from his evil way and live. To make the way clear for this turning, even to life, God made provision for magnifying the law, and making it honorable, in other words for being just to his law and government, and his un offending creatures, when He should justify, acquit, and accept, into His favor, all who do repent."

"And what was that promise? I burn to know it! It opens such hope to me."

"The Bible, which is the revelation of God's will to man, is also styled, the revelation of Jesus Christ. That is, it tells us about Him, and what does it say?" Why, that God sent His Son to be 'the propitiation for our sins,' That is, he sent Him to atone for the sins of sinners: to pay a ranson for them, purchase them out of the hands of the law, by furnishing, in their behalf, a satisfaction for that law's demands: and in this matter, he met literally, the law's demands against the sinner. He found the curse of that law upon the sinner. He became a curse that He might redeem us from the curse of the law. He bore our sins in His own body to the tree. He suffered for sins, the just for the unjust, and now, 'By Him, all that believe, are justified from all things from which they could not be justified by the law of Moses.' 'All things,' remember, so that the worst crimes are covered by this redemption of Jesus Christ. *Your case* is included, and to show it to you, He says, 'Come unto me, all ye that labor and are heavy laden, and I will give you rest.'"

"You speak of believing; what is that?" asked Paul.

"Let me illustrate. Suppose you had committed treason, the penalty of which is death. You are arraigned before the proper tribunal. When there, however, the king's proclamation is read; that proclamation declares that the king's son, by the sufferance of the very death denounced against treason, redeems all traitors, on condition that they, with sorrow for their crime, sign an instrument, accepting the Prince as their substitute, and declaring their readiness to accept, *as a free gift*, their acquittal, on the ground of his merits as the beloved Son of the king, and the heir to the throne; and to bestow on him, ever after, all the praise of their deliverance. You sign in sincerity; the king's promise is fulfilled, and you are free. Can you not, by putting God in the place of the king, and Jesus Christ in the place of the king's son, and sin in the place of treason, see into that believing? But let me say, there is a further requirement; what is not worth asking for, is not worth having. You are to ask God, in the name of Jesus Christ, and for his sake, to grant you this pardon, and to accept you with His favor. I speak thus to obviate the necessity of a further question for explanation from you. For this is prayer. Let me say, in conclusion, (for I must stop,) I know the reality of all this, and I pray you, just accept the facts of your case without quibbling, or doubt. Act, and you will reach an experience, that will do far more for you than all conversation with man. "He that believeth hath the witness in himself." I can say no more; I shall pray for you, but, dear Russell, let me beseech you, also, to pray for yourself."

CHAPTER IX.

DEATH OF MORELAND.

"Leaves have their time to fall,
And flowers to wither at the north-wind's breath,
And stars to set,—but all—
Thou hast all seasons for thine own, O Death.

Youth and the opening rose
May look like things too glorious for decay;
And smile at thee—but thou art not of those
That wait the ripened bloom to seize their prey."

DAYS sped on, and still Moreland gained strength slowly yet perceptibly. Dr. Bonnefaux, the skillful practitioner who attended him, warmly urged his passing some time in Italy; therefore Russell had offered to accompany him, and we now see them domesticated at the villa of Signora Fabretti, a friend of Moreland's, and a kind, hospitable person, a widow of intelligence, refinement, and wealth. Here they felt perfectly at home, and every attention was bestowed upon the invalid. For some time a great improvement was plainly visible, but as we see him the third week after his arrival, we find that the apparent strength that had been imparted by the change of air was gradually subsiding, and a prostration unaccountable, save by the rapid progress of his disease, had usurped the place of the first satisfactory effect.

Poor Moreland was confined to his bed once more, and in the sinking frame, the feeble tones, the labored breath, were certain signs that death would soon snatch him away.

Unweariedly had Russell watched beside him; for three nights in succession he had attended, with unabating care, his suffering and fast departing friend; and now, as another night approached with its round of duty, and as Moreland had dropped into a deep sleep, watched for a while by Signora Fabretti, who insisted upon relieving him for a few moments' rest, he softly stepped into his own apartment, and closing the door, seated himself at the piano and gently ran his fingers over the keys.

The touch was like the greetings of an old friend, and the fullness of the melody soothed his weary and worn condition. At first he played one of Mozart's stirring pieces; then, as the spirit of the tune thrilled his soul, his passion for composing came upon him, and he found himself extemporizing a death scene, beautiful, sad, mournful, and well suited to the hour.

It rested his weary frame to touch those keys, it strengthened him for the trying scene so near at hand, and as he still lingered over the melodious sounds, he felt at peace.

So he rambled on, drawing from the instrument such tones as inspiration dictated, and half an hour glided soon away, unperceived and unmarked by the absorbed musician.

Paul Russell's whole heart was in music; he loved it, he dreamed it, he composed it, as easily as he spoke his native tongue.

Rising at length, he wandered to the window, just in time to behold one of Italia's beautiful sunset scenes.

"Beautiful! Exquisite! Sublime!" he exclaimed, as

the full glory of the picture flashed upon his eager sigh "What a magnificent view! and Moreland, dear dying sain will soon be beyond the setting sun, at rest, amid infinitel more glorious beauties even, than this radiant cloudland.

But soon the sun had departed; and turning from his p sition at the open window, he threw himself upon a sof and passing his hand carelessly through his wavy hai pushing it from his brow, he enjoyed a few moments c the dolce far niente of Italian life.

But such restful repose was not long to last, for a hast summons from Signora Fabretti came, announcing that th sleep had passed, and Moreland seemed to be sinking while he asked anxiously for Russell.

Without a moment's delay, the young man again entered the sick room, and approaching the bed, clasped the out stretched and emaciated hand of the sufferer.

"Dear Russell," the dying one faintly articulated, "I feel that I am failing rapidly, fast going home to Jesus. Happy thought! peaceful rest, and glorious scenes are there! No sickness, no pain, no sadness evermore for me, after the dark valley of death is once safely crossed. Dearest Paul, I thank you for all you have done for me; no brother would have cared for me in my last hours with more devoted tenderness. I die loving you with a fondness that no brother's love could excel, and feeling this gratitude and affection swelling so deeply my heart, I cannot go without speaking to you *once more* of your eternal prospects. Let me, then, as from the gate of eternity and in the prospect of glory, of which man can have no conception, address you. How fare you now?"

"Oh Moreland, my precious, faithful friend, your conver sations have deeply impressed me, and led me to almost envy you! Would that I could see as you see! How shall I enjoy that gracious boon?" returned the agitated young man.

"Just as I came to it, so must you. Jesus Christ on my confession of my sin and earnest prayer for His mercy, 'gave me light,' and my soul had rest, because it could lean on his righteousness. I gave myself to Him, and He gave Himself to me, and being in Him, I found peace and joy. Now I am enabled to feel that though I am lamentably deficient in myself, and before the law stand yet a sinner, yet His righteousness, which by God's grace is accounted to me as mine, is the full requirement of the law, and His pardon is full clearance from all the law's demands, and my seal of eternal life."

"You spoke of confession of sin. That throws light upon the matter. But what does that involve?"

"Simply telling God all about yourself and your deeds, just as the case is, not hiding or coloring anything. Now I am convinced, you need but one thing, and that is action. I am going the way of all the earth soon. My strength is perceptibly failing. I hasten to ask you, will you promise me to do just what God requires immediately, and leave the result with Him?"

"I will, indeed I will," was the brief and emphatic reply.

"Well, then, go to God, tell him your sins, and your sorrow for them, because they are sins; tell him your willingness and desire to take His son as your substitute, before His law, and His atonement, as your justification, and ask him to "make you accepted in the Beloved, in whom we have redemption, through His blood, even the forgiveness of sins, according to the riches of his grace." Tell him you rely not on anything in yourself, or your life—and plead till the answer come. Will you promise to do this, my friend? Will you promise to attend to this, my dying request, thus preparing to meet me in Heaven?" The words came very faintly, yet distinctly from the pallid lips of the fast expiring one, while his eyes were fixed anxiously and intently upon the face of Russell.

"I promise faithfully, and from the fullness of my heart. Yes! oh, yes, dearest Moreland, I will do as you direct!" was the reply, that caused the dying man to smile in peaceful content.

"Thank God! I now die without one regret. I know you will yet be happy in the priceless riches of salvation. One word more; when you see your way clear, return to the scenes of your wrong-doing; make all the reparation required, and there consecrate yourself anew to the service of the Kingdom of Heaven. Farewell."

A pause followed the last words, broken only by the low sighs of Russell, who watched the closing eyes and failing pulse of his only friend, with deepest and most intense grief.

Ten minutes passed; no sound save the labored breathing of the dying man, and the sighs of the desolate watcher.

Ten minutes more, and the form was still—motionless—pallid—just breathing, alive, yet almost gone.

Colder and colder grew the hand that lay so silently in Russell's; shorter and shorter the fleeting breath, and leaning forward with tearful eyes, all seemed to think that the last fluttering of that devoted heart was passing, when suddenly the lips parted with a smile, the eyes opened, revealing a look of rapture, while the words came gushing forth to the astonished ear, as he rose to his elbow.

"Russell, it is Jesus! I see him! I hear the music of Heaven! Joy, joy! Praise be to God forever! Amen!"

He fell back, his eyes closed, and as Russell leaned for-ard to catch *one word more*, his spirit passed, in a gushing gh, to the "better land," the bosom of his precious aviour.

CHAPTER X.

FASHIONABLE LIFE.

"But if I live in the flesh, this is the fruit of my labor ; yet what I shall choose, wot not."—PHILIPPIANS—I. 22.

ESSIE BROWN and Minnie Morton left Cedar Lawn at the time appointed, and in company with Charles Percy, entered the cars, on their route to New York.

Bessie was in glad spirits, for a visit to the metropolis had long been a delightful dream, and her anticipations unusually bright and glowing.

They had a pleasant journey, Minnie being full of vivacity and fun, and Percy proving an interesting and gentlemanly companion.

As the cars flew over the track, Minnie's sallies of wit caused unbounded merriment; each amusing scene gave scope for good humor, and laughter, and Bessie was almost sorry when they reached Jersey City, so much had she enjoyed the society of the gay young couple.

Mr. Morton's residence was in twenty-third street, thus giving quite a ride from the Courtlandt-street ferry to the door. As the carriage rolled up Broadway, Bessie was delighted with the brilliant and lively appearance of the street, and the bright eyes of the many promenaders, who, regardless of the cold January atmosphere, strolled along, well enveloped in shining silks, and costly furs. Her res fairly danced with pleasure, as she glanced at the tore windows, so full of gay colors, and she well thought ne had never dreamed of half the sights afforded by even ne ride through this celebrated city.

In the hall of Minnie's elegant home, her mother, a fine ppearing lady, handsomely and becomingly attired, stood o greet them. She gave Bessie a warm kiss of welcome, while Minnie was overwhelmed with caresses, and conratulations upon her improved appearance.

Percy did not enter, but after seeing the ladies safely within the place of their destination, and promising very soon to visit them, he re-entered the carriage and rode way.

Bessie was very happy in Minnie's family; both Mr. and Mrs. Morton were kind and pleasant, and strove to place her at ease in every way, while Minnie caressed her one moment, and teased her the next, but all so good naturedly, that Bessie could not but enter into the spirit of the fun.

Minnie's apartment adjoined the one appropriated to Bessie, and communicated by a passage-way of closets. The appointments of both were truly splendid; black walnut furniture, English brussels carpets, and red damask curtains, with expensive falls of lace, and massive gilt cornices, formed some of the rich and tasty decorations, while elegant engravings decorated the walls.

Bessie was delighted; but as she gazed around, the secret thought would present itself, "what a contrast to my humble home! how could Minnie have seemed so contented and happy in so plain an abode?" She did not utter the thought aloud, nor foster it for one moment, lest she should bear a discontented heart back to her loving Father.

Closing the door of her apartment, Bessie changed he travelling dress for a simple black bombazine, while he luxuriant golden hair she prettily and becomingly arrange on her bright young brow.

She had but just completed her toilet, when luncheo was announced, and with their arms encircling each other' waists, the girls descended to the dining-room, where stylish and elegant lunch was spread, and where Mr. and Mrs. Morton were already waiting their appearance.

"Mamma," said Minnie, after all were seated around the table, "what has happened in the gay world, since I left? any parties, or entertainments to afford amusement?"

"Yes! Carrie Colman gave a very fashionable, although quite limited company, on Tuesday last. We were all invited, but declined, as you were absent. Then Wednesday evening, another of Mary Leslie's Private Theatricals came off very successfully."

"Ah! now I am sorry to have missed that! it must have been delightful! What piece was played?"

"The Lady of Lyons. Lucy Grey played Pauline to perfection, while Claude Melnotte was well personated by Joseph Miller. I think both these young people have a decided talent for the stage."

"So do I. I wonder how soon another will be gotten up?"

"Next week, I believe. Something was said about your appearing then."

"I wish I could! Really, I long to take a character!" returned Minnie.

Bessie was confounded; had she heard aright? Could it be Minnie Morton, her own giddy, yet loved companion, that longed to appear upon a theatrical stage, either public or private?

She made no remark, however, merely sipping her 1ocolate, while listening with deep attention to the ιother's reply.

"You will have an opportunity soon, I am quite sure. know you excel Lucy Grey in beauty and gracefulness, ad I think you have only to attempt the affair, to make decided impression. But would not Bessie also take a art?" queried Mrs. Morton.

A look of the deepest distress spread over Bessie's fair oung face, as she ejaculated firmly,

"Oh, no! I should certainly wish to be excused."

"Little Dork does not approve of these employments, iamma! Aunt Rebecca and Bessie have sentiments xactly alike in this respect. However, she has consented) go *once*, to each of our city entertainments, in order to ee for herself, of what they consist. If, after a fair trial, ie still clings to the belief that they are sinful, we are to rge her no more, but allow her to amuse herself with unt Rebecca, while we are absent, as she insists that I aall never stay at home on her account. But, Bessie, ie ball I spoke of, as coming off in Fifth Avenue, to which re received cards two weeks since, takes place next 'uesday, and as the invitation has been extended to you, s my expected friend, we will accomplish some shoping to-day. Sam," continued she, turning to the bony waiter, who had flourished around so briskly, uring their repast, but who now, at its close, stood like a tatue behind the chair of his mistress—"Sam, tell Pomp o bring the carriage to the door in half an hour."

"Sartain, Missy; the nabigation ob dis darkey will be nighty quick; dat am a fact," returned Sam, showing iis white teeth in true darkey style, as he left the oom.

Bessie laughed aloud at the sudden loquacity of tl negro, while Minnie explained to her, that Sambo ha been a slave in Georgia, and seemingly a great pet amor the children of his former owner. He was quite an ori inal character, and often amused them with his strang talk. He was very aristocratic in his feelings, woul never associate with persons of his own color, calling thei one and all, "dem debilish niggers." "Ise a spectib pusson," he often says, "and am allers gwine wid spectib folks. Ise a gemman of color here below, and when gets beyond Jordan, I shall go with spectibal people. I won't take long for dis chile, in tother world, to scrap acquaintance wid de Lord, dat am a fact; nor wid Mo ses and Aaron, nuther; so, as fur mixin wid dem debilis niggers aforehand, when I'm bound fur de land ob Ca naan, you'll not kotch dis chile a-doin it."

After a hearty laugh at poor Sambo's expense, they lef the dining-room, and hastened to prepare for their shop ping excursion. It occupied but a short time to do cloak, hat and furs, and then Bessie followed her frien into a handsome carriage, while its liveried coachma seized the lines, and drove the spirited horses down th crowded street, as easily as though no carts and carriage obstructed the way, so much had constant practice in dri ving, taught him the dodging skill.

Bessie was pleased with the elegant stores and fine array of beautiful goods, and her selections were soon made, as being still in black for her mother, she would wear simple white tarlatan, overskirt of same material, and for orna- ments, an elegant necklace, earrings, and pin, of rares pearl, which had descended to her from her mother.

Minnie's arrangement caused much more shopping and consultation. They passed nearly the whole afternoon oing in and out of stores, looking at laces, flowers and nery of every description.

When they reached home they found that they had ıly time to dress for dinner, which was always served unctually at six.

CHAPTER XI.

THE BEAUTIFUL WIDOW.

"Lady, we never met before,
Within the world's wide space;
And yet the more I gaze, the more
I recollect thy face!
Each feature to my mind recalls
An image of the past,
Which, where the shade of memory falls,
Is sacred to the last."

AS they approached the dining-room, Bessie fe an inward shrinking from meeting the sty and display of a fashionable city dinner, bu gathering fresh courage as she met Minnie loving gaze, and felt her gentle touch as she affectionatel passed her arm around her, she quickly recovered he composure, and quietly entered.

As she did so, she met the eye of a lady whose beaut in an instant riveted her attention.

"Bessie, allow me to present you to Mrs. Douglass, m dear Aunt Rebecca," said Minnie, as, after affectionatel kissing her, she led her friend towards the object of her ac miration.

"I am truly glad to meet one you love so tenderly Minnie," said Mrs. Douglass, in tones most musical, mos winning, as she took her hand softly, between both o hers, and drawing her towards her, pressed upon her lip kiss of welcome. "Bessie Brown and Aunt Rebecca am quite certain will soon be good friends!"

Bessie was charmed immediately with her sweet words, nd cordial greetings, while she could not but wonder at er splendid beauty; and as she admired that queenly ppearance at thirty-two, when sorrow and bereavement had harked her footsteps, she could not but wonder, what must he have been at eighteen, when life lay in all its alluring brightness before her. She was dressed in the deepest nourning, without ornament, save a jet pin, confining the imple crape collar, around a neck as white as the petals f the purest lily, and shaped in perfect grace. Her hair, he loveliest shade of chestnut, luxuriant and wealthy, was rushed becomingly from a brow whose shape bore promse of thought, and talent beyond the usual order, while he full hazel eye, fringed with long black eyelashes, was loquent in expression, gentleness, and deep mysterious eauty. Her lips were like the richest velvet, and when hey parted, revealed teeth, even, and pearly white, while he gentle smile was rare in sweetness and amiability. Tall, yet with a form of perfect symmetry, a bust of exquisite proportions, and a hand and foot whose whiteness and tiny shape could nowhere be rivalled, Rebecca Douglass was ndeed a woman of queenly grace, and peerless loveliness, and as the seat appointed Bessie was beside Minnie, and opposite hers, her eyes would wander with a look of bewildered fascination often to that beautiful face.

"I am glad your head is better, dearest Auntie," said Minnie; "we missed you at the luncheon hour."

"Yes, I was too unwell to appear, but feel quite myself, since a quiet sleep refreshed me. Had you a pleasant journey?"

"Delightful! we had a very charming companion in

Mr. Charles Percy, a young man residing in New Yo who was visiting his sister, near Cedar Lawn, and w escorted us home."

As Minnie spoke, the soup was removed and a fine turkey, with a multitude of delicate and delicio vegetables, were arrayed upon the table, by Samb who performed several characteristic flourishes in t effort, which caused Bessie to smile at the comic effect.

The girls were both hungry after their drive, and d good justice to the bountiful meal, so much so that wh the desert of lemon meringues, mince pies, etc., we placed upon the table, they felt little inclination for the nor the fruit that followed.

"Mamma," said Minnie, as, after the removal of th fruit, she sipped the coffee that had been placed befo her, "what are we to do this evening?—go to the theatr or to the opera?"

"Neither, my darling. Do you not intend to devo one evening to your parents after being absent? Certai ly, I must claim one!" replied Mrs. Morton, lookin fondly at her only remaining child, as she spoke.

"Then, Bessie, it is decided that we visit mamma th evening, that is, if you are willing."

"Willing? indeed, I am delighted to do so. I surel could not pass the hours more acceptably, than in a plea ant home circle. You know I am very domestic in al my tastes," returned Bessie, as she raised her blue eyes and encountered a gentle, approving look from the larg hazel ones of Mrs. Douglass.

"Aunt Rebecca, surely you will not leave us?" urge Minnie, as, turning from the dining-room, Mrs. Douglas seemed to be directing her steps towards her own apart ment.

"Dear Minnie, my head is not altogether well, therefore I will not risk meeting that 'charming Mr. Percy,' who, without doubt, will call this evening."

Minnie blushed the deepest scarlet, as her aunt made this remark.

She had not once thought of his coming so soon, yet she could not resist wishing that the prophecy might indeed prove true.

It was provoking, though, that she should color so deeply, and that Aunt Rebecca, of all others, should place her finger upon her crimson cheek. and smile at Bessie knowingly, as she passed on!

With a half pout on her rosy lips, the lively girl drew Bessie from the hall, into the superb parlors, Sambo had but just finished illuminating.

Bessie thought she should never cease admiring the rich velvet carpets upon which she then trod, and the costly and magnificent furniture around.

To her unaccustomed eyes, it seemed like a view of some enchanted castle, with its mirrors and curtains, its statuary and exquisite ornaments. Then how easy to dream the bright and lovely Minnie the queen of the palace.

Charles Percy did join the family gathering, and Minnie blushed again, as she met a roguish look from Bessie, while the whispered "charming Mr. Percy," made her bite her rosy lips at the recollection of her own thoughtless words.

The evening passed quickly, varied by music and anecdotes, and as Percy rose to withdraw, he invited both young ladies to accompany him to the opera the next evening, which invitation—Minnie graciously accepted.

Bessie's sleep that night, the first she ever passed in

a large city—was not very sound; the rumbling of the carriages and carts upon the pavement, which continued so late, and commenced so early, disturbed her, and then she was excited, after the varied scenes of the day.

When at last, however, she did drop into a restless slumber, the beautiful eyes of Mrs. Douglass seemed woven into her dreams, while her voice became a charmed Echo, for which she was ever seeking in vain.

CHAPTER XII.

THE OPERA.

"Be not conformed to this world.

BIBLE.

THE next night, at the appointed hour, Charles Percy and our young friends entered the Academy of Music, to listen to Madame —— in the Opera of Norma.

As Bessie's eyes wandered over the vast numbers of gaily dressed people who thronged the house, she was lost in amazement at the unexpected sight, and amid the display and beauty of the scene, the rustling of fans, and the flashing of diamonds, she felt sadly out of place, and a momentary pang shot through her pure heart at being present in such a scene of dissipation and allurement.

It was too late to retreat now; nor could she, were it not, after promising Minnie to see each scene of pleasure *once*, in order to judge from personal observation, as to the sinfulness or propriety of each. She felt sad and dejected until the curtain rose, and the music of the Opera commenced. Bessie was fond of music, and as the ravishing strains fell upon her ear, she was instantly enveloped in a maze of bewildered and intense feeling.

It was the first time she had ever heard such captivating tones, or beheld such exciting and wonderful scenes, and as she scarcely breathed through the whole performance losing no note of the singing, no motion of the troupe, she felt at its close a sense of relief, as though some great oppressive weight had been unclasped from her heart, while a sigh fluttered from her lips, which was a strange token of pleasure, and again in contradiction, of pain.

"Now Little Dork," exclaimed Minnie, as, when seated in the carriage, they rolled rapidly homeward, "tell me, did you not think the music glorious?"

"Glorious! No, Minnie, no. I could never apply that word to anything so perfectly worldly. But certainly, it was beautiful in the full sense of the word."

"Then you were pleased, dear, were you not?"

"I was pleased with the music, Minnie, undoubtedly, but its accompaniments I could not enjoy," returned Bessie.

"Not enjoy them! Now, Little Dork, do tell me why?"

"Minnie, I did not feel happy, as a Christian girl, to be mingling with such purely gay and worldly affairs. My conscience does not approve of such dissipations, and while I am exceedingly obliged to Mr. Percy for the kindness of extending to me the invitation of this evening, and while glad to have witnessed once, what enchants others so often, still I could never conscientiously again attend such a place."

"Of course, the theatre to which I was about asking your company, together with Miss Minnie's, does not come under this head?" said Mr. Percy, inquiringly.

"Oh pray do not be offended, Mr. Percy, if I declare that it does."

"Then I must understand that you will not accompany me next Monday evening?"

"Not, if you will excuse me."

"And you, Miss Minnie, surely you will not be equally cruel?"

"Not I, Mr. Percy. I shall most certainly enjoy being present, although politeness would say, stay at home with your friend.'

"Not for anything, Minnie, would I have you remain on my account. You know our agreement was, if after a trial of each pleasure, I thought it sinful, while you still thought the opposite, I was to remain with Mrs. Douglass."

"Yes, dear, I remember, therefore I am at liberty to accept your invitation, Mr. Percy; but really, Bessie, I wish you were not so particular," returned she, as Percy handed her from the carriage.

The next day was the Sabbath, and Bessie sighed as she opened her eyes that morning, bright and beautiful though it was, as she remembered the unprofitable mode in which the previous evening had been spent, almost infringing upon holy time. She strove to convince herself that she had sinned through ignorance, as she knew not the nature of the e:tertainment; but the recollection pained her, and throwing herself upon her knees she craved strength from heaven to protect her from every evil influence to which she must necessarily be exposed, by keeping a promise so rashly made, and now bitterly repented.

At the breakfast table that morning, Aunt Rebecca asked Bessie and Minnie to accompany her to St. —— Church, to listen to her loved pastor's eloquence and power.

The two girls gladly accepted the invitation, while Minnie regretted "that being in the city she would miss the 'meetin seed,' while the perfumes of peppermint and wintergreen would also be wanting."

She gave a roguish glance towards the demure face o sweet Bessie Brown as she spoke.

Dr. —— was unusually brilliant that morning. Powerful, grand, and deeply impressive were his remarks, and Bessie listened with the most devout attention and intense satisfaction. In truth Minnie had given her the greatest enjoyment, in thus bringing her where she could have an opportunity to listen to one of the finest orators of the day.

She was deeply impressed by the perfect stillness that prevailed—the reverence that seemed to fill all hearts for the time and occasion, so different from the bustle of a country church. Then the solemn tones of the organ, and the sweet voices of the choir, as they mingled in the chants of the Episcopal service, or united in singing the soul-felt hymns, all tended to gratify and please.

Beautiful indeed was the discourse that fell upon the ears of a silent and appreciative audience. Every sentence was filled with spirituality and thought. His descriptions of the abodes of the blest prepared by a loving Saviour, were replete with beauty and power, and the gentle invitation of Christ that all should come to him by faith, and obtain an inheritance among the blessed, was set forth with rare fidelity and sweetness. Then the tenderness with which he spoke to the impenitent, in concluding, the earnestness of this appeal to their hearts, was so fully evident that many an eye overflowed, and many a cold heart must have been touched.

Bessie left the church greatly refreshed in spirit; she had been hungering and thirsting after righteousness, and she had been filled. Feeling this, she silently thanked God 'or the instructions and comfort she had that morning re-ceived, and in an interesting conversation upon religious subjects with Mrs. Douglass, they passed the time until they once more reached Mr. Morton's residence.

CHAPTER XIII.

THE FIFTH AVENUE BALL.

SUPERBLY beautiful looked Minnie Morton on Tuesday evening, as, about quarter to eleven o'clock, she entered the parlor to wait for the carriage that was to take them to the long talked of party, given by Miss Susie Linden.

She wore a rich pink silk, with an overdress of point lace, while a necklace of pearls clasped with brilliants glittered upon her white and beautifully shaped neck. Her hair had been handsomely dressed by a skillful hair-dresser for the occasion, and white pearls contrasted finely with the rich dark folds of raven tresses in which they were entwined; while upon her round fair arms pearl bracelets also reposed, clasped with diamonds.

By her side, golden-haired Bessie Brown stood, arrayed in simple white tarlatan, with white half-blown rosebuds in her hair, and exquisite pearl ornaments also, upon her neck and arms. She seemed the personation of innocence and purity.

No excuse would Minnie allow against her accompanying her. One party she declared she *must* and *should* attend.

Mr. Morton was to attend Bessie, (Mrs. Morton not being able to go that night,) and a friend of Minnie's, a Mr. Oakland, was to be her escort, and as all were ready they entered the carriage, and in about five minutes approached the scene of festivity.

As it had commenced to rain about noon that day, and continued wet, an awning had been placed from the top of the front door running to the curb-stone, and a carpet also covered the pavement and steps. For several blocks the streets were crowded with carriages, and so great was the press that full fifteen minutes elapsed, before Pomp could approach to allow the ladies to alight.

The whole house was one brilliant illumination! As they passed into the doorway, the choice perfume of rare exotics greeted them, and on their way to their respective dressing-rooms, Bessie noticed here and there, stands, upon which were placed the most exquisite flowers.

Through the house, in every room, stood bouquets of these floral gems.

Leaving the dressing-room and rejoining the gentlemen, Bessie felt strangely timid at seeing so many bright faces; and such a display of rich attire, laces, flowers, jewels and ornaments of every description, quite dazzled her

Following the usher, they entered the crowded rooms, and after speaking to the host and hostess, and being presented to Miss Linden, they turned to a less frequented portion of the apartment.

Soon the band struck up a polka, and Minnie went whirling away in the fascinating mazes of the dance, encircled by the arm of Mr. Oakland.

Bessie watched them as they passed and repassed where she stood, and acknowledged that none excelled her friend in beauty of person, or gracefulness of motion.

Yet she shrank from seeing her thus clasped in the arms of that young man, whirling so recklessly around that crowded room.

It mattered not, that couple after couple of young m and maidens were occupied in the same manner; her pu heart revolted at sight of this disgusting, fashionab dance.

She was turning away with a sigh, when a voice at h elbow said—

"Good evening, Miss Bessie, will you not join th dancers, with your humble servant for a partner?"

"I do not dance, Mr. Percy, therefore will be but spectator to-night."

"Let us promenade in the hall, then, that is, if space wi permit. As we walk we can see into the room, and thu remark all that is worthy of notice." Placing her hand o his arm, he gently led her away.

"You must feel lonely here, a stranger among so many What shall I do to amuse you? I am entirely at you service."

"Tell me the names of some of these elegantly dresse ladies. For a beginning, the name of that queenly woma in black velvet, with point lace and diamonds," returne Bessie.

"That is the rich and aristocratic Mrs. Leland. She i a widow, and quite a shining light in the beau monde. Do you think her handsome?"

"Rather, but not to be compared with yonder exquisite little creature in white silk, with illusion overdress! She has quite a crowd of gentlemen fluttering in her train."

"That is Miss Colman, one of the most heartless and accomplished coquettes of the season. Many a young man has been dazzled by her beauty, captivated by her flatteries, and crushed after being won, by her scorn. Does she look so beautiful to you, now that you can read her true character?"

"Beautiful! No! far from it! Now, she is all glare and tinsel, her beauty has faded, and she seems merely a painted piece of vanity and frivolity."

"So I ever regard her," returned Percy. "A moth fluttering around a dangerous light, which must eventually *scorch* if not utterly *destroy.* See now her perfect antipodes! Notice that dark-eyed girl in blue; that is one of Philadelphia's sweetest gems. Retiring, pious, affable, and amiable, she is exactly *all* that the other is *not.* Very domestic in her tastes, she rarely mingles in the gay world. Nothing but her being on a visit of several weeks to Miss Linden could have induced her to make one in so gay a scene. Allow me to introduce you; I know you will be pleased with her; and then, as I see Miss Morton is disengaged, I will endeavor to secure her hand for the Lancers, just forming."

Bessie did indeed enjoy the companionship of Miss Dalton, and in an animated conversation that ensued she never noticed the lapse of time, until Mr. Morton approached to lead her to supper, at the same time that Mr. Percy offered his arm to Miss Dalton; Minnie, of course, being escorted, as etiquette demanded, by Mr. Oakland.

The supper was indeed a grand affair! Oysters in every mode, ice creams of every flavor, and confections of the choicest varieties. The centre pyramid was the admiration of all, and the smaller ones of frozen peaches and oranges proved equally luscious.

But to Bessie, the flying of the champagne corks, and the many glasses that were used of that fashionable beverage, by young girls and matrons, gentlemen of mature years, and the boy of sixteen, filled her with dismay and confusion. To her surprise and joy, however, she noticed that Minnie refused the sparkling drink, and also that

Percy did not join in the use of the dangerous liquo Mr. Morton, however, drank one or two glasses, whil young Oakland replenished his so often, that his mann changed perceptibly after its use, transforming him fro an apparently sensible young man into a silly rattlebrai foolish and disgusting in the extreme.

Poor Bessie was indeed shocked at this unexpecte phase of fashionable life.

And well might a pure unsophisticated heart shudde at the growing evil the love of intoxicating drinks is b coming in refined and polite society in our great citie especially in New York. The daily use of claret, cham pagne, and wines, upon a fashionable table, the free intro duction of this exciting poison to all kinds of festivities parties and weddings, is hourly increasing, and the effect are becoming more and more visible and glaring.

Young and old alike, often become infatuated with th social glass, and thousands of blooming youth, beautifu womanhood, and even the brilliant talents of matur years, are this moment fast hurrying to the drunkard's grave.

Can naught be done to stay the ravages of this dread destroyer, drink? Reader, is there nothing you can do to stop the current of this wrong? Are you a mother? have you no word of warning to utter to your heedless children, against the use of this infatuating poison? Are you a sister, or a brother, frequenters both of scenes of gay revelry and pleasure, and cannot your refusal to quaff the sparkling beverage, that passes so gaily from lip to lip, have its influence for good? Or, fonder still, are you the one chosen dear one of a noble heart—noble, yet rushing thoughtlessly to ruin, by a glittering yet slippery road, and can *you* not whisper one word of entreaty, before it be too late?

Reader, dear timid reader, let me earnestly entreat you to go and do what you can, to destroy this sinful practice. For the sake of God and of humanity, stretch out your arm, if it save but one poor deluded soul by the effort.

Be thankful if, by any chance, you save even *one* precious soul!

They returned to the parlor after supper, and then the band soon recommenced a lively air, and the German was the excitement of the next few hours.

Bessie became heartily weary before the party broke up, and she was permitted to bid Mr. and Mrs. Linden, with their daughter, good night.

As she re-entered the dressing-room to obtain her carriage wrappings, she looked at her watch, and was not at all surprised at the lateness of the hour.

It was three o'clock!

CHAPTER XIV.

MRS. DOUGLASS

"The heart knoweth its own bitterness."

"A merry heart maketh a cheerful countenance: but by sorrow of the heart the spirit is broken."—PROVERBS.

THE remainder of Bessie's visit passed more quietly, yet to her, far more pleasantly. At her urgent request, she was permitted to remain with the lady to whom she had taken such an unaccountable fancy. Many a delightful hour she passed in her quiet apartment, while Minnie attended matinées, or, of an evening, gay theatrical performances, both public and private; while many large parties, several of which were in fancy dress, claimed the thoughtless girl's attention. What an amount of time was consumed in collecting and preparing dresses for these different occasions, and what an outlay of money was necessary to prepare for each separate affair, could not but be observed by sweet Bessie Brown.

In the meantime she became deeply attached to the widow, so beautiful, intelligent and pious, and she looked forward to the daily visit to her apartment, as among the greatest charms of her stay. She found her a woman of the highest culture, uncommonly accomplished, and one gifted with conversational powers, unequalled by any person she had ever met.

Then she was a fine musician.

Often when the conversation would flag, to please her young friend she would seat herself at the piano, and play and sing until Bessie almost imagined herself in another world, surrounded by influences marvellous and holy; then wearying of that, she would take her guitar, and touch the strings, in strains exquisite, yet full of soul and passionate earnestness.

Often on these occasions would the eyes of Bessie wander from that lovely face, that delicately pencilled brow, and perfect features, so beautiful, so entrancing, to the portrait hanging over the mantel, which was a striking one, taken when but seventeen, and the exclamation "bewitching," had almost escaped her lips at meeting a half roguish look in the full hazel eye, and the smile that lingered around the most exquisite mouth and lips she ever painted even in fancy's dream. Yes, the beauty of that portrait was almost dazzling, and none that ever gazed at those sunny auburn ringlets, shading a brow of infantile purity, ever turned away without a second look, or low exclamation at its loveliness. But now, there was lingering about Mrs. Douglass a certain something Bessie could not account for; a sadness peculiar to herself, or a more thoughtful expression than is usual, together with this wish for retirement, that was mysterious to the young girl's buoyant spirits, and so, as she listened to her rich full voice, and marked her small white hand touching those strings, she felt that she was charming in her seclusion, charming in her quiet room.

"You are very fond of music, I see, dear Mrs. Douglass, and without flattering, I can say you are the finest amateur performer I ever listened to, *save one.* Oh, how I wish you could hear Cousin Paul in some of his enchanting arias. You are so passionately fond of music, I know you would be charmed."

Bessie did not notice the face of Mrs. Douglass, as she said these words, nor see the paleness that overspread her brow.

"Who is that cousin you speak of, dear?" at last issued from the paling lips of the widow.

"No relative in reality," returned Bessie, "but a dear friend of papa's. Paul Russell is his name. He is in Europe now, but I can never forget his exquisite musical composition. He composes nearly all he plays."

There was no reply! The head of Mrs. Douglass remained bowed over the strings of her instrument, but her lips were colorless, and her hand trembled as she sought to adjust the strings.

"Sometimes," Bessie continued, "his music is so mournful you would think it the wail of a broken spirit; then again so tender and so loving you would be sure he addressed some idolized being, some darling of his heart, yet it could not have been so, as Cousin Paul has never married, and this has continued for years."

No reply—save a long, distressed sigh; then suddenly Rebecca Douglass arose with a face pale as death could be, and throwing down her guitar, she slowly approached the window, which she sought in vain to raise.

"You are deadly pale, Mrs. Douglass! Faint, I fear! sit down and I will raise the sash!" Then hastily seizing some eau de cologne, she applied it to her pallid brow.

"I am better now, dear. It was but a momentary faintness to which I am subject! I am sorry to have alarmed you!"

"I am glad to hear you speak again! Ah! the color is

turning! Lie down awhile, will you not, until you are ıite yourself?"

"There!" said she, throwing a handsome affghan over ɜr reclining form, and pressing a kiss upon her white ırehead, "now I will leave you for a quiet sleep, which ill certainly restore you!"

She left the room as she spoke, and as the door closed pon her retreating form, the small white hands of Mrs. ouglass were clasped half distractedly together, while ith a broken sob, and a gush of tears, the words burst om her pale lips,

"O God! in mercy forgive thy wretched child!"

CHAPTER XV.

THE JANUARY RECEPTION.

"BESSIE," exclaimed Minnie, one day, as she entered her room through the passage leading from her own, "I claim your company a while this morning! It is Mrs. Oakland's January reception day, for ladies only, and of course we must go."

Bessie expressed herself pleased with the proposal—and one o'clock was the hour appointed for their leaving home.

One o'clock came, and both girls looked lovely as, dressed in exquisite visiting costume, their bright young faces radiant with smiles, they stepped into the carriage and drove to Waverley Place, there to pay their devoirs to the lady mentioned.

Several carriages had but just driven away to make room for others, after leaving their fair occupants at the door, so taking the place vacated, Pomp reined up his handsome horses at the entrance of an elegant residence, and the ladies, alighting, soon entered a parlor well filled with richly dressed, and some of them beautiful females. Passing quietly through each group, followed by Bessie, Minnie made her way towards Mrs. Oakland and her three daughters, Ida, Mary, and Kate.

After speaking awhile to each, they stood aside, Minnie recognizing, as she did so, several ladies of her acquaint-ice. Among the number were Mr. and Mrs. Linden, and iss Dalton.

Bessie was pleased to meet one she so much admired, id a few moments of pleasant conversation ensued, which as interrupted by a servant offering them chocolate and ke.

After partaking of these refreshments, Minnie and essie bade Mrs. Oakland and her daughters adieu, and -entering their carriage were soon at home.

On the whole, Bessie had passed a very pleasant morning.

In the evening young Oakland and Charles Percy ain called, and before they left invited the ladies to accompany them to Delmonico's for oysters and ice cream.

The walk down Broadway was delightful, well wrapped they were in warm cloaks, and furs. While walking eside Mr. Oakland, Bessie noticed the high spirits of Minie as she leaned on the arm of Charles Percy, and the ish filled her heart, that they might be chosen partners r life.

She imagined things verging that way, but of course ould not foresee the end, but anyway she wisely conuded to watch the course of events.

So time rapidly winged its flight, and the period of Buse's visit drew to a close.

She began to dread her journey home, as, being totally nused to travelling, she feared the lonely route.

Mr. Morton was to place her on the cars at Jersey City, nd her father, whom she now longed intensely to see, ould meet her at the station.

There was not the slightest source for timidity, yet she id feel a strange dread steal over her whenever she ought of it.

The morning came, cold, yet clear and cheerful.

Bessie was all in readiness, waiting the passage of b one short hour.

"Missy Brown," said Sambo, as he opened the door the sitting-room, thrusting first his woolly head, then l broad shoulders into the room, where he stood the pictu of indignation and injured self-respect, "dar am a gemm in de parlor gwine want for to see you. Mighty gra gemman too, I spect; couldn't gib a spectable culud puss he name, when he axed him. Spose he took me fur o ob dem debilish niggers, cos I got a black skin, and wool pate. Well, bress de Lord, hopes I'll be soon safe in glor and leave dis old carcass behind. Cussed old ting an how; dun kno what good it does to be so tarnal black- wish I had been sulted as to what culler I'd like to a be made; gess I'd a been white nuff den. Ki! yi!"

"A gentleman for me!" exclaimed Bessie, as sh smoothed her face after the laugh occasioned by po Sambo's explosion, and prepared to descend to the waitir person, whoever he might prove to be.

As she entered the parlor, a manly voice exclaimed, "M own darling!" and a pair of arms drew her in a fond en brace.

"Papa, you dear, dear papa," almost screamed the youn girl in her wild delight, as she clung to the neck of he loving parent. "O, how glad I am to see you!"

"And I to see my own pet once more! I have had lonely time without my Bessie." Then fondly kissing he again, he drew her to a seat beside him.

"So you came all the way to meet me instead of merel to the station, you dear good man?"

"Yes, I could not think of your returning alone, s supposing a surprise would do you no harm, I came on Are you quite content to turn your face homeward now my darling?" added he, passing his hand caressingly over her golden hair.

"Yes indeed, papa! I have had a delightful visit, but I am quite ready to return, and I know you are quite as ready to have me."

The Morton family all rejoiced in Mr. Brown's arrival, as they had noticed Bessie's timidity, and sympathized, therefore, heartily in her joy.

The adieus were soon spoken, Minnie promising to write often, everything that transpired, and amid kisses and caresses, they tore themselves away.

Their arrival at Cedar Lawn was warmly welcomed by housekeeper and servants, and as Bessie again entered her own neat and tasty apartment, she was happy in being there, and whispered to herself often through the day,

"Be it ever so humble,
There's no place like home."

CHAPTER XVI.

MINNIE MORTON TO BESSIE BROWN

"Thine own friend, and thy father's friend forsake not."—PROVERBS.

NEW YORK, *July* 15*th*, 1864.

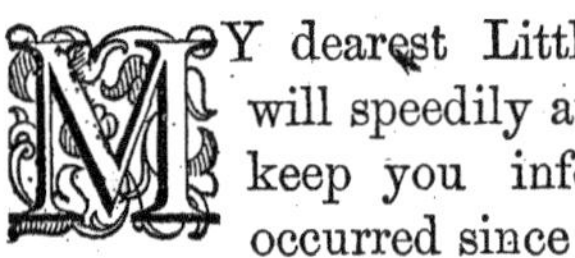

MY dearest Little Dork, according to promise, I will speedily answer your loving questions, and keep you informed of the events that have occurred since I wrote you last.

How can I tell you of mamma's declining health? She is anything but well! The protracted heat of June, so unusual, quite prostrated her, and Dr. Lee strongly recommends the sea-side and salt water bathing. Papa has decided, therefore, to leave this city for Philadelphia, pass a few days there, then on to Cape May.

I am to accompany them, and as several of my young acquaintances will be at the latter place during the season, I anticipate unbounded pleasure.

I wish dear Aunt Rebecca could be persuaded to make one of the party; but to all our pleadings she turns a deaf ear. Nothing can induce her again to visit a fashionable watering-place. You would be surprised to know how much she needs a change of air. She seems very feeble—not exactly sick, yet certainly she has undergone great prostration of strength, and general debility. Dr. Lee tried to persuade her to accompany us, but in vain, so she will remain in the home during our absence, and Mrs. Smith, an experienced nurse mamma has for years employed in sickness, will stay with her; thus, as the servants are long tried and faithful, she will have little care and perfect quiet, which last she thinks indispensable in her present state.

"Sambo," said mamma to that worthy individual this morning, "you will take good care of Mrs. Douglass while we are gone, won't you?"

"Yes ma'am, missus, sartin sure I will; and if one ob dem debilish niggers speak one disrespectful word to dat angel ob light, if dey don't see stars, its jus cause de arm ob dis yere chile has lost its cunning! dat's a fact!"

"Why, what would you do, Sambo?" asked mamma, simply to draw him out, for we all love to hear him talk.

"Do! missus, do? set em a-kiting as sure as my name's Sambo Johnson; make em beg for quarters down on dare nigger bones. Golly! if dey don't say prayers mighty quick den, I don't know beans, dats all. Ki! yi! But Missus, I specs deal ob trouble wid Pomp. Dretful sassy limb, dat Pomp, and pears to me he gets worser and worser ebery day. De imperdent dog told me dis blessed mornin, 'Sambo,' said he, 'you nebber get to hebben long as you lib!"

"'Specs not,' says I, 'but specs to when I die, fast nuff.'

"'Yes! nigger hebben, but not to white folks hebben let me tell you! You only see de cellar kitchen ob him."

"Now missus, I hit him a crack for dat, longside his sassy pate, but I keeps tinkin on it eber since, and pears like I can't stan it long. What *you* say now—is dare two hebbens up dare? cause if dere is, I don't know what's to become of dis poor chile; if I can't go wid de white folks, I'll neber go wid dem debilish niggers no how! so I specs I shall have to roost wid de chickens on de fence, all thro' eternity."

"No Sambo, not at all. Pomp did wrong to tease you. There is only one heaven and one God. You are just as welcome to go to that heaven as any one else," returned mamma.

"De Lord be praised for dat!" almost shouted the poor fellow, and he went back to the kitchen all smiles, singing,

"I'm bound for de land ob Canaan.'

As you may imagine, a jaunt to so gay a place, requires quite an outfit, so I can assure you I have been very busy; shopping, attending to dressmakers, and packing, requires time and patience. Happily I am through, only bringing such matters to a close, leaves me very tired. We start early to-morrow morning, and as I wish to tell you something of our arrival, I will place this sheet in my portfolio, my portfolio in my trunk, and finish at another time.

PHILADELPHIA, July 16th.

Seated in a large and cheerful room in the Continental Hotel, although late, I will occupy a few moments in telling my darling Bessie of our safe arrival. Mamma was quite fatigued when we reached Kensington Depot, and as several moments elapsed before the baggage had been attended to, and a carriage secured, I felt very anxious on her account. As soon as she was in her own apartment, however, she sought a short sleep, which refreshed her. Dear mamma! I hope I can soon write that she is well, perfectly well.

This afternoon we took a stroll down Chestnut Street, and were amply repaid by seeing the crowds of fair Philadelphia ladies, many of whom we considered very beautiful. We walked as far as Independence Hall, and entering, we ascended the winding stairs of this celebrated building, and from its top, obtained a splendid sight of Philadelphia and its surroundings, and certainly we could not but be pleased with this magnificent view, of a magnificent city. Returning, we strolled up Walnut Street, and were charmed with the neatness and beauty of this, the Fifth Avenue of the place.

July 17*th.*—To-day we visited the United States Mint, and papa was much interested in the process of coining. The gold room was especially attractive, and we held bars of that precious metal, worth 1500 dollars, in our hand at once. After registering our names, and examining the coins and curiosities, some of very great antiquity, there on exhibition, we left, much gratified with the visit.

On our return, we dropped into the Academy of National Sciences, on Broad Street, and spent about two hours, examining a most wonderful collection of stuffed animals and birds, while the mummies, skeletons, and skulls of different races of mankind, as well as skeletons of wild beasts, were strange and interesting. But by far the most entertaining specimens of the collection, were found in the room appropriated to ornithology. Here, thousands of birds, of every size and variety, delighted the eye, while their many colored and brilliant plumage was beautiful beyond description. Flamingo, swan, ostrich, and eagle, were but a few of the large kind, while of the smaller, from the magnificent bird of paradise, to *hundreds* of various species of humming-bird, a more rare or perfect collection of the "feathered race," can never be found, than is inclosed within those walls.

In the afternoon we rode to Laurel Hill, a sweet and charming spot on the banks of the Schuylkill, fully equal to our anticipations, but by no means equal, in natural scenery and manificence, to our own favorite Greenwood.

So you see we have been busy indeed, sight-seeing,

during our short but pleasant stay in Philadelphia, the City of Brotherly Love!

I am very weary, Bessie dear, so much so, that I would fain bid you a fond good night. To-morrow, we have a few more spots of interest to visit, such as Girard College, Moyamensing Prison, etc., and then—ho! for the old Atlantic.

MINNIE.

CHAPTER XVII.

MINNIE TO BESSIE

"Where does the water dwell, powerful and grand?
Here where the ocean foam,
Breaks, in its rock-ribbed home;
Dashing and lashing, up-bounding, wrath-spanned,
Anon, sweetly sleeping,
Soft dimples o'er creeping,
Like a babe on its mother's breast, soothed by her hand."

By the Sea, *Aug.* 1*st.*

ARE you angry, pet mine, at my long and unaccountable silence? Two weeks in this charming spot and not one whisper to Little Dork, to remind her of my unwavering love, or to tell of my deep and soul-felt happiness.

"Yes! darling. I have something sweet to tell you; something that causes my heart to flutter, and my cheek to flush, as I write.

Dearest, can you guess the secret?

But why anticipate? I will chronicle the facts as they have transpired, and then leave you to imagine my deep joy.

We arrived at Cape Island safely, and soon felt at home in Congress Hall.

Our apartments are very small, yet comfortable, facing the ocean.

The view of the mighty sea, from my window, is superb and the roar of its dashing waves nightly lulls me to repose.

Sometimes I sit entranced, watching the huge swell of the billows, as they gather in the distance, coming nearer, and nearer, the white foam on their crested heads glittering in the sunlight like so many brilliants, then curling themselves for one grand effort, they rise higher and higher to dash upon the shore with a mighty leap, and in a moment disappear, only for another equally large, equally sparkling, to take its place.

Then the charming walks upon the sandy beach, at the hour when the moon rises so grandly, hovering in a ball of clear bright brilliance in the starlit sky, throwing the most beautiful rays upon the rolling waters, making long streams of amber, sparkling jewels, and dazzling light as they stream around, how can I describe them?

Sometimes the ocean seems a sheet of liquid gold, then again one solid chain of diamonds, and once more, green, blue and orange, rival each other on the bosom of the waves, while afar off, gleams a light from Cape Henlopen, over the sea, and a little farther down the beach the beautiful revolving light, from the Light-house on the Island, sheds its mellow ray.

Sometimes, weary of wandering, we turn to the beautiful Columbia House Pavilion, and ascending the steps, seat ourselves to watch the splendor of the night, and the majesty of the starlit sea.

Oh, Bessie, my friend, how I wish you were here! I know your pure, pious heart would swell with gratitude to God, while gazing at his wonders on the deep. I imagine exactly what you would say. I can see exactly the holy light that would illuminate your brow, could your eyes but rest upon these scenes.

Ah! why am I so different? Why so reckless, and so absorbed by fashion and frivolity! To night. I would I were a Christian!

The bathing is delightful, and as all the hotels are crowded, the beach presents, at eleven, a gay and striking scene.

Crowds of carriages filled with spectators are standing around, while hundreds stroll on foot to enjoy the sight.

Out as far as the Bar, are myriads of bathers, laughing, shouting, and full of merriment, while the grotesque and varied costumes make the spot a perfect carnival. On the beach, some in bathing dresses gaily trimmed, are running towards the water; one laugh, one spring, and the waves clasp them in their close embrace. Then again some bather is just emerging from the sea, dripping, laughing, with streaming hair from which big drops are falling; ashamed, yet full of fun they scud along to the bath-houses, glad when the gauntlet of hundreds of eyes have been safely passed.

I love our daily dip in Neptune's foamy bed! I love to feel the water dash over my form, to give the spring with each heaving billow. Mamma enjoys it also. She is gaining strength rapidly, and each bath invigorates and renews her hitherto sinking system.

Yesterday about four, after we had enjoyed our bath, had a refreshing sleep, dressed and dined, I met papa upon the hall of the second story, who requested me to repair to the parlor, as a friend wished to see me.

Little dreaming of the glad surprise in store for me. I tripped lightly down, but not before I caught a quizzical look in papa's dark eyes.

As I entered, for a wonder, the parlor was vacant, with the exception of a single gentleman who stood with his back toward the door, by the piano, looking at some music.

I had nearly reached his side before he turned, and then I saw——Charles Percy.

How bright and happy he looked, as he took my hand in his, not seeming to notice the deep blush, I felt was sweeping over my cheek and brow.

"I was so lonely without you, Miss Minnie, that I could not refrain from following to this distant spot. Am I welcome?"

"Indeed you are; I cannot express my pleasure and surprise," I returned, in tones scarcely audible, for my heart was in a strange flutter, and my voice trembled with excitement.

He had never clasped my hand so tenderly before, never had I seen the look that then met mine in other days, and a thrill of joy rushed through my soul, at the thought that now he felt, as I had long wished that he might feel! Bessie, darling, was I not happy?

Others entering the room, we seated ourselves for awhile conversing on events that had transpired since we parted in New York; then, as the grounds looked shady and inviting, he proposed walking around their large and extensive limits.

That night there was to be a hop in the ball-room of our hotel, and as I was to be present, Percy promised to be there. As I re-entered the hall, Percy again took my hand in parting, and again a gentle pressure was felt upon my fingers, and a deep, earnest, tender look, flashed from his eyes to mine as he turned away to return to the Columbia House. where he was staying.

I dressed for the hop with uncommon care that night, and as I clasped my white silk, with its fine lace over-dress around my bounding heart, a sigh of deep satisfaction burst from my lips.

My fingers trembled too, as I placed white flowers within the black folds of my hair, and fastened ornaments upon my wrists and neck.

They trembled, but not in grief! no! what then?

Could the emotion that caused that fluttering, be love?

I enjoyed the evening vastly; Percy was my partner in almost every dance; he was by my side from the moment of my entrance, and I was contented that he should be there.

Once, as we whirled in a gay mazurka, he whispered in my ear,

"Would that my arms could ever be your support, sweet Minnie, as now, in the mazes of this dance!"

Dear Bessie, I can never describe the glad joy those words occasioned, for be it softly whispered, I have long *loved*, Charles Percy.

"Will you ride to Diamond Beach with me to-morrow, at nine, Minnie?" whispered he, as I bade him good night at the close of the entertainment.

I consented and drawing my hand from his, I ran eagerly to my room to still the tumult that reigned in my bosom, in solitude, and silence.

The morning came bright and sunny, and as Percy handed me into the buggy and lightly sprang to my side, he gathered the lines in one hand, but the other stole into my lap, and mine was a prisoner.

Scarcely one word was spoken in that four miles drive, but I knew that there never was a happier heart than my own, nor am I wrong in adding, that *his* also was filled with deep and heartfelt joyfulness.

He tied the horse at the top of the hill after lifting me to the ground, and drawing my hand within his arm, we descended to the beach, that justly celebrated spot.

And there, with the white waves dashing, singing, chanting on the one side, the high bank, with its countless millions of diamonds and many colored stones covering its whole front on the other; standing on a sandy beach, with myriads of shining Cape May gems under our feet, we whispered our first vows of love and devotion, and solemnly plighted our troth.

Yes, Bessie, I have promised to be Percy's wife, and when the hour comes that unites us, may I not claim the fulfillment of your promise, given in our school days, that you would be my first bridesmaid?

Remember I shall look for you there.

MINNIE.

CHAPTER XVII.

LEONI MARETTZI.

"For with what judgment ye judge, ye shall be judged; and with what measure ye mete, it shall be measured to you again."—ST. MATTHEW.

"AUNT REBECCA," said Minnie, one day about three months after her return from Cape Island, as she bounded into Mrs. Douglass' room, where that lady was sitting engaged with her needle-work, "how I wish you could have seen Charley just now! he had the blues so dreadfully, and as you could never guess the cause, I will tell you. Last night we passed the evening at Mrs. Austin's, in Twenty-second Street, and just to see how the 'green eyed monster' would affect Charley, I flirted desperately with her son, that handsome Arthur. All for sport, you know, for I do love Charley dearly; only a harmless flirtation! The effect was splendid, I assure you—the poor fellow was as jealous as I could wish, and he has not recovered his spirits yet."

Laughing heartily as she spoke, at the remembrance of the sad face she had parted with, a few moments before, Minnie, glanced at her aunt, but her gaiety was instantly checked by seeing that her face was colorless as marble, while her frame was in a perfect tremor, so deep was her emotion.

"Aunt Rebecca, dear Aunt Rebecca, what is the matter? What have I done to cause this agitation?" exclaimed Minnie, as she bent over her, alarmed at the singular emotion of her usually calm, although pensive relative.

"Minnie, my dear child," said Mrs. Douglass after awhile, when she had governed her feelings to a certain extent, "you know not the horrors that one word flirtation ever throws over my heart; the long train of remorseful recollections it ever brings to my mind. Minnie, never, as you value the love of Charles Percy, as you value your own happiness through life, never again suffer yourself to be led into a flirtation. If you would avoid the misery that must ever haunt the life of Rebecca Douglass, if you would avoid the nights of sleepless remorse, the years of agony that have withered her heart and feelings, despise being a flirt! despise what you have just styled 'a harmless flirtation.' Harmless! it has been the bane of my existence! harmless! yet the willful wounding of another's affections have made your aunt *twice a murderess.*"

She paused, while large tears stood upon her eyelashes, as she leaned her pale cheek upon her hand, then motioning for her to go, she whispered.

"Come to me in one hour;" and with her words and looks still vividly before her eyes, Minnie withdrew, until the appointed time.

The hour had passed, and twenty minutes more glided slowly on, before the door of Mrs. Douglass' room opened to summon Minnie to her side again; but as she entered, the traces of tears, as well as the pallor of her cheeks, told that her agitation had been of no trifling character.

"Minnie dear," said she, as, after seating her by her side, she had placed two miniatures upon the table before her;

"I know your curiosity, as well as surprise must have been excited by the words I uttered a little while ago, and although it will be a painful task for me to unfold the history of my past life, still it may prove a warning, and save you many sad hours; therefore I feel that I must sacrifice my dread, and relate those events for the sake of the good that may result from the history. Oh, remember, darling, when you see me in a new and guilty light, remember that from the depths of a burdened soul, from the recesses of a broken heart, I have repented—bitterly repented; and I trust that guilty though I have been, God, in his great mercy, has forgiven me. While, therefore, I relate the distressing recollections that cluster around me, my prayer shall be that the future life of my niece may bear the imprint of no such dark clouds, and that not even a shadow of jealousy may ever glide between her future husband and herself."

She paused, and after a moment of deep thought, continued:

"I was, as you already know, an only daughter, and many years had passed away after the birth of my only brother and your father, before I saw the light, and when I did, it was to become the pet and darling of the whole household. My parents resided then, and indeed until my eighth year, in the lower part of New York city, as this was in those days its most fashionable portion. At that time we removed to St. Mark's Place. I was still very young when I began to receive attention as a young lady, from the numerous visitors at my father's house, and when not yet sixteen, I had made several conquests; for even at this early age, I gave evidence of being a decided coquette. I had flirted with my cousin, Albert Graham, a young student at Columbia College, until I had brought him in despair at my feet, only to laugh and ridicule his distress, as I told him I had no love for him. I had glanced at a handsome youth, living directly opposite our residence, and had carried on a long flirtation with him from my window, until, after bowing several times in Broadway, he had joined me in my walks, and attended me home, and after visiting the house every day for two weeks, he had made me an offer of his hand and heart, only to be refused, with great apparent indignation at his presumption, but in reality with secret triumph at my own success in winning hearts. But, Minnie, those were as nothing to the deep, dark flirtations of my after life, when, although but eighteen, I was the acknowledged belle and beauty of New York.

I was leaving the breakfast table one morning when my father detained me a moment by asking—

"If I ever saw the young Italian singer, Leoni Marettzi?"

"No, papa," was my reply to the question; "but I have often heard him spoken of, with the warmest praise."

"Well," said my father, "I engaged him yesterday, to give you lessons on the guitar. Poor fellow! he labors hard at his profession, and supports his mother and two sisters by his musical talents. He is not long for this world, I suppose, as he has bled at the lungs several times, and the hectic on his cheek, with his hacking cough, tell too plainly, that consumption has already a deep hold upon its victim. I could not but feel sad, as a friend related to me his history, and so I sent to engage his services for you! he will be here to-day to give his first lesson."

I smiled as I left the room, and was very happy all that morning, for I had often heard of the young Italian, of his splendid musical powers, as well as the singular beauty of his face, and the hours seemed to hang heavily on my hands, so eager was I to meet my new teacher. I could not account for the interest I felt in the young man's story, or for the care I bestowed upon my toilet that morning, or the many times I consulted my glass, to see if every ringlet was placed in the most becoming position, and if every article of my dress was in the most exquisite taste.

He came, and my heart beat tumultuously, as I met the deep beauty of those lustrous eyes, and marked the pale, yet perfect face of the young stranger, and even in that first glance, the determination stole into my heart that Leoni Marettzi should love me. I did not regard his feeble health, I did not heed the pale cheeks and hollow cough of the young man. I did not think of the mother and sisters left alone, in a strange land, of the effect a disappointed affection might have on his already weakened frame. I thought not of all this. I only thought of the triumph of making a conquest of the handsome stranger; I only resolved, nay vowed, that he should pay the homage of his love to my beauty.

I will not tell you how, day after day, I dressed and labored for this object; how, day after day, I sought to ingratiate myself into his affections, and all apparently in vain. He appeared to be above my reach! his thoughts seemed to be too far from earth, to think of the fascinations of a beauty; too high and elevated to be touched by her enchantments; and with a bitter disappointment, did I confess, at the end of two months, that but once or twice had I seen him give the least evidence of feeling my power, and then it was but in a passing glance, or his heightened color, as, in placing my guitar, he accidentally touched my hand, and that was all.

I was baffled, but I did not give it up.

I had gone down sooner than usual one day, after he was announced, and entering the room, I was surprised and inwardly delighted at his occupation. He stood with his back towards me, in front of my portrait, and seemed to be lost in thought, for he did not notice my entrance, or see me at all, until I stood beside him and had placed my hand softly upon his arm, and then he blushed painfully, and stammered, as he bade me good morning. It augured well, and my spirits rose in proportion. His visit that morning was unusually long, and I exerted every nerve to follow up the impression I saw that I had made. I sang my very prettiest; I gave him some of my softest looks, and sweetest words, and before he arose to leave me, I invited him to make one at my birthday party, that evening.

"It is my eighteenth birthday, and you must help me celebrate it," I said, in a low tone. I paused for a reply; it came, and I was disappointed.

"My place, Miss Morton, is not amid the rich and happy!" he said, with a deep sigh; "I am but a poor music-teacher, and my station is at my humble home, with my mother, and my sisters. No, lady! I must not come!"

"Leoni!" said I, in a reproachful tone, and blushing deeply, as I pronounced the name, for I had never called him this before—"Leoni, then you will mar the happiness of my whole evening. How cruel!" and my eyes filled with tears as I spoke, for I was bitterly disappointed.

"Miss Morton—Rebecca!" said he, seizing my hand, and pressing it passionately to his burning lips, "if I dared to think that my poor presence was—" he stopped, for my father's step was heard, but the look of joy he gave me, as I returned the pressure of his hand, before withdrawing mine, can never be forgotten.

"You will come to my daughter's party to-night, Mr. Marettzi?" said my father, a few moments after, as he arose to go.

"Oh yes, certainly—with the greatest pleasure!" stammered the young Italian, as, bowing gracefully, he left the room.

"Poor fellow!" said my father; "his lot is so sad, I could not resist inviting him! Do be polite to him to-night, Rebecca! see that he enjoys himself for once, at least."

I was polite! yes, cruelly polite! I walked with him in the promenade! I spoke to him in my most winning manner, and I even declined dancing several times, for the sake of being beside him. Thus did the evening pass, and the happiness that sparkled in the eyes of Leoni, and the violent beating of his heart, which I could feel as my hand lay upon his arm, whenever his eyes met mine—told me he was happy, and also told me what I more wished to know, that he loved.

It was late, and I was standing in a recess, by the window, conversing gaily to my poor victim, when I saw my father approaching with a stranger, who had just arrived, and as I looked for the first time upon the manly and intellectual beauty of your uncle, (continued she, as she placed the miniature of a noble looking young man in Minnie's hand,) my heart bounded, and my color deepened, and from that moment, poor Leoni Marettzi was forgotten.

"Rebecca, allow me to introduce to you, the son of an old and valued friend! My daughter—Mr. Douglass."

I blushed again, as I bowed in return to his respectful salutation, and when, in another moment, I stood among the dancers with my hand in his, I was in a perfect tumult of excitement; for, from the first time I saw him, I resolved to win Clement Douglass. An hour passed away in his company, and while I listened to his words, so full of intelligence and thought, not once did I remember, or even turn my eyes towards Mr. Marettzi, who was still standing in nearly the attitude and place he occupied when I left him, eagerly watching my every movement; nor was it until, when standing alone for a moment, after the supper, he approached, and asked me to promenade, that I even recollected that there was such a person in existence. We walked up and down the splendidly lighted rooms a few times, and then, unnoticed by myself, for my thoughts were with Mr. Douglass, he turned from the crowd, and led me to the cool piazza, which was vacant and still, and after traversing it silently, for awhile, my companion surprised me by an eloquent and thrilling declaration of his love. He told me how he had come to me in poverty and sorrow—how from the very first he had loved, but how he had struggled against the feeling, knowing that the difference of our station and position in society would make an union impossible. Then, when he had succeeded in smothering his feelings into subjection, as he supposed, he told how I had bidden him hope, by my manner, and my smiles, and how, feeling that he was not indifferent to me, he had been led to tell of his devoted love, and to sue for a return.

Never could I describe the feelings with which I listened to those words, so long desired, yet now so worthless. Pride, remorse, triumph, and indignation, all struggled together in my bosom, and for an instant, prevented a reply; then, snatching away the hand he had taken, I gave him a look of the deepest scorn, and commanded him to cease, bidding him never again *insult* me by such words, and ended by asking how he dared misconstrue the kindness arising from the pity I felt for his *low condition*, into encouragement and love. Yes! I said those very words! I, Rebecca Morton. I forgot myself so far as to taunt a fellow creature with his poverty, after injuring him so deeply as I had done, and he, too, fast passing to the grave. Never shall I forget the look of agony he gave me, or the heart-broken tones of his voice, as he said,

"May God forgive you, Miss Morton, for trifling as you have done, with the feelings and affections of another, and may He spare you from ever undergoing such anguish as you have inflicted on me."

His face was almost ghastly as he ceased speaking, so deadly was his paleness, and with a quick motion he placed his handkerchief to his lips and turned away, but not before I saw that it was stained with blood. I could not speak, so deep was my alarm, but I sprang forward to detain him;—too late, he had gone, and I never saw him more. A couple of weeks passed by, and then I read his name among the deaths in a daily paper, but I was so deeply interested in Clement Douglass, that I could breathe but a passing sigh of regret, and then the sad and early fate of Leoni Marettzi was thought of no more.

Days glided on into weeks, and yet hourly was I becoming more and more infatuated with the intelligent Mr. Douglass, whose place was daily at my side, and who seemed to be equally pleased with myself; then, when the first words of love fell from his lips—when he first told me I was dear to him, it was with a proud and happy heart that I placed my hand in his, and whispered a blushing consent to be his own forever. Those were happy days that followed, for there was but one thought to cast even a shadow upon our hearts, and that thought was his unavoidable departure for South America, to be absent eighteen months previous to our marriage. The hours passed swiftly on, and then the day came that parted us for so many weary months, and with tearful eyes, and a heavy heart, I received his last embrace and kiss, and then he was gone, and I was sad, and oh, how lonely.

My parents had been much pleased with my acceptance of Mr. Douglass; they had become so accustomed to my "affairs of the heart," as they termed them, that they hardly knew what to expect as the result of my present infatuation.

Had I not not seemed equally infatuated with a dozen others to say the last?

When Mr. Douglass, however, waited upon them, formally requesting the hand of their daughter, assuring them that he had obtained her consent, they were delighted, as of all the gentlemen that had ever visited at their house, he was the only one they desired to call by the name of son.

He was in truth all they could ask for their idolized child. Of excellent moral character, son of one the first families in the country, and very wealthy, it was with unbounded delight that they had given their consent to our union.

They regretted exceedingly, however, his early departure for so long a time; they knew the failing of their child, and trembled when they thought of that separation, and with anxious and foreboding hearts they bade him adieu.

CHAPTER XIX.

LUCY RANDOLPH.

"Standing with reluctant feet,
Where the brook and river meet,
Womanhood and childhood fleet!"
LONGFELLOW.

"Softly!
She is lying,
With her lips apart,
Softly!
She is dying
Of a broken heart"

"YES, I was very lonely," continued Mrs. Douglass, "after my affianced husband left New York. My engagement had been quite widely known among my gentleman acquaintances in the city, therefore, one by one had left off visiting me, making quite a void after he sailed. In consequence of this falling off, I could not mingle much in the society of the sterner sex, and so found no opportunity to commence a new flirtation.

You look surprised! Could it be, you would say, that you would so forget yourself had you such an opportunity?

Ah, Minnie darling, how can I tell you the evil that lurked so many years in my guilty soul, the passion that caused such dreadful desolation? How true are the words of inspiration "the heart is deceitful above all things, and desperately wicked."

I had thought my love for Clement Douglass a pure and devoted affection, but after-events told that I was mistaken. His position in society—his great wealth, and excellent family, had not been without their weight. I respected him, and thought I loved him, but it was not the wild, consuming passion, that afterward overtook and enchained me.

Alas, poor Douglass!

A few weeks after his departure I received a pressing invitation from a young lady friend, to pay her a visit at her home on the banks of the Hudson; and as in the autumn she was to be united to a gentleman to whom she was ardently attached, making this my only opportunity of meeting her in her beautiful home, I gladly consented.

It was then on a lovely morning in June that I found myself upon a steamer, gliding through the waters of our own beautiful and far-famed Hudson, casting looks of wild and enthusiastic delight upon the magnificent scenery around; for I was a passionate admirer of the varied leaves of the book of nature, and was ever on the watch for the picturesque and the beautiful. But I will not linger to describe the well known scenes that meet the eye on a passage up the Hudson, nor will I stay to picture my arrival at "Silver Lawn," as the beautiful residence of Mr. Randolph was called, or the wild joy with which Lucy sprang forward to meet me.

Poor Lucy! I can see her now as she was then; the same sunny ringlets, the same blue eyes, and perfect smile, that you see in the miniature before you.

Ah! she was beautiful, and so pure and gentle in her manners! but poor child, could she have read the future, when she welcomed so warmly the arrival of Rebecca Morton, could she have seen the tears that arrival would cause, and the early grave—but I will not anticipate the evil that comes but too swiftly at best; so will return from my digression, to the Lucy that strove to entertain me, on that first day at Silver Lawn. She told me of her pleasures and amusements; she led me over their charming mansion, and then guiding me to a beautiful bower of roses, that stood near the centre of the garden, and commanded a view of the whole landscape around, she pointed to all the beauties that surrounded their home.

It was indeed a matchless scene that met my eye, when, following the direction of her finger, I gazed upon the pure white village church, where, from the tall old spire, the sweet toned bell announced, each Sabbath day, the hour for prayer and praise. It was a sunny afternoon! so calm, so still! the very blue upon the sky seemed to my excited fancy more pure and deep than ever; while the long rays of sunshine, as they quivered from that white spire to the green below, seemed to the heart that had bathed in its golden light, almost to burst from Heaven. But we could not linger long to gaze upon the sunshine by the village church, but turned our eyes to the grand old woods, that rose in lordly majesty behind it. Never, never did I see anything more charming than the contrast of the deep blue canopy, and the dark green shade that rested upon the waving leaves of the beech, and the ash, the walnut, and the mulberry, whose many branches were twined gracefully together, while

> "Mysterious whisperings,
> And sounds like half heard voices, dwell among them !"

How swiftly did they sway to and fro in the gentle breeze! how perfect was the form and color of each tender leaf, and then their shadows, as they were reflected on the tall grass, were truly beautiful!

"I love the leaves—who would not love such silent monitors?—
They wake a thought that far above all earthly feeling stirs;
They spring alike on fertile bowers, and on the barren tree,
Let others grasp the fruit and flowers,—the leaves, the leaves for me."

But we turned away from the old woods, too, after a long, lingering gaze, and allowing our eyes to wander down the road, passing the beautiful residences, that were sprinkled here and there; we lingered in ecstasy upon the splendid water-view so widely spread before us. Oh, how the water sparkled in the sun as it dashed along, now pausing in its course, lying peaceful and still for a second, then dancing up into graceful waves as they rushed onward, while the white foam quivered in the sunbeams, as they played upon the rising billows. Then came a vessel, with its snowy sails floating in the air; how gracefully she glided, like a white spirit through the water, riding upon the waves, while the spray played up against her sides, then dashed away as if in delight at their own airy movements. One could not help knowing, as he gazed upon the calm beauty of the scene, and the noble swell of the waters, that he was looking at the Hudson, —the beautiful Hudson, whose Highlands and Palisades have a place in our warmest affections, and to which the historian turns a glance of love and gratified ambition.

All this, did Lucy show me! all the beauties of the spot did she point out for my entertainment, and then, when all were seen, and the last word of delight had been spoken, then she passed her arm around me, and told of her love for one, whom for various reasons of my own, I will call Fay Leslie, although, dear Minnie, that was not his name. Yes! she told me of her deep trusting love; how he had won her by his gentle words, and low fascinating tones, and of the happy hours the future had garnered up for her when she should become his own dear wife. Then, when on glancing down the road, she saw the well known form approaching, her blue eyes sparkled with delight, and the rosy blush spread over her pure cheek as she welcomed the one she loved, and introduced him to the friend to whom she had given such strong proofs of confidence and trust.

Sweet Lucy Randolph! how was thy young confidence misplaced, and how cruelly was thy love and trust requited!

Shall I stop for one moment to describe the splendid man that now for the first time stood before me? Shall I tell of the very first thrill that went through my heart, as those large expressive black eyes were first bent on mine.

I cannot! O, I cannot! Would there were no more to tell! Would to God, Fay Leslie, that we had never met!

We walked back to the house together; Lucy and I both leaning on the arm of Mr. Leslie, who proved fully as interesting and intelligent, on acquaintance, as her loving heart had described him. I was delighted with this new companion, and the fund of information he possessed, with his polite endeavors to amuse the friend of his betrothed, made the day and evening pass rapidly away, and when I retired for the night, I lay awake some time thinking how pleasant it would be, to carry on a flirtation in that romantic spot, with the elegant lover of my friend, and how amusing to see poor Lucy jealous. I did not think of the consequences that might follow; I only thought of the amusement it would afford me during my stay, and with the firm resolve that I would carry out the thought on the following day, I fell asleep.

The morning came, and with it Mr. Leslie, and then my

sport commenced. I laughed, I talked, I sang, I played, throwing around me all the charms I had wielded so successfully to captivate Leoni, and exerting every effort to please, until I saw with delight that Mr. Leslie was beginning to be charmed, and that poor Lucy's eye began to look sad, and her young cheek to lose its bloom. Then, day after day, I followed up my well laid plans, overcoming every obstacle, employing every power, until I had the gratification of reaping some of the fruits of my endeavors, but sad to relate, I then made the discovery, that for the first time in my life, *I loved*. Yes! I, the affianced bride of another, fell passionately, deeply in love, with the future husband of my trusting friend.

Oh, the blindness of my folly! Oh, the perverseness of my frail heart! Why court the agony that has blasted my life forever?

At first the young man seemed to resist the snare that was woven to entrap him, seemed to gird himself in an armor that was invulnerable, but that only served to make me strive the more to conquer. Then the melancholy that had hung around him was dashed away, and like Leoni, he yielded, like Leoni, I knew *he loved*. If I sang, he was leaning enraptured over me. If I spoke, his eyes told the interest he felt in the most trivial word. If riding was proposed, I was the one lifted tenderly to the saddle, while Mr. Randolph attended to Lucy, and by my side, instead of hers, was the young man's station. If we were in the row-boat on the lake beyond the hills, to fish, it was my line that was attended to, my hook that was so nicely baited, while Lucy's success was unwatched and uncared for. Then, when upon the blue waters for the purpose of sailing, it was my head that was sheltered from the bright rays of the sun, and my smiles that were sure to please.

Thus weeks went by, and Lucy's cheeks grew paler, and her smile more and more sad; then we went out and came in alone, for Lucy was not well, and could not endure fatigue. Her head ached often now, while her step grew languid, but none could account for the change, none but myself. Leslie did not notice it; he did not look at the injured girl often, for his eyes and thoughts were ever with another.

At all this I rejoiced. It added to my triumph, and besides, I could flirt on now, without her pale face and sad eyes to reproach me, and the effect was full as apparent on our return.

We were sitting beside a window that opened on a piazza, one summer evening, watching the shadows the moon was throwing on the grass, while Lucy sat on the sofa a little distance from us, and although silent, with her hand supporting her head, I knew that she was listening to our words with eager attention, and with a fiend-like love for tormenting, I was unusual gay and agreeable. I had been singing, and my guitar lay silent on my lap for a moment, when Leslie suddenly took it and swept his fingers over the strings with a masterly touch that enchanted me. I was not aware that he played, or sang, and my delight and surprise was intense, while I hung enraptured upon the delicious sounds he drew from the instrument. He played several airs, until I was almost intoxicated with the bewitching melody, then pausing for a moment before he again touched the strings, he fixed his deep expressive eyes on mine, with a look full of meaning, which was distinctly visible by the light moon without, then sang with a voice full of thrilling beauty and power, these words:

Would I might tell thee, beautiful lady,
All the bright visions, I cannot control!
Would I might picture Love's fairest feeling,
Its lowest sigh, as it floats o'er my soul
Would I might tell thee, beautiful one,
How every heart throb is only thine own.

Dearest, I love thee! Dearly I love thee!
Scorn not the heart that is beating for thee:
Whisper one word, one little word only,
Lady, sweet lady, oh, listen to me!
Give one fond *look*, love, in answer to mine,
Dearest! this fond heart, is thine! only thine!

I knew not what I did! I was bewildered, fascinated! Lucy—Douglass—everything was forgotten, but that passionate look and song, and when, as the last word died away, Leslie leaned forward, as if to arrange the strings of the instrument, and whispered, "thine—only thine, Rebecca!" I could not still the violent beating of my heart; I could not keep the crimson color from my cheek, or withdraw the hand that he drew in his; and moment after moment passing, saw that hand still trembling in his own, and those dark eyes still bent upon my burning cheek. At length lights were brought in, and rising hastily, I changed my seat to one beside Lucy, and as I did so, I almost exclaimed at her brilliant color, and the singular brightness of her eye. "Come Lucy," said I, to cover my own confusion, "you have not played yet; it is your turn now; will you not sing one song, dear?"

I laid my hand on hers, as I spoke, but wondered, as I did so, for it was burning hot, and so was her breath. I drew back my hand again, in alarm, as I felt that feverish heat, and turned to ask if she were ill, when she sprang up with a low, excited laugh, saying,

"Music! sweet music! gay songs for the happy, and

love lays for the loving!" then crossing the room she seated herself at the piano, and sang in a clear full voice, a lively negro melody, then suddenly changing the notes, she sang, in a softer strain, one verse of "The Dream is Past," but her voice trembling, over the sad and truthful words, she paused—pressed her hand on her brow as if to soothe its throbbing, and then again, that clear, powerful voice rang on our ears, in the thrilling words and air of "Then you'll remember me!" Lucy's voice was always sweet, but never had I heard her sing like that before; usually it was low, and full of melody, but now, while all the melody remained, it was firm and powerful. Wilder it grew in its singular depths—stranger in its thrilling force, until Leslie and I both left our seats and stood spell bound by her side. Yet still those white fingers passed over the keys, still those piercing tones filled the room, and as the last words,

"Then you'll remember, you'll remember me,"

fell from her lips, she arose from her seat, and without even a glance at her wondering listeners, she glided from the room.

We did not notice where she went; we could not think of anything but that voice—and for some time, both were silent, but then Leslie spoke, and in a gay conversation that ensued, poor Lucy—her song, and her love, all were forgotten.

"What a charming evening," said Leslie, about half an hour after she had left us, "and how brightly the moon is shining through the trees of the garden! come Miss Morton, what say you to a stroll in its pleasant shades?"

I was pleased with the proposal, and we were soon walking arm in arm among the roses and the honey-suckles, enjoying the moonlight, and conversing in low tones, until weary of the winding paths, we turned in the direction of the rose-bower, and entering, sat down. We did not see the white form that was but a little distance from us, in the shade of the drooping vines; we did not hear the throbbing of that bursting heart, or see the wild eager gaze of the blue eyes that were fastened upon us, as we sat fully revealed in the bright moonlight. No, the words he was saying were too deep and thrilling; the ear they fell upon, too strangely infatuated with their guilty meaning, to heed all this; and there, encircled by his arm, with my hand in his, my head resting on his shoulder, and his dark curls almost touching my cheek,—did I sit, listening to those words of love, forgetful of my plighted faith to another—the breaking heart of my friend, everything but the heart beating so near my own, and the passing pleasures of the moment.

"And Lucy?" said I, in reply to something he had been saying.

"Lucy! ah, true! I had forgotten her; she will feel grieved for a while, probably, but she will overcome it, and perhaps eventually will marry young Morris Clay, who has loved her from boyhood. But think not of her, dearest; she shall not come between us, now that I know I am not indifferent to you. Oh, Rebecca! words cannot tell how I love you, words cannot paint— "

He stopped, for a loud, long, hysterical laugh fell upon our ears! another, and another followed, and whiter than the dress she wore, the form of Lucy Randolph stood before us, pale, motionless, and silent, save those strange, wild laughs, that burst from her bloodless lips.

"Lucy!" exclaimed Leslie, his voice trembling with alarm at seeing her thus; "Lucy, dearest, forgive me, and do not look so dreadfully!"

Yet still those laughs rang on.

"Lucy!" said I, filled with remorse at what I had done; "do listen to me! Indeed, indeed, I did not intend to wound you thus! You must not laugh so frightfully! Do stop, Lucy, and I will go to my home to-morrow, and never see Mr. Leslie again!"

In the greatest terror, I threw my arms around her, but she shuddered at the touch, and would have fallen, had not Leslie caught her in his arms, and thus borne her to the house.

I will not linger upon the week that ensued, nor tell how all that night, those wretched peals of laughter filled the house; how the next, a burning fever set in, and she, in her ravings, called repeatedly the name of Rebecca and Leslie, and wringing her hands frantically, screamed in agony, "Don't let them kill me! don't let them kill me!"

I will not describe the stupor that followed that wild delirium, nor my wretched feelings of remorse and despair, when, a week after that never to be forgotten evening, I stood weeping over her, and saw her pure, grieved spirit take its flight, leaving only a cold, white corpse in the place of the beautiful, injured, and heart-broken Lucy.

Oh, how I suffered then; how I wept and groaned in the bitterness of my spirit, and how I hated the very name of the man for whose sake I had become the murderess of my friend! Yes, her heartless, cold-blooded murderess!

I would not allow him to come near me! I would not listen to one word, and before the ground had hardened over her still grave, I returned to my home, there to weep anew, over the desolation I had wrought in a kind, and once happy family.

Minnie, it was a long, long time before I forgot poor Lucy, and that cruel flirtation!

CHAPTER XX.

THE MARRIED FLIRT.

"Unless you can swear, 'For life, for death,'
Oh, fear to call it loving!"

WAS married on my twentieth birthday; for Clement Douglass returned at the appointed time, and in making such a brilliant settlement, I was happy.

The three first years of my wedded life were passed in the country in retirement, and seclusion. No clouds marred their flight; no flirtations took place to disturb the happiness of either, and save the sorrow the remembrance of Leoni and Lucy caused me, I had nothing to give me a pang.

Those were happy days! too happy to last, for a change came, and then the passion that had but slumbered, burst forth anew.

Business made it necessary that my husband returned to New York; therefore a splendid mansion was erected for our accommodation on Thirty-first street, and I again became a resident of the city. But with my return to my native place, my love for display and admiration took their places once more in my bosom. The past was forgotten, and Rebecca Douglass was the gay, the brilliant, and the accomplished belle! but that was not all; she was that most despicable of characters—a married flirt.

At first, my husband accompanied me to the opera, the theatre, and the fashionable party, but now he remained at home with his books and studies, and young fops were seen beside me, and conceited Broadway frequenters were ever my attendants.

Thus two years more swept by; two years of dissipation—two years of folly—and two years of coldness and indifference, lay between my heart and my husband's.

I was at a splendid entertainment given by a fashionable friend, one evening, two years after my return to New York, and six since poor Lucy's early fate, and as usual, I had been surrounded by a host of admirers. I had been dancing, and feeling weary and warm, I stood for a moment near an open window, conversing with a young military gentleman, who had been extremely polite in his attentions throughout the evening; when, suddenly raising my eyes to the opposite side of the room, I met the glance of a tall, elegant gentleman, and with a start, I recognized the expressive features of Fay Leslie. It was the first time I had seen him since we parted at Lucy's grave, and my heart throbbed painfully, as my eyes fell beneath his look, while my face flushed to a perfect crimson when he approached and addressed me; but all the time he was speaking, it seemed as though Lucy's laugh rang still upon my ear, while her face, pale in death, lay before me, and my tongue refused its office, for a moment, so deep was my agitation.

"May I have the pleasure of your hand in the next cotillion?" asked he, in his own musical tones, after the first greeting; and in taking our places, I somewhat recovered my self-possession. We danced the quadrilles, then waltzed, and when, weary with the exercise, I motioned to leave the airy groups of pleasure-seekers, he led me to a vacant corner, and seated beside him, with his low, familiar voice in my ears, and his deep, expressive eyes on mine, returned my old fascinated feelings when in his presence, and my old love, and desire for his admiration. He referred not to the past! he never alluded to our former acquaintance, and yet, with all the assurance of an old friend, he gave a glowing description of his travels in a foreign land during the last six years, and of the different scenes he had witnessed, and the nations with whom he had mingled, and once more was I charmed and fascinated with Fay Leslie.

Days, weeks, passed on, and Leslie was ever by my side; at the opera, the theatre, in my rides, and in my walks, he was my shadow, and his presence was still to me a spell. Yet I was not happy, for my husband's care-worn face, and sad, thoughtful look, haunted me forever, and seemed always to follow my steps.

I was sitting on the sofa, one day, in my own parlor, and Douglass was beside me, reading. He had been more like himself that day, I thought, more affectionate towards his erring wife, for his arm was around me as he read, as in our early life, and ever and anon he looked kindly upon me, as of old. As we sat thus, silent and almost happy, in raising his arm to turn a leaf of the volume he held, a button of his sleeve caught in the gold chain I wore; but my mind being occupied with other things, I did not notice that the sudden jerk, had loosened a small locket I had in my belt, or that Douglass had perceived, and detained it. He arose soon after, and was leaving the room, as Mr. Leslie entered, and in turning to greet him, I caught a glimpse of my husband's face, as he disappeared, and was struck with its deadly pallor, and the peculiar look he gave me; but Leslie proved unusually entertaining, and I soon remembered it no more.

I had been playing, and was still seated at the piano, while Leslie was bending over me, when he surprised me, by saying, "Rebecca, I cannot endure this wretchedness longer. I cannot linger here, so cold and distant, while the songs you used to sing, and the voice I used to hear, still have the same power to thrill my heart, it had in days gone by! I cannot, must not bear it, and to-morrow sees me depart for distant lands, there to bear alone my lot so full of bitterness. I cannot be silent, dearest! I cannot conceal my love, even if you are the wife of another! Then chide me not, but suffer me to breathe it *once*, only once, before we part forever. Oh, Rebecca! the love I felt for you in times gone by, I feel with tenfold power still, and could I but hear you say, as once you said, that I was dear to you, could I but hear one word of love, to cheer my exile, I would leave almost happy! Rebecca, my idol, my all, tell me, do you still love me?"

I was startled at his words; I was overcome with agitation at the thought of his leaving me, yet a low murmured "Yes!" escaped my lips, and in a moment his arms were around me, and I was clasped in a passionate embrace, his lips meeting mine in a first fond kiss. We did not see the pale face that was gazing at us through the half open door, (as a pale face had gazed six years before;) we did not see the bowed form that rushed up the stairs, a moment after, and yet I knew that I was doing wrong, and with a shudder at my own folly, I drew myself away from his arms, and bade him leave me, adding:

"I never will see you again, Mr. Leslie, nor suffer another word of love from your lips!" Then, when he threw himself at my feet, imploring me "not to leave him thus, but to speak *one loving word* to cheer his absence," I burst from him with a sudden impulse, and fl d up the stairs; but before I reached the top, the report of a pistol from my husband's library made me dash forward with a wild scream, and throwing open the door, I stood horrified at the sight before me. My husband, my noble, my injured husband, lay covered with his own blood, *dead* on the floor.

I saw no more, heard no more, but with one wild cry of anguish, I sank back insensible into the arms of Leslie, who had sprung after me, when he had heard the report of the pistol, and my scream.

I knew nothing of the scenes that followed, for I was raving in a brain fever, for many, many days, and when, at last, reason was restored, and I began slowly to recover, the agony of my mind can never be realized, on opening a small package addressed to myself, and found in his room, containing a locket, in which was the miniature of Fay Leslie, and a note in which I read simply these words:

"I saw this locket fall from your chain: I saw you a moment since clasped in the arms of its original. Rebecca, I forgive you! Farewell!"

Minnie, I was a second time a murderess!

(Mrs. Douglass paused, while the great tears of sorrow fell from her eyes upon the miniature of her husband.

It was some time before she spoke again.)

I recovered, but I could never forget that awful scene! I wandered about like one stricken with years, and for a long time I prayed for death.

My brother, grieving over the state of his unhappy sister, persuaded me to make my home with him. Gladly I accepted the offer, as I had no father's roof to shield me, as both parents were sleeping in the quiet shades of Greenwood. Yes! gladly I left my lonely house, and came to this loving home, and here, in seclusion shall I pass the remainder of my days.

I said, a moment since, I prayed for death. God in his mercy did not hear the impious petition; although I often wonder that he did not strike me dead in an instant in just retribution for my mighty sins.

No! he suffered me to live! He suffered the pangs of remorse to cut so deeply into my heart that in an agony of repentance, I cried, "Lord what shall I do to be saved?" Then he led me to a faithful servant of Christ, who told me of the "Lamb of God, who taketh away the sins of the world;" who painted the Saviour, in his wonderful love, dying for my guilty soul, and from the bottom of my longing heart I cried—

"Lord, save, or I perish!'

Yes! he did forgive me, he did stretch out his hand for my salvation, and applying my Saviour's precious blood to my sin-sick heart, and throwing myself entirely on Jesus, I became, in believing, comparatively happy.

"And Leslie, dear aunt, what became of him?" asked Minnie, as she paused once more.

I never saw him again; but I received a letter from him about a year after my husband's death, offering me his hand and heart. I need not say that both were refused, and from that time the memory of my sinful trifling with poor Lucy's affections, and of my erring married life, served to banish from my heart every thought of his love of the world, or its pleasures.

I have now told you the history of my sad past, dear Minnie; I have laid open all my sorrows and temptations, and my prayer shall be that its reproachful records may prove a warning to protect you from the sin of trifling with the warm affections of another, and forever guard you from the dangers lurking in what the world so often styles, "a harmless flirtation."

CHAPTER XXI.

THE ANSWERED PRAYER.

"The eyes of the Lord are upon the righteous, and his ears are open unto their cry."—PSALM XXXIV. 15.

AFTER the death of Moreland, Paul Russell grieved as he had never before, over the death of any friend. Short as their friendship had been, it was warm in tenderness and love, and now, as he bent over the coffin of the only being on that side of the Atlantic, for whom he felt a deep attachment, a feeling of utter desolation and despair swept over his heart, and bowing his head upon his hands, he gave vent to sighs, mingled with tears.

"Oh Moreland," he uttered in his distress. "Where shall I ever find again, so faithful a friend? Who now will feel an interest in my poor soul?"

Pausing, the dying words of the departed came flashing back to his memory, together with his promise to immediately throw himself upon the mercy of God.

"Where," he exclaimed, "could I better perform that promise than by the silent body of the one who begged me to fulfill it? Oh Saviour," he added, throwing himself upon his knees by the side of the coffin. "Oh blooding, dying, Lamb of God, listen to my earnest cry for help, in this my hour of need. Poor, wretched—wicked, though I am, I cast myself entirely upon thee! Oh wash me in thy saving blood, and blot out all my sins, for they are full of blackness. Lord, I am sorry for those sins, and I do desire to lead henceforth a better life! Grant me, then, a knowledge of thy forgiveness—grant me a hope in thy salvation. Save me, oh blessed Saviour, for my only hope is in thee!"

So full an hour went by, yet still upon his knees wrestled the young man, in an agony of prayer, while the heaving bosom and tearful eyes bore evidence of his mighty earnestness.

Full an hour upon his knees, pleading for mercy by the coffin of his friend! then suddenly rising, with a new and holy light upon his brow, a joyful peace within his heart, his face radiant and hopeful, he exclaimed—

"Bless the Lord, oh my soul: and all that is within me, bless his holy name.

"Bless the Lord, oh my soul, and forget not all his benefits.

"Oh, I am forgiven; the Saviour, the precious Saviour is my own. Moreland, dear Moreland, how can I ever thank you? Here by thy coffin, dearest of friends, I solemnly consecrate myself to Jesus; solemnly devote myself, in body and spirit, to the work of my Heavenly Master. Oh God! I thank thee for this great peace that is filling my heart, the first this poor heart has known for years." Then again, throwing himself upon his knees, he poured out his soul in thanksgiving and praise, renewing his consecration of himself to the service of his Lord forever.

According to the dying request of Moreland, his remains were taken back to London, to be buried from the Church of which he was a member; the funeral services to be performed by the pastor from whose hand he had often received the sacramental bread and wine, and from whose lips the words of salvation had so often brought joy to his soul.

Paul accompanied the remains, never leaving the cold corpse of his now doubly prized friend, until he saw him lying peacefully by the side of his father and mother, brother, and young sister, the last on earth of a loving family, now fondly united upon the bright shores of an eternal heavenly home.

Russell returned to his hotel after the last sad rites had been performed, full of varied and solemn feelings. The words of the funeral service had deeply impressed him, while the deep affection and glowing terms with which the servant of Christ, Dr. Hartley, had spoken of the departed one, had brought tears to his eyes, and this wish to his heart:

"Oh that my last days might be like his! Oh that the mantle of Moreland might fall upon me, even poor unworthy me!"

He now seated himself beside a window, in his lonely apartment, to think over his future course, striving to plan the best way in which to work for Jesus, for this was now the first and foremost wish of his soul. Had he the means he would study for the ministry! In this pursuit he felt he should be happy. He could then divert his mind by his theological studies from any earthly vexations and trials that might beset him, and in due time spend his whole strength and energy in laboring for the salvation of souls. But now he realized sadly his limited means, and want of friends. He had but the very small income of a few hundreds, that had been left him by his parents at their death, and a travelling agency to which he had attended while in this strange land, had amply supplied his wants. Were he to commence the study of theology, this agency would have to be relinquished. What then would be done for his support? What would pay for his board and clothing?

Sadly revolving these thoughts in his mind, he again remembered the dying counsels of his friend, his earnest prayers for his salvation, and the firm belief he always indulged that he would eventually be brought to Christ. Thus dreaming, he casually remembered a small box which Moreland had placed in his hands about a week before he died, requesting him to keep the key safely, never opening it until after he was buried; then, when all was over, he wished him to examine it carefully, and act according to its wishes.

Rising as he remembered these charges, Paul opened his trunk, and taking from it the little box, he tremblingly applied the key.

As he raised the lid a splendid miniature likeness of Moreland first met his gaze; this he grasped with an exclamation of pleasure, and gazed long and tenderly into the loving blue eyes, now all that remained to symbol to his mind the features of his cherished friend. The small pocket Bible from which he had read the holy word of God, upon that never to be forgotten night in France, now lay beneath his hand, and lifting it with a tender smile, a business document next met his eye.

Upon opening this paper he was startled at these words. "The Last Will and Testament of Ernest Moreland."

What was the surprise and deep thankfulness of Paul Russell as, upon reading this legally drawn up document, he found that his cherished companion had bequeathed to him, his dearest friend, in the absence of all other heirs, the handsome fortune of two hundred thousand dollars, the remainder of his vast estate, he having made bequests to many different charitable institutions, all of which were named and specified in this last will and testament.

A letter also remained in the box, directed to himself, in which he again urged upon him the necessity of immediately becoming reconciled to God.

"Scripture has said, my own dear Paul," it continued, after thus pleading, "that the effectual fervent prayer of a righteous man availeth much." Remembering this, I have a full assurance that you will become a true and devoted Christian. I have prayed with tears for your salvation. I have wrestled hours in the silent watches of the night; pleading that my death may be the means of bringing you to Jesus, and I know that my prayers *will be answered.* My faith in Christ's ability to save is firm. He has promised, and He *will* perform. 'Ask and it shall be granted!' I have asked for the salvation of my friend, and I am certain God will hear my prayers.

Paul, I leave to you a small return for your kindness and devotion to me in my suffering sickness, and in the hour of my death. I leave it to *you*, because I love you, and because I feel that you will yet love and labor for my Saviour's precious cause.

My dear friend, when you obtain a full assurance of faith, when you know that your name is written upon the Lamb's Book of Life, will you not dedicate yourself to the work of the gospel ministry? Will you not obey the Master's commands, and "Go, work in His vineyard?"

With your pleasing address, your full, sonorous, musical voice, your eloquence and power in the use of language, and the devoted love for Jesus which I know you will yet possess, surely you will be a successful minister of God, and will labor acceptably for the salvation of souls.

Happy would the thought make me, that my portion of this world's goods would help educate and sustain one of my Saviour's faithful ambassadors.

If the day ever comes when you desire to enter the ministry, and I feel it is not far distant, consult freely my much loved pastor, Dr. Hartley, 24 —— Square, London, who will give you all needed advice and counsel.

Your devoted friend,

ERNEST MORELAND."

"Now God be praised!" exclaimed Paul, as the last word was read, and the last affectionate sentence examined. "How manifold are all His mercies! Dear precious Moreland, to pray for my salvation so earnestly, to pave the way so kindly for my following the desire of my heart, and the dictates of my conscience. Noble man! Surely this splendid fortune shall ever be dedicated to the work he loved so well, the Master's holy cause."

That very day saw Paul Russell in close consultation with Dr. Hartley, in reference to his being received into the church, by making a public profession of religion, and also in regard to the best course to be pursued for his immediate preparation for the ministry.

As it was now the summer vacation, when all the institutions were closed until later in the season, Paul, taking the advice of his old friend, Dr. Hartley, concluded to avail himself, by means of his late wealth, of the opportunity afforded by the interval that must elapse, before their reopening, to gratify an earnest desire to travel; therefore, after a few days spent in attending to the business of preparation, he started to make a tour of the Holy Land, and also of other parts of Europe which he had never seen.

CHAPTER XXII.

THE GIPSY CAMP.

"A moment may yield us a bliss without ending—
A moment consign us to darkness and woe!"

N the Eastern Continent, as well as upon the Western, large numbers of the gipsy tribe rove in small bands over the country, lurking on the borders of cities, where from their encampments they daily stroll to the city pavements to beg, steal, tell fortunes, sing ditties, or pick up a living, the best way they can. England is not exempt from the unprincipled rovers, and many a farm-house has been left minus turkeys, chickens, and ducks, when these people lurk around, while even the larger thefts of cattle, sheep, and horses, are of no rare occurrence.

On a bright, lovely afternoon just before sundown, in September, 1864, a party of gipsy travellers were passing over a rather lonely road, leading towards the city of London. Three large covered wagons, drawn by very jaded, weary looking horses, composed the train, while a number of swarthy men, and dark, coarse appearing women, dressed in fantastic, yet time-worn garments, were seated within.

Children, also, were there; for, as they passed along, fretful cries of little ones would be heard now and then, followed by sharp words and often blows, from the wretched parents, mingled with curses and bitter imprecations.

The centre of these vehicles could not but demand attention for its unusual and rather pretty appearance; it being, in reality, a small house upon wheels. It was well lighted by windows, and also possessed a neat little door, while at one end stood a comfortable looking bed, upon which lay a little girl in a deep sleep, unbroken by the jolts the wagon wheels gave as it passed over the rough road. The child seemed about seven years of age, although very small in stature for even those few years, and was a perfect model of infantile loveliness, despite the coarse calico of her dress, and the wretched appearance of her place of abode. Her little cheek, as it lay upon the soiled pillow, was smooth and fair; but tears had dried upon its surface, and tear-drops—even now, trembled upon the long, black eyelashes, that drooped so gracefully over it. A wealth of light brown curls flowed across the pillow, and among their sunny clusters, a small, exquisitely shaped hand was lingering, upon which the brow so beautifully pencilled reclined. One little-snow white shoulder lay exposed to view as the child slept and sobbed, for every now and then a sob checked her breathing, while the poor little back had evidently been cruelly beaten, for long ridges of swollen flesh were perceptible, and here and there the shoulder bore marks of a heavy whip.

Poor little creature! hers had been a hard and severe trial, before sleep caused her to forget, for awhile, her wretched lot.

By her side sat a woman, whose pinched features, and bowed shoulders, as well as a hard racking cough, told of disease and sorrow. She was about thirty-two, and had been a good looking, indeed handsome, woman, for one of her swarthy race. She sat in great dejection, with a few broken branches of a locust tree in her hand, with which she waved the flies from the sleeping face of the child, and as each sob fell upon her ear, she would start, then throw a glance of hatred and indignation towards a brutal-looking man who sat driving the tired horses.

Once, she rolled up the dress-sleeve of her right arm, and looked at two or three deep cuts, evidently received from the same whip that had lacerated the back of the moaning child; then again a vindictive, furious look, was darted towards the man, while the clenched fist, and muttered imprecation, told of a deep revenge plotting. No word, however, was spoken, and silently the three wagons rolled onward, until the shades of evening began to deepen, and the stars to appear, one by one, in the sky.

At last the city lights loomed in sight, while sounds of busy life seemed even at that distance to fall upon the ears of the silent occupants of the middle wagon. At the same time a beautiful grove of trees rose to view, but a a short space in advance of the train.

"Hallo, there!" shouted the man already alluded to, addressing the driver ahead; but the language he used was Italian, and this seemed to be the common dialect of the whole party; "halt, I say! here is a first-rate spot to encamp; good water near, fine shade, and close to the city."

So saying, he jumped to the ground, and fastening the lines to the top of the wagon, he passed to the other vehicles, seeming to consult the men within. After debating with each a few seconds, he returned, and taking hold of the horses' bridles, he led them and the wagon to a comfortable place, by the road-side, in the masses of weeds and grass. Thus, also, did the men in company dispose of the other wagons, while from each, the horses were detached, and being unharnessed, were allowed tc graze around, and roll in the long grass. Out of both other wagons, descended quite a large number of men, women, and children, the women immediately commencing to make preparations for lighting a fire, with which to cook their evening meal; while the men attended to the vehicles and horses, bringing water from a neighboring spring, also watering the dry and weary animals.

All this while, the woman we have described as seated in the centre wagon, which evidently belonged to the leader of the band, from the fact of his being the one to issue orders to the rest, and also from his being the occupant of the best and least crowded ambulance—all this while, she sat in the same spot, never stirring, while her face was still covered by her wasted hand.

"I say, Costanza, you fool!" growled the man we particularly speak of, as he strode to the door of the little apartment, "what do you mean by pouting there? Get up this minute and set to work cooking supper, or I'll put this over your back, worse than I ever did before. Sullen—hey!" said he, flourishing the large horse-whip he still grasped, as the woman slowly arose to obey. "Sullen, because I licked that infernal brat! Look here, woman, I'll be the death of that lazy young 'un yet, if you don't stop interfering with what don't concern you!"

"It does concern me, though," returned the woman, vehemently; "that child is mine; you brought her to me yourself, when our little Caterino died, and told me she was mine. I love her, and so help me heaven, I won't see her abused like that again. What had she done, that you need have whipped her so savagely?"

"Done! ha! ha! that is a good one! Never earned a dollar by her begging all last week, and she such a good singer, she might have earned double that, if she had tried! Let her see what she will get, if she don't do better here!"

"You will not strike that poor child again, Alfonso; promise me you will not," exclaimed the excited woman, as she clung to his arm in her earnestness. "Please promise not to hit Margherita again, and I will do my best to earn money while we stay."

"I won't promise! I tell you now, if the brat don't look out, I'll break her bones, if I don't her head. As for you, you jade, you stop your impudence and go to work, or I'll make the blood roll down your own carcass. There, take that, to begin with!" then raising his arm, he gave her a cruel blow with the whip he held, which caused her to jump aside, and, without another word, hurry away, to prepare something for them both to eat.

Half an hour afterwards, the whole party were seated on the ground, enjoying their evening meal, while the savory smell told that it consisted of something substantial, and palatable, while the bones that were thrown away, whispered of some devastated chicken coop.

After a hearty supper, the men, with Alfonso at their head, all turned towards the city, for a ramble and a drink, while the women, with their children, threw themselves in their wagons, and fell into a deep sleep, for they had travelled far that day, and were very weary.

Costanza, however, as soon as all were quiet, drew from a hidden place a plate of the choicest bits of chicken, a few boiled potatoes, and a bowl of sweet milk, which she had managed to secrete, then entering her wagon home, she softly aroused the sleeping child, and begged her to eat.

With a moan and a start, the poor forlorn little one,

opened its beautiful brown eyes, and gazed at the woman who stood beside her, holding a small piece of lighted candle, and pointing to the tempting food she had placed on a bench by the bed.

"Come, Rita. Alfonso has gone; nothing shall hurt you now. Eat a little supper to please mammy, won't you? See, here is chicken, potatoes, and sweet milk. Come, darling, eat now, for mammy."

"I will, mammy, but are you sure Alfonso has gone?" The little creature shuddered as she pronounced his name, while her cheek paled with fear.

"Yes, dear, he went to the city, and there he will be sure to stay until morning, if he finds his way into a rum-hole once! Curses on him for beating my lamb!" muttered Costanza.

"Mammy!" asked the child, as she devoured the food placed before her, for she was very hungry, Alfonso not having allowed her a morsel to eat the whole of that long day: "Mammy, how did you get me this nice supper? Did he let you?"

"Not he!" answered Costanza. "I stole it from the pot and hid it among the bushes, until he left the place. For the milk you are indebted to a cow that was going home from pasture. I stopped the good old creature, and milked a good supper for myself and you."

She did not add that the milk was all that had passed her lips that night, as the chicken was what was assigned to her, which she had hidden for her pet, instead of using for her own benefit.

"Mammy," again spoke Rita, "where are we now?"

"Near London; why do you ask, child?"

"Is that far from my home, good mammy?" asked

the girl, fixing her eyes upon the woman's face as she spoke.

"Your home, where is that, I would like to know?" surlily returned Costanza.

"In the sunny land I dream of—where the flowers bloom so brightly, and the blue waters of the Arno leap and glisten. Where a lady, beautiful and lovely, clasped me in her soft white arms and called me 'her lily-bud, her darling.' Are we far from that noble house where I used to play, far from my own dear, darling mamma?"

"Rita, cease!" exclaimed the woman, sternly. "Am I not your mother now? Do I not love you? do I not care for you as well as I can, with such a dreadful wretch for a husband? Why are you always grieving and talking of another mother, and another spot, fairer than the one you are in? Will you never love me?"

"I do love you, mammy; but oh, mamma, mamma!" the child stopped; she had finished her supper, and now threw herself back upon the bed, while, as the wail floated from her little lips, the tears gushed forth anew from her closed eyelids, and a wild heaving was again perceptible in her troubled bosom.

Costanza threw herself also upon the bed, after extinguishing the light, and clasping the tender form of the child in her arms, she soothed her at last, once more to sleep.

But for the woman there was no slumber. Through the long watches of that dreary night, her eyes never closed, her thoughts never stopped their wandering.

Once she muttered, as the little girl sobbed the word "Mamma" in her sleep—"Poor Rita, she will never cease moaning for her mother! I wonder who and where her mother is? I ought to know before I die, for I feel I cannot live long, and what will become of my lamb if I die and leave her among wolves? Strange, he never told me! Poor little thing! all my life would I give to see her happy and safe out of this dreadful trouble. Ha! ha! he would murder me, truly, if I placed the child out of his reach, but I could only die if he did, and death will come *very* soon anyway.

"He struck me again to-night! Yes! and for that I will be revenged! He makes a deal of money out of this poor babe's sweet singing, and begging! I will stop that income! I will plot something before many days roll by, to save my darling from his clutches;—the mean, black-hearted wretch, to beat her as he did to-day! Yet I loved him once. Ha! ha! how strange that seems! those days have gone, long, long ago, and now let him beware. Yet it is strange—how changed he is since he brought home to me this poor babe; before that, he was kind. When my sweet Caterino died, he tried to soothe me in his rough way, and then one night he came with Rita in his arms, and told me he had stolen her, to comfort me; that now, *she* was my own. But ah, I shudder when I think how bloody were his hands, and how his shirt and pants were clotted with gore: he said no word when he saw my eyes fixed inquiringly upon the stains, but giving me a dreadful look, went alone and washed out every spot himself.

"Yes! yes! there was murder somewhere, for Rita shuddered ever after, when he came near her, and never dared say one word; when I urged her to tell how he came by her, and what happened at the time, she would shake as if going into convulsions, and only whisper, 'Hush! he will kill me! he will kill me!'

"I fear I never can fathom that mystery! four years have passed away, and Alfonso is nothing but a brute since! no kindness now! nothing but curses and blows for Rita and Costanza.

"Yes, she is mine now. My darling. All I have to love and cherish. But I must part with her; I must place her somewhere before I die. See!" she still murmured, holding up her shadowy hand for the moonlight to fall upon, "see, it grows thinner every day, and my strength is almost gone. Oh, what would become of Rita if I should die before I get another place for her. I am certain he would murder the innocent lamb!" then she folded the sleeping form to her bosom, and wildly kissed the sweet lips, which caused the child to smile and again whisper, "Mamma!"

A frown passed over the woman's face as the word fell upon her ear, followed by a sigh, "Ah! she dreamed it was mamma, that kissed her—her dear mamma, not her poor "good mammy," as she ever calls the gipsy. No, she will never forget the mother that bore her, poor pet!"

Hours passed after these words, but Costanza's black eyes still remained wide open, fixed upon the star-lit sky, seen through the windows of the wagon.

Hours passed! then the stars disappeared, one by one, the moon also went down, while the grey dawn lit up the trees and bushes of the grove, and the gipsy camp was soon visible by day.

Costanza was now the first one to stir, and passing out, she began to gather sticks to re-kindle the fire, with which to cook some breakfast. She was soon joined by the other women, and a large fire sent forth in a few moments its bright and welcome blaze.

By the time the breakfast was prepared, and Costanza had fully fed her waiting child, the men returned, much the worse for the bad liquor they had taken through the night.

As soon as Costanza heard them wrangling in the distance, she seized Rita, and hurried to secrete her behind some bushes, a short distance down the road, thus thoughtfully placing her away from Alfonso's drunken sight.

After the men had finished eating what they wished, they tumbled into the wagons, or stretched under the trees, and soon fell into a deep sleep, much to the relief of the women and children, who, while they were in that condition, could but regard them with terror and dread.

Costanza lingered around, until she was certain Alfonso was sleeping to waken no more for hours, then stealthily entering her little home, she approached a small chest kept exclusively for her own use, and taking a key from her pocket, turned the lock, and raised the cover. Casting every now and then a cautious glance at the sleeping form upon the bed, she drew forth a moderate sized paper box and proceeded to examine its contents. A scowl of anger and malignant hate swept over her face, as she raised the beautiful needlework it contained, examining each article of a small child's wardrobe, that lay within, seeming to seek anxiously for some particular object, which yet remained undiscovered. Twice she unfolded and shook a finely wrought, white dress, made apparently for a little girl about three years of age; also, all the tiny undergarments that accompanied it, together with the broad blue sash, of expensive ribbon, the dainty white merino sack, and various small items, but the object for which she searched, did not present itself.

"Good heavens!" she whispered to herself, "can it be that Alfonso has meddled with this box? Can he have discovered that I did not obey him, when he ordered me to burn every garment Rita wore that day, when he stole her from her mother? It must be that he discovered this box yesterday, when he was so long alone in the wagon, else how could that golden chain and those pretty armlets have disappeared? Probably by this time they are far off in some distant pawnbroker's shop, where the eyes of my poor little darling can never rest upon them. I must be certain, though; perhaps he has not yet parted with them. I will by some means examine his pockets, but I must use the utmost care, for terrible would be the consequences if he should awake, and see my movements."

Casting around her a look of caution, the woman proceeded to screen the windows, and fasten the door, after which she advanced on tiptoe, to the side of Alfonso, who lay in a deep, drunken sleep, upon the bed. Bending over him, Costanza stealthily inserted her fingers into each capacious pocket of the loose gipsy coat, that enveloped his burly frame. One after another of those pockets she softly examined, but so light had her touch to be, so cautious her every motion lest he should awaken, that some time was occupied in the search. At length all was examined without success, save a small pocket in his vest, which was by far the most difficult for her fingers to in vade, on account of the position of his arm, which rested upon it, as it lay across his breast. Costanza feared, if she attempted to move this member of his body, that he would open his eyes, and perhaps give her a furious blow; there was no other way, however, and she bravely resolved to make the trial.

Passing her fingers gently, then, under his arm, she gave it a soft shove downward, which left the pocket exposed, but which caused him to mutter some inarticulate curse, then throwing both arms over his head, he once more passed into a deep unbroken sleep. The pocket was within reach of her long thin fingers now, and again she leaned over the unconscious man, and proceeded to inspect its contents. A small knife, and a quill toothpick, first presented themselves, then a tiny paper box met her touch, which was quickly drawn out and opened.

The lost treasure was there, safe and unharmed!

Gently replacing the other articles, Costanza retained these, muttering to herself—

"He will think, if he misses them, that he lost them in his drunken spree;" then placing the recovered treasure underneath the needlework, and securing the cover of the large box with a stout string, she slipped the whole under her shawl, and taking from a nail, upon the side of the wagon, a small instrument of music, she left the spot, closing the door behind her, and turned towards the bushes where she had hidden the trembling, obedient child.

"Come, Rita," she whispered, "all is safe and quiet now; the men are sleeping soundly, and it is time for us to commence our daily work. Here is your instrument; now you must play and sing your very best to-day, that we may please Alfonso, by earning a deal of money."

"He won't whip me then, will he, good mammy? I am so lame I can hardly walk," she added, as Costanza clasped her little hand, and turned towards the city.

"Poor lamb! I know it is hard to take you out to-day! but cheer up—there may be good luck for us, after all this exertion. I too am weak and feeble, and can scarcely drag myself along. But let us press onward, for once within the city, we can sit down upon some door-step and rest.

A long pause ensued, during which time they must have passed over half a mile, when suddenly, a hard turn of coughing seized poor Costanza; so severe did this become, that Rita was obliged to support her trembling frame to a seat under a tree, upon the green grass, by the side of the road.

The little one was frightened at the ashy paleness that had settled over her companion's countenance, and the short breath that oppressed her, after the coughing had ceased.

"Mammy, don't you feel better now?" she asked, with quivering lips, and trembling voice, more to arouse the poor sufferer, who sat leaning her head against the trunk of the tree, with closed eyelids and cheeks white as death. 'Mammy! Mammy! speak to Rita! she is so lonesome, mammy dear!"

No answer came to the imploring voice of the little girl. No answer! for Costanza had fainted from exhaustion and debility.

"Mammy!" still pleaded the child. "You look so white and strange, I am afraid! Why don't you speak to Rita? I love you, indeed I do, good mammy! Oh dear! I am all alone, and something dreadful has happened to mammy."

Here the poor little girl burst into tears, and wildly kissed the pale lips of her only friend, as if, by these affectionate caresses, she thought to arouse her.

The kisses seemed at length to have the desired effect, for Costanza opened her eyes and smiled faintly upon the weeping child.

"Oh mammy, you are not dead! I was so frightened—I thought you had died and left poor Rita all alone. But you did not die, you would not be so cruel, would you, mammy dear?"

"God forbid, my darling! I think I must have fainted! I shall soon be better. Can you see water near?"

"Yes! there is a stream close by, but if you wish a drink, I have no cup," returned Rita, sadly.

"Take my handkerchief and wet, then, darling! You can bathe my head a little, then we will hurry on."

Rita did as she was directed, and returning, she applied the wet cloth to the head and face of the gipsy, which seemed to revive her.

Plucking a large leaf from the ground, under a horse chestnut tree, she folded it in such a manner that it formed quite a little cup, from which Costanza quenched her thirst.

Thus refreshed, in about half an hour she again arose, and once more proceeded towards the city.

"Take a good look behind us, darling, to see if any of our people are coming. Be very watchful all the way, for I do not wish to be followed. My eyes are dim and uncertain, this morning, so I must trust to you."

"Never fear, mammy! I will surely tell you, if any person appears in sight. Oh mammy, poor little Rita will be very good, and mind every word you say, if you will only keep well, and not look so strange and white, as you did just now. What would Rita do, if you were to die, good mammy? Alfonso would kill me then, I know he would!" she added, with a shudder.

"My poor pet!" was all that Costanza could reply, for tears choked her utterance, and she strove mightily to repress them, lest Rita should be yet more alarmed at her weakness.

CHAPTER XXIII.

THE STREET SINGER.

"Speak gently to the young, for they
Will have enough to bear—
Pass through this life as best they may,
'Tis full of anxious care!

* * * * *

Speak gently, kindly to the poor—
Let no harsh tone be heard;
They have enough they must endure.
Without an unkind word."

THE feet of the gipsy woman and the brown haired child tarried not a moment, until the pavements of the great city of London were reached, and the high walls of the buildings covered them from all eyes that might be peering from the camp.

Costanza knew not why she was so fearful of being detained, except it were her great anxiety to find a hiding place for the little girl, whose lot was daily growing worse and worse, and for whose life she often trembled.

She was pursuing no unusual course in thus leaving the encampment, for it was the wish of Alfonso that she should take the child to every town, village, or city, through which they passed, to sing, and thus obtain the money which he spent in drink and carousing. The thoughts that had filled her mind all night she knew had made her nervous, and strangely excited, and this inward disquiet but lent speed to her feet, and a chilling dread to her bosom.

Passing rapidly, then, down one street, and up another, she paused at length, before a high brick dwelling, and bidding Rita play and sing, she sat down upon the stone steps to rest, for she was very weary, and she was also unwontedly sad.

In meek obedience, the little creature placed her instrument in the right position upon her arm, and commenced a plaintive tune, while her timid, trembling voice, full of beauty and of power, floated out upon the morning air.

The words were sweet and sad, but the voice of the child was sweeter far, and the melody she threw around, was truly wonderful in one so young.

A crowd soon collected near the tiny songstress, and when Costanza went among them, gathering the pennies they readily bestowed, she was astonished and pleased at the unusual quantity.

"Cross my hand with silver, lady," she said, as the child ceased singing and prepared to travel on—"Cross the gipsy woman's hand, and she will tell you a nice fortune. Come now, bonny lady, cross the fortune-teller's hand with silver, and you will hear something of your sweetheart and your wedding-day."

The young girl she addressed hesitated a moment, then placing some small coins in Costanza's hand, she stretched out her palm for the promised fortune.

"I see," said the gipsy, "lines, that picture wealth and plenty—lines, again, that say your path is to be crossed for a while, for two suitors will be pleading for your love. One is rich, but he is not to be the chosen, although trouble lies between the favored of your heart, and success. But never fear; the clouds will by and by disperse, and you will marry the man you love. He is a fair-haired, light complexioned man, and he loves *you* as he does his life."

The girl laughed, and drawing away her hand, with a look of deep satisfaction, ran gaily on, while Costanza, equally pleased with her good luck, passed into a wider, and more frequented street, where once more she paused, while the voice of the little one swelled and trilled melodiously upon the ears of the passer-by.

"Stop, Bennett," exclaimed a tall, handsome gentleman to his companion, as, arm in arm, they were hurrying through the crowded thoroughfare; "hark! what a splendid voice! where can that singing be?"

"I do not know; but it is very sweet! Why, Russell, it surely cannot be that little child, standing before yonder house?"

"It certainly is!" exclaimed the first speaker; "I never heard anything so wonderfully beautiful before, from such a mere child. Let us go nearer. What a charming face! did you ever see such eyes, and such perfect features? What a pity so much beauty, and such musical talents, should be wasted upon a street singer."

The two gentlemen paused by the side of Rita, until her song was finished, then the one addressed by the name of Russell, placed a piece of money in her hand, and gently inquired her name.

"Margherita, sir," was the answer, as the beautiful eyes gazed sadly into his own.

"Where do you live, little one?" again asked the gentleman, who was deeply interested in the little singer, he knew not why.

"I stay with the gipsy mother," murmured the child,

pointing her tiny finger to the form of Costanza, who stood with her back towards her, busy telling fortunes to as many of the crowd as would cross her hand with money.

"Is it your mother, little one?" once more questioned the stranger.

"It is my gipsy mother, not my own sweet mamma! She is far away, where the blue waters dash and foam."

"What is her name, poor child?" still asked Russell, gazing kindly into the timid little eyes, raised to his so pleadingly.

A low sob was the only answer, as a burst of tears followed the question.

"Poor little thing! Can you tell us mamma's name, now?" said Russell, as the tears flowed less freely, and the agitated bosom ceased to heave.

"I do not know her name; I only called her mamma, and she called me her lily-bud—her darling."

"Where is she now?"

"I do not know! Far away where the Arno dashes and quivers in the sunshine."

"Italy! I'll be bound!" exclaimed Bennett. "But she is not an Italian child, I know from her looks. I should not wonder if she had been stolen by those thieving gipsies. But come on, Russell, or we shall be late; the seminary bell must have rung before this."

"I hate to leave the poor little outcast, but I suppose I must," returned Russell, and slipping another piece of money into the hand of the little girl, he passed on; but all day the voice of the street singer sounded in his ear, and those beautiful brown eyes seemed gazing into his own.

"Mammy! see here, mammy! what a splendid gentleman gave me!" said Rita, as Costanza once more came to her side, at the same time exhibiting a gold piece, and the smaller coins, to the eager gaze of the gipsy woman.

"Where is he? how came he to give you such a treasure?" asked Costanza, grasping the gold, the first she had touched for many a weary day.

"He said some bell must have rung and he must go. He gave me this for my sweet singing—those were his words; and oh, he asked my name, and who my own mother was, and where she lived. But mammy, I wept, because I could not tell him."

"Oh, if I could only have seen him, if I could but have spoken to him! Which way did he go, child? tell me, and we will hurry after him."

"Down that street, mammy; but he has gone now, and I do not know where."

Seizing the child's hand in hers, the poor gipsy hurried along, in the direction taken by the gentleman; but with all her speed, she could not overtake them; and disappointed and anxious, she sat down upon some steps, once more to rest her weary frame.

While seated there with Rita by her side, she revolved in her own mind, what should next be done. When she had left the encampment that morning, she was flushed with the hope that something would happen before nightfall, that would rescue Rita, and save herself. She had allowed herself to dream that she had looked her last upon that tribe, made hateful in her sight by the brutal treatment of Alfonso to herself, and her fondly loved charge.

Now she realized her disappointment.

Night would soon cast its shadows over the city; she had no resting-place within its broad environs; no shelter for her weary, fainting frame, in all its countless dwellings.

Among the vast number of its inhabitants, who would shield, even for one night, a strolling gipsy?

These thoughts filled her with sadness, but she could not shake them off!

She saw that necessity compelled her to return to the encampment of her people; so, opening a well-worn purse, she counted over her gains. The sum it contained far exceeded her usual success, without counting the golden treasure, given by the kind stranger, in the morning, which she much desired to conceal for the benefit of Rita. But would the amount satisfy the greediness of Alfonso's appetite? Would it save her darling from his dreadful whip?

Long she sat and studied! Then taking the gold piece from her purse, she fastened it in the remotest portion of her dress-pocket, by folding over a corner, and securing it firmly with a pin; then charging Rita not to mention to Alfonso that this had been given them, as she wished to hide it, for the purpose of buying shoes, to replace the worn ones on her little feet, she arose, and once more turned sadly into a street that led from the city; but she paused once, before she gained the open fields, to purchase a substantial supper for herself and child, fearing that, being late in their return, Alfonso would again deprive them of food.

It was well she had this forethought, as after events fully testified.

She had a long road to pass over, after she left the crowded streets and lordly dwellings; long for her feeble footsteps, and the stars were in the sky, but the moon was shedding scarcely a ray upon the grass and road, so dark and dismal had it become, before the wagons of the gipsy camping-ground arose before her.

She had not intended to be so late, and she trembled as she thought of the anger of Alfonso at her unusual delay, for she well knew that he was entirely out of money, (her search through his pockets in the morning had proven that,) and she feared that he would wait for her return, to seize the proceeds of their weary toil, to spend for his nightly pleasures in the city.

The sound of his angry voice, as she drew near, proved that her fears were well founded.

Alfonso did await their return.

CHAPTER XXIV.

FURTHER CRIMES.

"YOU baggage!" exclaimed a rough voice, as Costanza approached the fire around which the gipsy crew were seated, taking their evening meal. "You lazy, good for nothing pest, what made you crawl along so slowly? You ought to have been back, an hour and a half ago. Where is that snivelling brat, I say?" he added, for Costanza had advised Rita to hide herself in the wagon, instead of advancing with her, by which means she hoped to shield her from trouble. "What have you done with the imp? tell me, or it will be worse for you;" he exclaimed, seizing her by the arm, and shaking her roughly as he spoke.

"Let go of my arm, if you wish me to speak. I have done nothing with the child, unless making her sing herself to death, be a sin. See, I have brought a good stock of money, gained by her sweet songs. I could not break away sooner, when unusual luck was ours. Darkness came almost too fast, to-day, money seemed so plenty."

"Plenty for all but us," growled the man; "money is scarce enough in this camp. Give me the change quick, for I would count this famous luck. Mind, I expect at least three pounds for this late tramp.

Costanza's heart beat quickly at these words; she knew there was not half that amount in that worn and faded purse, and she knew, also, that Alfonso was in so terrible a mood, that fifty would not satisfy him.

Tremblingly then, she awaited his next words.

"Ha! ha! great luck truly! the whole of one pound. Look here, woman, I won't stand this! There, take that," said he, giving her a blow that felled her to the earth, "and that, and that," he added, kicking her prostrate form with his heavy boot. "Now bring me that brat, and let me give her what she deserves, for this paltry sum. Get up, I tell you," he exclaimed, giving her another kick, "and hunt up that girl."

Costanza arose with difficulty, for she was stiff with bruises, but she made no movement to place the poor little child within his reach.

"You won't stir, hey! then I will make you," exclaimed the wretch, springing towards her, and grasping her long black hair, which had become loosened by the rough treatment she had received, he dragged her several steps by these sweeping locks.

A piercing cry burst upon the ear at this moment, and little Rita, who had witnessed the whole scene from a window of the wagon, came flying to the spot.

"Stop! stop! for heaven's sake!" she cried. "Stop, don't kill my mammy! She has been sick all day. Don't hurt her. Please don't, Alfonso."

"Ah! here you are, you imp of Satan!" exclaimed the infuriated man, releasing Costanza, and catching the trembling child by the arm. "So you hide away when you come back, do you? Afraid of a thrashing, were you? It is well you know what you deserve. How does it feel, hey?" continued the brute, as he gave her blow after blow with a heavy stick he had picked from the ground, upon her already sore and wounded back. "Curses on you! I could tear you limb from limb!" he muttered, while fast and thick the blows fell upon the unfortunate child.

"Stop now, I say, Alfonso! That is quite enough in all conscience!" interfered a rough dark man, starting up from the fire: "I believe in whipping, when it is deserved, but I don't see the sense of killing what is of value. If you strike the girl another blow, she cannot sing to-morrow, and a pound to-day and another to-morrow, is not so bad to my mind. Let her go, I tell you, we have had enough of that, for this time."

"Ah! for this time, mind you both," said Alfonso, pushing the bleeding child toward Costanza. "If more money comes not to-morrow I doubt if you see another day. Out of my sight, now, if you know what is best. Not a morsel of supper do you have this night."

Slowly, for both were bruised and sore, the poor creatures crawled towards their wagon, and dragging themselves within its shelter, they threw their weary bodies upon the bed, and there, exhausted and suffering, they sobbed in each other's arms.

"My precious darling! to think that mammy could not save you!" sighed the poor woman, as she pressed kiss after kiss upon the tearful little face beside her.

"Good mammy!" sobbed the child, "you did all you could. I was glad he left you, even if it was to whip me. I nearly died, when I saw him kick you and drag you so savagely by the hair. Oh, mammy, it was dreadful! But you won't let it kill you, for my sake; you will live longer for Rita, won't you, dear, good mammy?"

"God grant that I may!" murmured the gipsy. "Dreadful indeed would be your lot with such a brute, my precious brown-eyed birdie."

At this moment they heard Alfonso's voice, under their window, saying to some companion,

"Come this way Bob, let the other fellows get ahead, while we follow slowly to the city. I want to talk as we go along, for I have a grand scheme to tell you—but mum is the word. First though, let me go back to secure old Betsy's butcher knife, as we may need it before daylight. Wait here one moment; I will soon be back."

A pause ensued, and Costanza held her breath lest she should lose a word of this strange conversation.

"All right, Bob!" she heard Alfonso whisper on his return; "Bess was easily gulled. I told her I might need the knife to kill a sheep, for we must be in want of meat. All right, come on!"

So the two passed away, and as Costanza drew aside a small curtain from the window, and gazed after them, she distinctly saw a female figure creeping softly after their receding forms, seemingly intent upon watching their motions, and overhearing their words.

"What can this mean?" thought the gipsy woman, as she dropped the curtain after they had disappeared, and again rested her aching head upon the pillow by the side of the now sleeping Rita. "What terrible deed does that guilty wretch contemplate amid the darkness of night! Oh, Alfonso, how fast are you plunging on to ruin!"

Closing her eyes, she sought to compose herself to sleep, but it was some time before she succeeded in chasing the fearful visions from her mind, that was suggested by those dark and meaning words. Horror upon horror flitted through her brain, imaginations full of blood and death, in which Alfonso stood prominent, presented themselves, until weariness and excitement prevailed and fitful slumbers, mingled with broken dreams, visited her exhausted frame.

Turning from the encampment, let us follow the two men in their nightly tramp towards the city, and listen to the villainous scheme, unfolded to Bob, by Alfonso.

The night was very dark, the road very lonely and quiet, and the two seemed to have not the slightest fear of being overheard, in the deep solitude of the spot and hour.

"Well, Al, what is in the wind?" asked Bob; "what good job do you calculate on? Something to line our pockets, I hope! Mine is as empty as a cuss!"

"Line our pockets, did you say? Darn me if it don't! I tell you, Bob, I am tired of this grinding poverty; a fellow can't get a decent dram now-a-days because he is so wretchedly poor. I vow I can't stand it. I will have money! I don't care how it comes. I will have it! The world owes me a living, and if it don't give it to me, I will steal it!"

"Bravo say I to that!" returned Bob; "this snailish way of getting along don't suit my composition either. Thunder! how I long for some great haul, some good dive into somebody's money bags!"

"Ha! ha! bully for you, Bob! Bully for you! I thought you would do, to help a fellow in a ticklish job! I see, I did not mistake my man. Well, to business! but let us rest a bit under this tree, while I tell you my plan, for there is plenty of time, as we must keep sober until this work is over; then, hurrah for a jolly spree! Now listen."

So saying, the two rascals threw themselves into an easy posture upon the grass, and drawing out their pipes from a huge pocket, they proceeded to fill them with tobacco, and puffed away, in order to ignite the contents of the well-filled bowls, while they applied a ready match to the surface.

So intent were they upon this occupation, and their guilty plans, that they did not notice the stealthy form that crept to the spot, and glided behind a clump of bushes, not an arms length from their side.

"Well, Bob," said Alfonso, after drawing several long puffs to make sure that the smoking operation would be a success; "well now for my story! Last night, as I was about passing into a drinking saloon, I heard an old tippler, who stood on the steps, say to another, "there goes Mr. Cleaveland! I wish I was half as rich! Why couldn't he give a chap a lift, I wonder; he don't know what to do with his jink."

"I looked at the person old Stephen pointed out, then, instead of entering the saloon as I had intended, I followed the rich man as he passed up the street.

"He had not far to go, it seemed, as in a few moments he ascended the steps of a splendid house, and taking a dead latch-key from his pocket, he unlocked the door and entered.

"I was certain, now, that he had reached his home!

"Oh how I panted to steal softly behind him, secrete myself until midnight, then help myself to the gentleman's gold, or perhaps to some of his prime silver, for this I know so wealthy a person must possess.

"I could not accomplish this then, however, but I chuckled as a thought crossed my brain: so marking the house that I might be sure to find it again, I walked back to the saloon, laying my plans as I went, for a future visit to the rich man's home—a secret pull at his well filled coffers. Hey boy!" added the villain, giving his companion a hearty slap on the shoulder. "A thousand pounds would not be bad, would it, these devilish thirsty days? What say you to paying the chap a visit to-night, filling our pockets, then going shares with the spoil?"

"Agreed! it will be prime fun! But how shall we get inside the premises?"

"Nothing easier! where there is a will there is a way! We can cut a panel from the back door, after we scale the fence of the dooryard, then insert our arms and undo the fastenings. This accomplished, we can take off our boots, go in stocking-footed, unlock the front door in order to escape readily, if discovered, and then search the premises."

"But what did you want of the butcher-knife?" asked Bob.

"Use it in cutting the door, or perhaps run it into Mr. Cleaveland's heart, if he happens to discover us. Nothing like being ready for a contingency, you observe."

"Yes! yes! Al, that is a fact, shall we jog along now? it must be getting late."

"I suppose we might as well. I wish it was not so deuced dark."

"Pshaw! what a wish! It is the best thing that could happen, with such a piece of work in hand," returned Bob.

"I believe you are right there. Come on!"

Once more the two men arose, and travelled towards the city, never halting again, except occasionally to refill and light the pipe, they considered so essential to comfort and happiness.

CHAPTER XXV

OLD BESS.

> "Woman, I have a secret—only swear,
> Before I tell you—swear upon the book
> Not to reveal it, till you see me dead."
>
> ENOCH ARDEN.

AS they left the spot where Alfonso had developed his well laid scheme of villainy, the same stealthy form that had crouched behind the bushes, again glided away, but this time her feet turned towards the gipsy camp, leaving the guilty plotters to pass unwatched and unharmed on their way to the scene of burglary and plunder, if not of murder.

As the person advanced, placing a safe distance between them, she raised herself to her usual height, but that was not being very erect, as age had bent her shoulders, and even amid the darkness, her snow white hair might be distinguished by a close observer.

It was Bess, the same old crone that Alfonso supposed he had deceived in regard to the butcher-knife.

"So ho!" she muttered, as she hobbled away, "that is the game, is it? Precious scamps you are becoming, to be sure! Breaking into houses, plundering, mayhaps murdering the innocent inhabitants. Who ever supposed a gipsy would stoop so low? Stealing cattle, and poultry is not against our principles, but burglary is not in our line often. Well, well, what is the world coming to, I wonder? Wanted my butcher knife to kill a sheep, did ye? thought to pull wool over the eyes of old Bess, hey? Well, all I have to say is, you did not do it this time, and it is strange to me, if you do get a chance to do that pesky thing. Bess is no fool, if she is nigh eighty years of age. No—no! 'tis not so easy to catch old birds with chaff, my boys! No! no!"

So muttering, the old woman jogged onward, heedless alike of distance or darkness, and in about some fifteen minutes she found herself crouching beside the low embers of the fire, holding over the feeble blaze which she had succeeded in fanning, her withered hands, for the night was chilly and her aged fingers were blue with cold. Casting now and then a handful of chips upon the blaze, the old crone succeeded at last in getting herself thouroughly warmed, then creeping into her accustomed sleeping place, in one of the canvas-covered wagons, amid half a dozen other forms, she rolled herself into a warm, thick, comfortable, and was soon asleep, but the last thought that filled her mind, before she closed her eyes, was, "I must be up by the first peep of day, to see Costanza, before the others stir. Ah, me! what will she say to this? Poor thing!"

It was still dusky around, although daylight was beginning to light the horizon, when Bess again opened her eyes, and softly arose to her feet. Very cautiously, she moved among the sleeping forms, as she passed to the end of the wagon, and slid to the ground. Standing still a moment, gazing back to see if any one stirred, she was satisfied that her catlike movements had been unobserved, and that all were still sleeping soundly.

As she paused beside the wagon, the feeble light of day

glimmering around, revealed yet more perfectly her withered features.

The hollow cheeks, furrowed by deeply set wrinkles, the toothless mouth, the snow-white locks, all combined to tell her many years and frequent exposures to hardships and storms, but her black piercing eyes, spoke still of energy and fire.

Passing softly to the rear of the wagon, she approached Costanza's resting-place. Gently opening the door, she entered, and carefully closing it after her, she crept towards the bed, and placing her hand upon the sleeping woman's shoulder, she whispered,

"Wake up, child, wake up! It is morning, and time to stir yourself"

"Who speaks?" asked Costanza, opening her heavy eyes and gazing around.

"Hush, speak low—it is nobody but old Bess!" whispered the crone.

"Why Bess, what started you so early? It is hardly day yet! Is anything the matter?"

"Matter enough, I should say! I wish to talk to you. Is the child asleep?"

"Yes, soundly. She was very tired and exhausted, but she sleeps well now," replied Costanza, rising, but seating herself upon the edge of the bed, making room at the same time for Bess beside her, who gladly took the proffered place. "What has happened that you seek me thus early?"

A pause followed before Bess offered to speak, and then her words were, as if she had not heard the question just asked.

"It has been a dark night, and many a dark deed has probably been transacted."

"Do you know of any in particular Bess?" again queried Costanza.

"Ah, yes, do I! What would an old soul like Bess, be doing in the darkness, ferreting out mysteries, when young forms sleep and dream?"

"Come, Bess, tell me what you mean? Is danger threatening our encampment?"

"Danger! yes; but it is of a kind you little dream. Mayhap a prison cell, or hangman's rope, for some of our party."

"Bess, what do you mean?"

"Pretty doings was there last night, girl! Are you certain the child sleeps?"

"Yes, Bess, Rita never wakes easily. Go on, I am curious to hear what has happened."

"Well," resumed the crone, "last night, after Alfonso had vented his rage upon yourself and the pretty baby, and had seen you disappear, he once more counted your hard earnings and chuckled,

"'Not so bad after all, is it Bob? better luck than we have had in many a day. Come on, let us go to the city!'

"'Yes; quite a heap of jink they brought, I think. The young one is a great windfall, with her fine singing. I counted it strange in you to beat them so, when they had done so well; what possessed you?'

"'Curse them!' returned Alfonso, 'I did it to make them do better yet. The whining fools! Let them know once that you are satisfied, and there they stop! I know their infernal pranks. Yes, sir! the licking will make them all the sharper, and to-morrow they will double this. You mark that.'

"'And get whipped again, after doing it, I suppose;' said I, for I could not keep still.

"'What if they do, old grizzly head? It is none of your business. Shut up now, and speak when you are spoken to,' growled Alfonso fiercely, shaking his fist at me.

"I concluded to obey, as he seemed so savage, but it required a great effort to keep from telling my opinion of his conduct and words."

"Good Bess, returned Costanza, laying her hot hand upon the old woman's, "then you did sympathize with us last night?"

"Yes indeed!" was the answer, "he was a brute. I thought so then, but I am certain of it now. Only hear the rest of my story. As they stood talking, most of our men had risen, and started off, but Alfonso yet lingered, telling Bob to wait for him. In a few moments they also turned away, but I heard Alfonso speak some strange words about wanting to tell Bob something, but I pretended not to heed their talk. Presently Alfonso returned to the fire, and coming to my side, whispered,

"'Let me have that knife you used awhile ago, to disjoint that chicken; do now, Bess, won't you?'

"'What for?' asked I crossly, for I thought his manner odd.

"'To kill a sheep if we find one, old woman. Our stock of meat must be low!'

"'That it is,' said I, handing him the knife. 'One tires of fowls, very soon. Some mutton now would be a perfect godsend.'

"I said this innocently enough, but I well knew some different thing from sheep killing was intended by the rascal, and I resolved to find out what it could be in good time.

"Old Bess is not easily baulked!

"They passed on into the darkness, and folding a heavy shawl around me, I passed behind the wagons and followed, dodging their footsteps.

"They threw themselves upon the ground about a quarter of a mile from here, and lighting their pipes, Alfonso proceeded to unfold his wretched scheme. As I had crawled behind some low bushes, close beside them, I heard every word of a conversation that caused me much indignation and horror.

"'Last night, Bob,' said Alfonso, 'as I stood on the steps of a drinking saloon about to enter, an old tippler exclaimed to another, 'there goes Mr. Cleaveland, one of the richest men around. I wish I had some of his money.' I did not enter the place after hearing these words, but followed the rich man home. I saw him ascend the steps of a splendid house and disappear within, and marked it, so that I could find it again. I propose to cut a panel from the back door, to-night, go in, in our stocking feet, unlock the front door, so that we can escape that way if discovered, and then help ourselves to money, silver, or any other valuables that may present themselves. If detected, the butcher knife shall find its way to the old chap's heart, right soon.'

"Bob agreed to the proposal, and promising to divide the spoils, they passed on, while I hurried back to the camp. I was very weary after my unusual exertion, therefore could not arouse you, as I well knew that nothing we could do, would prevent the burglary. This morning I awoke thus early, in order to tell you the story before others were abroad."

"Oh Bess, what is this thing you tell me? Can it be possible that Alfonso has become so depraved in villainy?" exclaimed Costanza. "To become a housebreaker, a burglar, perhaps a murderer, really, the horror is dreadful—dreadful!"

A convulsive motion passed over the poor creature as she spoke, and throwing her apron over her face, she rocked her body to and fro, in extreme agony of mind."

"Don't child! Don't take on so!" murmured Bess, striving to comfort her. "Perhaps they will not be discovered! Perhaps they are yet safe!"

"Safe! Oh Bess, safe did you say, with a State Prison offence hanging over their heads? Oh Alfonso, Alfonso, how could you do this fearful deed? But Bess, what can we do? Have you thought of anything for their deliverance?"

"No, child! nothing can be done. It is daylight, and the crime has been all completed before this. The rascals are now in the hands of the police, or off on another spree. But I must go, as I see signs of life in yonder wagon. Keep still about what I have told you; never let it pass your lips. If they are in prison, we must do something to release them. I will study out what that something shall be, before night."

Here the old crone disappeared, leaving Costanza alone with her sorrow.

She still sat weeping on the bedside, her apron over her head, her body rocking to and fro, when she was startled by a pair of soft arms encircling her neck, and a musical voice, whispering in her ear.

"Don't cry, mammy darling, you have Rita yet! Your poor little Rita loves you, indeed she does, mammy! Don't cry, any more, please don't!"

Pulling away the apron from her face, the little one kissed again and again, lips, cheek, and brow, of her friend.

"My precious birdie, you are my only comfort!" exclaimed the gipsy, catching the child in her arms and fondly caressing her.

"Then you won't cry if Alfonso is bad, will you? What made old Bess tell you all that long story, mammy, when you can do nothing to prevent the dreadful sin?"

"Rita, were you awake? did you hear what was said just now?"

"Yes, mammy, nearly all?"

"But you must not tell it, you must never breathe it to a human being. I am sorry you overheard us, my pet!" exclaimed Costanza.

"It will do no harm, for I shall certainly keep the secret. Surely you can trust your Rita, mammy."

The child laid her head upon Costanza's shoulder as she spoke, one arm still encircled her neck, but with the other hand she patted the poor woman's pallid cheek, caressingly.

"Trust you? Yes! yes! my star, my blossom, my pretty, pretty flower!" sighed Costanza, pressing her lovingly to her bosom, and wiping away her tears.

"Shall I sing the song you taught me, mammy, before we go out? Listen to my pretty song. Maybe it will chase away your tears."

RITA'S SONG.

I'm a poor little waif, floating down the stream of Time,
Far adrift, from my parents, and my home.
Most beautiful, and fair, was that early home of mine,
Where loving glances, *only*, met my own.

No angry voices chided, no brutal whip was there,
No cruel tramps required, in that spot;
Affection's sweetest pleasures, unchequered by a care,
And joy alone, was mingled in my lot!

My father I remember, a noble gentleman,
Who ever looked with fondest pride on me.
Alas! how can I finish the picture so began?
Or tell how I no more his face may see?

He showered kisses on me, his only precious child;
And ever bought me presents rich and rare;
I sat upon his knee,—as I prattled, how he smil'd,
Or smoothed with loving touch my curling hair.

But ah! I see before me another gentle one,
Whose spirit hovers near me day and night!
Her face of mournful beauty, her voice of tender tone,
Seem ever bursting on my ear, and sight.

That face, I often saw bending o'er my cradle bed,
Soft lullabies that voice would ever sing:
Upon her loving bosom I nestled my young head,
And to her clasping arms, would gladly spring.

O precious, darling, mother, I cry for thee, in vain!
My heart is nearly broken, with this grief!
They tore me from thine arms, heeding not the bitter pain,
And leaving not a shadow of relief.

I wander now a gipsy! The green-wood is my home!
The gipsy camp my shelter through the night.
Each day I earn my bread, in the towns through which we roam,
By songs that fill my hearers with delight.

Amid my lonely exile, while tears fall fast and wild,
One ray of comfort *only*, fills my breast!
One voice alone speaks kindly, to soothe the weeping child!
One person only pants to give me rest.

It is the gipsy mother, who cares for me each day;
Upon whose loving bosom oft I weep;
In peril she has shielded, in sorrow been my stay,
And in her tender arms each night I sleep.

To soothe her weeping anguish they brought me to her side,
For in the grave, her only darling lay.

"Won't you love your gipsy mother, precious girl?" she cried.
While tears from my sad eyes, she kiss'd sway.

Yes! I'll love my gipsy mother, all Life's journey through,
For care bestowed upon me every hour!
I find her ever faithful, I find her ever true,
I find her *ever watchful* of her flower.

"Oh my darling, what would life be to poor Costanza without your love?" sighed the gipsy, as she pressed her yet closer to her bosom, and wildly kissed her cherub lips. "Yet all this joy cannot be cherished long! Once more must I think of my darling's welfare, before my own pleasure in her love. Come, Rita, we must travel on without our breakfast this morning. We must be off, before Alfonso or the men return, for it may be, if they find all here, that after last night's affair, he may order us to leave this spot, to fly from pursuit, and I cannot go until I see that gentleman, who was so kind to you yesterday. We must search well for him to-day, and maybe we shall be successful! We can buy some bread as we walk along, and thus satisfy our hunger."

"But mammy, we shall surely meet Alfonso returning as we go along," remarked Rita, timidly.

"True, child, I had forgotten that! We can take, however, a different route. We will go across the fields, instead of by the main road.

Taking the child's instrument of music from its accustomed place, and once more placing the paper box containing the tiny wardrobe under her shawl, the poor woman took the little girl's hand in hers, and passing down the main road until beyond sight of the encampment, fearing that prying eyes from the wagons might observe their movements, she struck into the fields, when it could safely be done, and as swiftly as her feeble feet would allow, she hurried towards the city.

Hour after hour they walked up and down prominent streets, looking in all directions for the form of their benefactor of the previous day.

They did not pause to sing, or to tell fortunes once, so eager were they in this search; and Costanza knew, that if obliged to return again to the camp, she had the gold piece in her pocket, which she could easily get changed into small coins, in order to exhibit as the proceeds of the day.

But as she travelled on, she determined on no account to return. No! better rest upon some doorstep all the night, than meet the abuse she knew would await their appearance.

Then again the thought came that Alfonso might be obliged to fly that night; if so, of course, if she was with them, she would lose all chance of finding the person for whom she searched.

Oh how weary she felt! Would she never see the kindly face of the stranger!

Noon had long since passed, and the afternoon was far advanced and as yet no success.

Her head swam! Her eyes grew heavy! she felt that she should fall if she proceeded another rod.

Gliding to the steps of a church they were at that moment passing, she sank upon them, and leaned her giddy head upon her hand.

"Mammy! I hear lovely music!" exclaimed Rita; "it comes from this church! there is a little side door open yonder, may I creep in, and listen to the beautiful sounds, while you rest here?"

"Yes, darling, go! I feel sick and strange, and therefore

cannot go any farther yet awhile. Go, listen to the melody."

"Do not stir, then, mammy, I will soon be back."

So the child arose, and softly following the music, disappeared within the open door.

CHAPTER XXVI

THE BURGLARY.

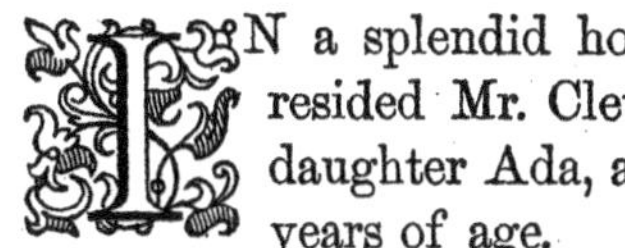N a splendid house, fronting Trafalgar Square, resided Mr. Cleveland, with his wife and only daughter Ada, a sweet young girl, about fifteen years of age.

Very amiable, and affectionate in disposition, as well as beautiful in person, was this darling daughter of the wealthy, pious, and truly benevolent Mr. Cleveland. Her blue eyes always beamed fondly on her father; her sweet words always comforted the heart of her mother; and to her they ever turned as the delight of their earthly existence, the brightest gem of all their vast possessions.

What to them would be earthly riches, if Ada were not there to enjoy it with them? what joy could money purchase, if deprived of her pure young affections?

So often said these loving parents, as they proudly watched their only child's development, in gentleness, purity, and beauty.

Ada was indeed very beautiful! Her hair was so luxuriant and so rich in its chestnut brown shades—her eyes were so "deeply, darkly, blue," and were fringed with such graceful lashes—her skin was so delicately fair, revealing so clearly the rosy tinge of her cheek,—while her pearl-white teeth and ruby lips were so ripe with beauty, that one could not but admire the charming girl.

Then she was so good, so lively, and so full of girlish enthusiasm, that she was a general favorite with her relatives, her teachers, and her schoolmates, as well as with the many visitors to her father's stately house.

Sweet Ada Cleaveland would soon have been spoiled by adulation and flattery, were it not for the judicious instructions of her parents, who, amid all their devotion to their "one ewe lamb," never forgot to train her for some more definite purpose than to be admired, fêted, and caressed.

Mr. and Mrs. Cleaveland sought early to inculcate religious truths in the heart of their daughter, sought, both by example and precept, to lead her to place her affections "on things above, not upon things below." Well had they succeeded in their endeavors, and Ada, to their great delight, early gave her heart to Jesus, and found happiness only in the earnest desire to do right.

The night in which we followed Alfonso to the city, listening to the explanation of his criminal intentions to his accomplice, found Mr. and Mrs. Cleaveland attending to the wants of Ada, who had been slightly indisposed all day, caused by a nervous headache, to which she was somewhat predisposed. She had taken cold a few days before, and this had aggravated the usual symptoms, causing more fever to accompany it, and consequently much more pain.

Faithfully had both father and mother attended to the suffering child, bathing her head, and administering soothing remedies, until about eleven in the evening, when they were gladdened by her assuring them that she felt much better, quite comfortable in fact, and as she inclined to sleep, she urged them to retire.

"'You are weary, mother dear, and really I feel so much relieved, it is not necessary for you to linger beside me. I shall sleep well, I am convinced, and by morning, shall in all probability be fully restored.

" 'Well, daughter, if you think so, we will retire, but we shall leave the communicating door from our room to yours, ajar, and if you wish anything you have only to speak, and I shall surely hear.

" 'That is all that is necessary, I assure you, darling mother. Please fill the silver cup with water, and place upon a chair beside my bed, then kiss me good night, and be sure to sleep soundly and well!' "

"Good night my daughter!" said both father and mother, kissing her fondly before entering their own apartment. "I trust you will be quite well by morning."

"I know I shall;" returned the young girl, cheerily, "good night!"

Ah! it was a long good night that issued from those fresh young lips! a long, long kiss—never more to be repeated in this world of sadness and of sin.

Poor father! poor mother! God keep thee in the agony that will be yours, before many hours pass over your now peaceful home!

May God, in his great mercy, sustain and comfort thee, poor, stricken ones, as, before the morning light, you look upon the still, cold corpse of your precious child!

Twelve o'clock had sounded, and all was peaceful and quiet in the rich man's dwelling!

One o'clock—and the young girl with her parents slept sweetly and well!

Two o'clock! still sleeping! No sound save a low, strange, cutting noise below, so cautiously guarded, that not one of the sleepers were disturbed in their peaceful dreams.

Three o'clock! still sleeping! but a crouching form is

gliding on hands and feet around the chamber of the unconscious parents! the hideous face of a man has been close beside their bed, the watches of both have been taken from beneath their pillows by a stealthy hand, and now rest in the villain's pocket, while the drawers of the bureau in the room have been ransacked, and a roll of money also finds its way into the burglar's possession.

Stooping again, to walk upon his hands and feet, the rascal glides through the open door, into the smaller room beyond.

A pair of blue eyes open at this instant and fix themselves upon the approaching creeping figure.

"Oh horror! what can it be? what fearful thing is drawing near?" thought poor, shuddering Ada.

"Father! mother!" burst from her livid lips. "Mother! father! there is a monstrous dog in the room! Mother! mother! it is close by the bed! Oh heavens! it is no dog, it is a man!"

A scream followed these words, and as Mr. and Mrs. Cleaveland sprang to their feet, they distinctly saw a man spring from the bedside and run into the hall, then down the stairs.

Pausing one moment to see if their darling was wounded, imagine their terror and surprise, at finding her in a fearful convulsion occasioned by this dreadful fright.

Neither thought then of pursuing the flying thief! neither thought of property stolen, or fugitives to be brought to justice.

So Alfonso and his companion, who had been equally busy below, succeeded in making their escape, and chuckling over their good fortune, they hastened to a distant grog-shop, and in a secluded corner divided the spoil, which amounted in all, to four hundred pounds besides the two gold watches, and a quantity of silver forks, and spoons. Delighted at their well accomplished scheme, the wretches called for glass after glass of bad liquor, and before the morning dawned, were in a beastly state of intoxication.

Poor Mrs. Cleaveland and her husband, in the meantime, hung almost stunned with fright and anguish over the convulsed form of their precious child some moments, before either thought to arouse the servants, and thus obtain assistance. When at last they did bethink themselves of this source of help, they touched a bell that communicated with their apartments, thus giving the alarm, but it was some moments before the maids, or the coachman, made their appearance.

Hastily dispatching the man for a physician, the agonized parents stood in wild suspense beside the bedside, striving by soft touches and affectionate words to restore poor Ada to consciousness.

In vain! No mother love could arouse her to reason,—No father's agony could render the least assistance, and before the arrival of the nearest physician, a frightful heaving of the chest, a tighter clenching of the soft white hand, was succeeded by the rigid stillness of death, and the beautiful Ada Cleaveland was safe in Heaven.*

Why linger on this harrowing scene? why picture the despairing grief of these stricken hearts, or, paint the tears that fell upon the fair, cold brow of their almost idolized child?

It would be useless! Nothing in this world could restore to them their jewel, therefore, with a pitying glance, a fervent prayer for the consolations of heaven to fall upon their chastened spirit, we leave them weeping sadly over their dead.

---

* The above incident is strictly true.

CHAPTER XXVII.

THE CHURCH ORGAN.

PAUL RUSSELL'S studies during all the day in which he had seen the gipsy fortune-teller, and the singing child, were, as I have said, strangely interfered with by visions of those sad tearful eyes, coming constantly between his own, and the page over which he bent. Then the exquisite voice of the little one kept ever recurring to memory.

He regretted exceedingly that his friend had urged him away, before he had asked her where he could see her again. He felt sure, the more he thought over the mournful words of the poor little musician, that she had been stolen from some loving mother's arms, who might be even then grieving for her "lily-bud,—her darling!"

The more he reflected upon each circumstance connected with the scene of the morning, the more he longed for the hour when he should be at liberty to leave the Seminary, and strive, by walking in frequented streets, to again see the object of his solicitude.

With a hurried step, then, he turned from the place of his mental labor, and passed rapidly through street after street, listening to catch the voice of the child, or to see the fantastic dress of the fortune-teller. But his efforts were all in vain, no woman or child of that description greeted his sight. As night was drawing near he at length passed disappointedly homeward, resolving not to mention the circumstance to any one, but to spend as much of the following day as was not devoted to study, and the Seminary, in continuing the search. The next morning he therefore arose early, and passed some time before breakfast, walking around the city.

But still he met with no success.

After the Seminary had closed for the day, Russell once more sallied forth, but it was with a fainter heart, and fast waning hope of meeting those he sought. It grew late, and disappointedly he again turned towards his residence, but as he passed along, he found that he was nearing the church in which Dr. Hartley, his pastor now, officiated, and as he voluntarily played the organ, while the true organist was absent for a few weeks, he took the key of the church from his pocket, hailed a small boy who was lounging near, to blow the instrument, for a few farthings, then passed in, not noticing that he had left the door ajar, in his haste, and preoccupied state of mind.

He would rest himself now, he thought, by wandering in the paths of the music he loved. He would revel in the tones of that fine old instrument, until his soul was imbued with the spirit of the beautiful, and his heart was soothed by the magic spell of the power of melody.

So he played on! Soft, low cadences, wild, stormy passages, mellow, glorious anthems, until his heart throbbed, as his fingers swept over the keys, and the color mounted into his pale face, and the fire flashed in his fine black eyes—the fire of inspiration and of genius.

So often, had he played in all the grand old Cathedrals of Europe; so had he lingered entranced, over the organs belonging to St. Peter's in Rome, the splendid Duomos of Florence, and the grand Cathedrals of Cologne, and Dantzic in Germany, pouring out his soul in exquisite harmony, and chasing sorrowful remembrances from his heart, by refrains of unequalled splendor and beauty.

So had he glided over the marble paved aisles of Notre Dame, up into the choir, and so called forth the notes of the immense organ there, drawing inspiration from the rich and varied tones of that celebrated instrument, and pouring out his heart in melody, as he bent over the keys.

Then again, he had swelled the notes of the organ in St. Paul's Cathedral, had composed many a stirring overture upon that noble instrument, but none did he love so well, as the unpretending, fine-toned one, in the church where Moreland had worshipped; never did such visions of heaven, such hymns of rapture and sweetness, roll over his spirit, as when seated by that organ, with his fingers passing lightly over its keys. So he played on, never seeing the little form that had entered the half open door, that had glided up the stairs, passing through the choir-seats, and that now stood breathlessly by his side, drinking in the grandeur of the music that swelled from his fingers and his soul.

He saw not the tears of delight that filled the large brown eyes, he heard not the wild throbbing of the poor little heart, as, heaving a deep sigh, she sank upon her knees, crossed her hands upon her bosom, and listened, awe-struck, to the charming notes.

But he did hear that long, low sigh, and half turning his head, although never pausing in his occupation, what was his surprise to see, kneeling beside him, with awe upon her face, and rapture in her look, the little street singer of the morning.

She did not see him turn his head, so intent was she upon the music, and wonderingly, he watched her speaking features, through many a prolonged note and swelling chord, which he then played for her benefit.

At last he spoke, and the little girl sprang to her feet with a cry of delight, and seizing his hand, exclaimed—

"Oh good sir! good sir! is it you that have made such heavenly music? All day Costanza and I have looked for you through the dusty streets, and now I have found you in this splendid house!"

"You looked for me, little one? Why I, too, for hours, have been searching for you. But where is the gipsy mother?"

"She is sick, and rests upon the steps without, while I followed the music. She wanted so much to speak with you; may I bring her inside the door, and will you listen while she tells you something?"

"I will indeed, dear child. Let us go down," continued he, taking her tiny hand in his, and descending to the entrance. "Now go and bid her come in; but close the door, Rita, when you return, so that we shall not be interrupted."

Paul Russell waited but a few moments, before the child appeared, supporting the feeble steps of the woman, who did indeed seem sick and faint, caused by her long tramp that day.

"Oh, good gentleman," she exclaimed almost before she reached him, "have I indeed been so fortunate as to find you? You spoke kindly to my poor Rita yesterday. You gave her this golden treasure. Oh may I tell you her story, and interest you in her welfare before I die? for, sir, the grasp of death is on me, its cold chill is even now spreading over my heart."

Paul saw in one look that the gipsy woman's words were true, for an ashy whiteness was around her lips, and a short catch was in her breath, that told truly of approaching dissolution.

Opening a pew door, he bade the poor creature lie down upon the soft cushions, while she related the story, in which he assured her he took a deep interest, adding, that he would assist her in her trouble as far as it lay in his power.

CHAPTER XXVIII.

THE GIPSY'S STORY.

> "Life hath not laid her hand upon me lightly;
> I have known sorrow, disappointment, pain;
> Have seen hope clouded when it burned most brightly,
> And false love fade, and falser friendship wane."

MY name, kind sir, is Costanza, and all my life has been spent with my tribe, travelling from place to place, camping in the woods, and picking up a living by telling fortunes, begging, and indeed the best way we could find it. My mother died about the time I was married to Alfonso, which is now ten years ago. I loved Alfonso devotedly, and then he seemed very fond of me. He courted me under the green trees of the wildwood, with sweet flowers, wild roses, and honeysuckles blooming under our feet. I was very happy in his love, and asked for nothing more in the wide world, than I then possessed. He told me I was beautiful, and I think I was; my form was plump and round, my cheeks rosy and brown, while my black eyes were full of the ardor and sprightliness of youth.

Alfonso was a great man in our tribe, and became a leader of the race. He was looked upon by all with admiration for his bravery and strength, and I was the envy of all the gipsy girls around. He built me a nice little room, which he placed upon wheels, and thus I was carried from town to town, in much greater comfort than were the other women, for they had only canvas-covered wagons, while my home was dry, and well protected by windows and door.

He never sent me out on tramps in those days, in the villages we passed through, to beg, or tell fortunes, but I was regarded as a sort of gipsy queen, and nothing laborious was put upon me.

Thus time sped by, until I became a mother. One day, a dear little daughter came to my nest, and in the light of my Caterino's eyes, I was as happy as the day was long. I loved my child with a passion that few mothers feel. She was my star, my flower, my beautiful, beautiful babe! I idolized her, and thus three years of joy passed over my head, three years of unclouded bliss, fed by the purest mother-love, swept past my bosom. Such happiness could not last! sorrow must lurk somewhere in the path of the living, and sadly did I discover, that it would not pass me by.

It was a bright summer morning, and our encampment then was near Florence.

Italy had ever been our favorite stopping-place; indeed it was in that sunny land Alfonso as well as myself, first saw the light of day, and there my precious babe was born. At the time of which I speak, we were camping in a lovely grove near the city, and all seemed prospering finely, when one day my darling drooped. I saw her little face grow flushed with fever, I saw her loving eyes grow dim, and in an agony of terror, I gathered her in my arms, and started for a doctor's residence in the city. He shook his head when he saw her, saying she was very ill with scarlet fever; he gave me some remedies, charging me to administer them faithfully; I need not say, I obeyed him. All day and all night, I watched her, while Alfonso also stood sadly by, to see if any change would appear for the better. It came not—but fearful convulsions came on, in one of which dear little Caterino breathed her last. Yes! she was gone, and I was wild with sorrow. Alfonso did all he could to soothe me, but in vain, I would not be comforted! We laid our darling to sleep in the shadow of the grave, where the birds sang, and the flowers blossomed, and there I sat day after day, for we lingered a much longer while than usual in that place, Alfonso was so strangely engrossed by some attraction in the city.

So day by day I wept alone, broken-heartedly, by the grave of my lost idol; night after night I felt in vain for the little arms that had been wound so lovingly around my neck, and for the curly head that had slept so sweetly upon my bosom.

One evening, just as the stars were making their appearance in the sky, I was lying on the grave of my departed Caterino, gazing sadly, at the broad canopy above, when I heard Alfonso call my name; jumping to my feet, I ran hurriedly to meet him, for he had been quite impatient the last few days, and I disliked to irritate him by the least delay.

"Costanza," said he, as I approached, "now I must have no more weeping! See," said he, throwing back a shawl from the face of a child he held in his arms, "see, I have brought you a little girl to take the place of our dead baby."

I looked at him in mute amazement, but he spoke truly; a little girl about the age of Caterino, the most beautiful little creature I ever beheld, lay shuddering frightfully in his" —— the poor gipsy stopped; she was about to say bloody arms, but with a shiver, she paused, and added, almost in a whisper, "in his arms. Take her," said he, "I have stolen her to comfort you! She is yours now, so keep her and stop grieving."

The poor little thing held out her arms imploringly for me to take her from Alfonso, and as I did so, she clasped them tightly around my neck, whispering in my ear, in Italian, for she dared not speak aloud, "Oh take me to mamma! please take me to mamma!"

"What is her name, Alfonso?" said I, "whose child is she and where is her mother?"

A horrible look, the first I had ever seen, but by no means the last, fell upon me from Alfonso's eyes, as he growled, "Shut up on that! Never dare ask me that again. Call her after your mother, Margherita; the child is yours, I told you, now say no more."

I was frightened at his savage tones, as well as his looks, and taking the little one in my arms, I entered my wagon home, while Alfonso gave immediate orders to move on, night though it was. I heard him hurry around, I saw the confusion of the men, and the bustle of the women, as I sat holding and soothing the almost frantic child, who kept imploring me to carry her to her father and mother.

Poor dear! in a few moments the horses were harnessed, the camping ground destroyed, and in the starlight and in the moonlight, I looked through the window, towards the little mound under the trees—my last look—for the wagons moved on, and from that time to this, we have never more visited Italy, the bright land that I loved.

"Take off that child's finery, and put on Caterino's clothes; do you hear?" came the rough words of Alfonso from the driver's seat, as morning dawned, and I still sat clasping the poor pet to my bosom. I could see her brown eyes dilate with fear, as he spoke, shudder after shudder passing over her frame. Sweet innocent! she has never recovered from her horror of that man's presence, although four years have passed since that fatal night.

I took the child's beautiful clothing from her little form, replacing them by the coarse garments of my own lost babe, but notwithstanding Alfonso ordered me to burn them, I carefully preserved the little articles in this box, thinking they might be of use some day. "Here the gipsy paused, and drawing forth the box from under her shawl, she offered it to Russell, who took it carefully, and raising the lid, gazed at the beautiful needle-work with unfeigned interest.

"There is a golden chain and armlets in a smaller box, underneath, with the initials L. L. engraved upon their clasps. I loved the stolen child," continued she, "from the moment she clasped her arms around my neck, moaning so piteously for her dear mamma. I thought of the mother's anguish, for I knew what it was to lose a babe, and could I have restored her, gladly would I have done so. But Alfonso never told me one word of her history, giving me but *blows*—yes *blows*—when I questioned him. From the day he stole that child, he became a brute; he took to drink, sent us both out to beg, and Rita to sing, while with a heavy whip he often beat us until the blood poured over our flesh from the wounds, because we did not earn enough to satisfy his passion for liquor."

"See," said the poor woman, exposing the deep cuts upon her arms, "these I received while striving to defend my poor little pet from his cruel blows the other night. Look, good gentleman, at her wounded back," then turning down the dress from the tender shoulders, Paul Russell uttered a cry of horror at the fearful ridges of lacerated flesh that met his gaze. Then gathering the tearful little one in his arms, he exclaimed,

"God helping me, my good woman, she shall never suffer thus again! from this hour I shall protect her; she shall be my child."

"Thank you, oh thank you! now I can depart in peace. As for me," added she, with a sort of gasp, "I dare not return to the camp. I will die by the wayside sooner than be murdered; but oh, to die in this great city, and not be buried in the rich green woods, that is so hard! so very hard!"

Sinking back, she closed her eyes over her pallid cheek a moment, then opening them with a sigh, she cried again,

"You will certainly care for my Rita; you will save her from the gipsy tribe, for they will surely kill her after I am dead? Your wife and little children will love and cherish the motherless one?"

"I will protect her, fear not. No gipsy crew on earth shall ever drag her from me," replied Paul; "but while I have no wife, nor little children, I board with a noble woman, who will be a mother to her, until I find her own."

"I am content, I give the child to you—and now, I have nothing to do but die," moaned the poor gipsy.

"No, mammy, do not die! do not die!" exclaimed Rita, leaving Paul's arms, and kneeling by the woman's side, "I love you, for you were always kind and good."

"Yes, I know, darling,—but—I must go—kiss me once!—close—closer! Caterino—I come!"

The words ceased, a slight shudder, and the poor fortuneteller, was no more.

CHAPTER XXIX.

THE CHILD'S NEW HOME.

"I am far frae my hame, an' I'm weary often whiles,
For the langed for hame-bringin," an' my Father's welcome smiles;
I'll ne'er be content, until my een do see
The gowden gates o' heaven, an my ain countree."

PAUL gazed with astonishment upon the body of the gipsy, after all was over. He had seen that she was in the last stages of consumption, but that she was so *very* near her end, he had not dreamed. He hardly knew how to proceed under these peculiar circumstances, but gently closing her eyes, he stood for a little time, lost in deep contemplation.

At the moment he had closed the organ, he had dismissed the boy who had blown the bellows of the instrument, therefore he had no one to dispatch for assistance, and he could not leave the child. On reflection, he was glad of this, as he feared some of the gipsy band might be prowling around, and thus obtain a clue to her whereabouts, and he was well convinced, that whatever was done, must be done with great secrecy and care.

Arranging the body, then, as comfortably as possible, upon the cushion of the pew, he wrapped carefully around it a large cloth that had been used to cover the velvet of the pulpit; then taking Rita by the hand, he led her into the vestry-room, and there sought to comfort her in her grief at the loss of Costanza, by talking of the probability of his soon restoring her to her father and mother.

Thus he beguiled the time, until darkness covered the earth, then carefully folding a large, dark table cover, he took from a table in this room, around her, he raised her small figure in his arms, and bidding her keep perfectly quiet, he softly unlocked a small side door, quietly fastening it after him, and passed swiftly through the streets on his way to his pastor's residence, which was but a couple of squares distant, for it was in his family he boarded, while pursuing his studies.

The good Doctor and his wife were seated in their parlor, enjoying a quiet chat, after the cares of the day were ended, when they were startled by a sharp ring at the door bell.

"Some sick person in haste sends a message, I think! I will open the door and not wait for the servant!" remarked Dr. Hartley. "Ha! Russell, is that you? what in the world have you there?" he added, as Paul stepped with his burden hastily past him, quickly closing the door as he did so.

"A precious charge, Doctor, and to you I turn for counsel. Can I see yourself and wife alone in my room a few moments? There we shall be free from interruptions."

"Certainly!" replied both, following his footsteps to his own private apartment and carefully closing the door.

"I have met with a most singular and thrilling adventure to-day, Doctor Hartley. I hold in my arms a poor little girl, who was stolen four years ago from her parents in Italy, by a band of gipsies. To-night she is rescued from their clutches, and I have been in part the instrument. Seeing how providentially she has been thrown upon me for protection, I would cherish her until I find her parents. Look!" cried he, throwing back the cover and revealing the tiny form, sleeping soundly in his arms from sheer exhaustion. "Did you ever see such perfect beauty, such a fairy face? Do you wonder that I am interested in such a little gem? Oh, if you could see her eyes and hear her sing, you would exclaim, indeed!"

Then placing the sleeping cherub gently upon the bed, he related to his eager listeners the story told by the gipsy, and finally ended by the sad scene of her death, explaining where he had left the body, and asking counsel as to what had next best be done.

But the box containing the poor babe's clothing, have you that with you?" asked Mrs. Hartley.

"Yes! thanks to a capacious pocket, intended for conveying a book now and then to and from the Seminary," replied Paul, drawing it forth. Placing the box in her hands, the simple, yet beautiful garments were carefully examined, while the initials upon the chain and armlets were also studied, but no farther clue could be obtained to her parentage, than the letters engraved thereon.

"It is very evident," at length said Mrs. Hartley, "that her parents belong to the upper class of society. What must have been their anguish at her loss. Dear Mr. Russell, you are perfectly right in thus protecting her. Glad am I, that by bringing her hither I can love and care for her also. Poor little creature!" added the kind hearted lady, as in bending over the sleeping face, a tear fell upon her lovely brow. "She shall never know the want of a mother's care while I live. Never! never! To think of that brutal wretch, whipping so cruelly such a tender babe." Then shudderingly she examined the sore and mutilated back and shoulders of the little sufferer. "I wonder if the child is hungry as well as torn? I suppose she has had no food for hours."

"She is not hungry," replied Paul. "I asked her while I waited in the vestry for nightfall to fold the city, before I ventured out, and she assured me Costanza had purchased her a good supper, just before they reached the church. All she needs now, is a quiet, refreshing sleep."

"Then, Mr. Russell, pray go to the dining room yourself, and take some refreshments there awaiting you. Not reaching home at the tea hour, you must need food. I will watch the child while you are absent. Never fear: I will see that she is not left alone."

"I have no fears for her welfare now, since kind Mrs. Hartley is her friend," said Russell, as he left the room after gazing one moment tenderly upon the little waif thus thrown upon his bounty."

After partaking of a hasty meal, Paul and Dr. Hartley left the house, in order to notify the coroner that an inquest ought to be held over the corpse lying in the church, and to make preparations for having her interred as secretly as possible.

It was decided best not to disclose the fact of a child having been with her to any one, nor did they think it necessary to mention that the woman belonged to the gipsy race. Passing first to the church to view the corpse, and to see that all was right, they lighted a small jet of gas, and then removed from her dress, without stirring the position of the body, all the fantastic decorations, denoting her profession of a fortune-teller, and placing them in a safe hiding place, they thus gave her the appearance of but a poor dead beggar. Re-covering the body after a pitying gaze at the wasted features, they turned down the light to a mere glimmer, and relocking the door, pursued their way to the coroner's. It was then only half-past eight, but they could not succeed in obtaining an inquest and permit for burial until sometime next day, but as it was early in the week and Dr. Hartley was certain the sexton, nor any other person, would have occasion to enter the church before the following Saturday, it was determined to allow the body to remain as it was until the morrow, when farther arrangements could be made, and deliberations taken as to its final disposal.

CHAPTER XXX.

POOR BELLE.

"Death!—death! do I see thee with weapon dread?"
L. H. S.

MRS. HARTLEY was a woman of much energy and character; with her to think, was to plan and to act. As she sat therefore that evening by the side of the bed, gazing at the poor swollen shoulder of little Rita, and listening to the moan of pain that followed the least touch, she saw that she would need a woman's care and attention. She must be taken immediately to her own room, for what would Mr. Russell do with her there, never having had the charge of a child in his life? With her, I say, to think, was to *act*, therefore ringing for her chamber maid, she quietly waited her entrance.

"See here, Rose," she exclaimed, as the tidy looking girl entered. "See what Mr. Russell has kindly rescued from the city streets, a poor homeless little girl. He brought her here with him, to-night, and intends to take charge of her always."

"The dear, illigant man!—what a darlint it is though! and as beautiful as the daylight. I niver saw sich a splendid child indade!" uttered the astonished, yet kind-hearted maid, as she bent over the sleeping form.

Mrs. Hartley knew the girl she was dealing with. She

had been in her service twenty years, had nursed her children in childhood, had seen each one marry and leave her home, and she knew that her sympathies would be immediately enlisted for the motherless one before her. She was not mistaken,—nor in the fidelity of the cook Bridget, another faithful servant of eighteen years. Both these women—for Rose immediately summoned the other, by Mrs. Hartley's orders—listened with intense interest as their mistress related the history of the stolen child. Then promising strict secrecy, they both kissed the fair little cheek, and set themselves to work in good earnest, to complete the preparations Mrs. Hartley wished made. A small single bed, that had once been used for a similar purpose by her own children, now watching the slumber of theirs, in their distant homes, was brought from the garret, and placed in her own apartment; the snowy sheets, pillow-cases, and counterpane were soon adjusted, and everything was ready for its new occupant. Opening a huge trunk in which unused articles were kept, Mrs. Hartley took therefrom some night dresses and undergarments, once belonging to those same children, and again turned to the slumbering child.

How quietly, now, she seemed to sleep!—what a pity to disturb her! but feeling that it was for her good, she gently aroused her.

"Will my dear little girl let me undress her and wash her, then sleep nicely in a beautiful white bed?"

"Mammy, is that you? Oh, I remember," exclaimed the startled child, gazing around her with a surprised and bewildered look. Where am I, and where is the kind gentleman, mammy gave me to?"

"You are in his home, darling; this is his room, and I am his dear friend. He has gone out for a while to attend to your gipsy mother! Won't the little girl let me wash her, and put on these nice white clothes?"

"Yes ma'am!" almost sobbed Rita, "but you are not mamma, and he promised to find my own, dear mamma!"

"So he will, poor lamb, in a short time, I hope. No! I am not mamma, but I will love you very—very much!"

"You won't let that dreadful man get me, dear lady, will you?" exclaimed the child, as the thought of Alfonso crossed her mind, while she clung to the hand of her new friend.

"No, never, darling, never!" Then taking the little form in her arms, she entered the bath-room, and soon refreshed the weary body by a nice tepid bath. The little one smiled as the soft garments were placed upon her, and she was gently lifted into the snowy bed, in that spacious room; then, with one hand clasped in Mrs. Hartley's, who sat beside her, the beautiful brown eyes soon closed, and "tired nature's sweet restorer," once more folded her in its welcome embrace.

"Sleep quietly now, poor innocent, and oh may God soon lead thee to thy mother's longing bosom!" murmured Mrs. Hartley, pressing a loving kiss upon her ruby lips.

Often through the silent hours of the night, might Mrs. Hartley have been seen leaving her own bed to bend over the sleeping child, for she had discovered, before she retired, a slight tendency to fever, and a restlessness that seemed to whisper of approaching sickness, and before morning dawned, the good woman found, indeed, ample room for anxiety, for little Rita was in a burning fever, caused by ill usage, excitement, and over fatigue.

When daylight came, however, the cooling remedies given so wisely, had somewhat relieved her, and although still sick, she seemed bright and cheerful.

"Can I see that nice gentleman that made such heavenly music, and will he let me hear such beautiful sounds often, dear auntie?" asked Rita, for Mrs. Hartley had told her thus to address her.

"Yes, darling, lie very quiet in the bed to-day, and he will soon come to you! Did you know that he kissed you as you slept last night, after he came home?" replied the lady.

"Did he? that gave me those sweet dreams, I know! I love him very much already, auntie, and I always shall," murmured the child.

When Mr. Russell entered, and approached her comfortable bed, little Rita's eyes sparkled with pleasure, and her outstretched arms were ready to wind around his neck, as he stooped to kiss her.

"Oh, sir! I love you so much for taking me away from those cruel gipsies, and for that sweet music. Will you play again for Rita sometime, and will you find papa and mamma?" asked she, still clasping his hand in hers, as he took a seat beside her.

"I will often play and sing for you, dear one, and you will sing your beautiful songs for me when you get well. Some day also I hope to find your friends, for I shall try very hard. But did your own mamma call you Rita? Think, darling!"

"Oh no! She called me her lily-bud, her darling!" murmured the child, tears instantly filling her eyes at the thought.

"But what did papa call you! can you remember?" asked Paul.

A look of deep thought followed, a few moments' silence, then clapping her hands together, she exclaimed,

"I remember! Yes, I remember! it was Liza. Papa and poor Belle always called me Liza."

Delight flashed in Paul's eyes at this pleasant information. This answered to one of the initials, and was most likely the real name of the desolate child; therefore, much encouraged, he continued questioning his tiny friend.

"Then, dear, if papa called you Liza so shall we; the gipsy name of Rita you will hear no more. Now tell me, who was poor Belle?"

A shudder, fearful to behold, followed that question; a look of the greatest terror dilated her brown eyes, as, with a frightened whisper, she cried as she clung to his arm, "Don't—don't,—he will kill me if I tell! he said so, and I know he will!"

"Who, darling? no one can harm you here. Do not be afraid; won't Cousin Paul always take care of his sweet pet? Who said he would kill my birdie, that wicked Alfonso?"

"Yes! oh yes! Are you sure he won't come here?"

"I know he can never find you. Tell me all about poor Belle. It may be I can find mamma sooner, if I know of her."

Winding her arms around his neck as she drew his head to the pillow, she whispered,

"Belle took me out to walk! Alfonso met us and said he would take us on the pretty Arno for a sail. We went —but, oh dear, I dare not tell!" shuddered the poor child.

"Do not fear, Liza, tell me *all*, for I will take care of you," soothingly replied Paul.

"He took a sharp knife and stabbed poor Belle! Three times he cut her. Oh, I saw him kill my Belle and throw her into the dark blue river; "added the child, hiding her face in Paul's neck. "He caught hold of me then, and raised the knife; I thought he was going to kill me too, but he did not; he said he wanted me to be Costanza's child, and to sing, (for he had often heard me sing when he came to see Belle,) and make money for him. If I did he would not kill me, but if I ever told what he did to Belle, he would kill me the next moment. I promised to be good and not tell, if he would not cut me. Then he took me in his bloody arms, and carried me to the gipsy camp, and gave me to Costanza. I have been good, kind sir; I did sing and make lots of money, but he said it was not enough, and used to whip me, and I was so afraid he would kill me."

Paul's look of horror may well be imagined as he heard this story of cruelty and murder, but clasping the child to his bosom, he kissed her sweet lips, and told her she *was* a good girl, and now, he would go out and buy her some beautiful clothes, new dresses, new shoes, and ribbons, and some pretty toys too, all that could possibly please a little girl: then bidding her lie still, and try to get well, by thinking how much Cousin Paul loved her and how he would soon find her own mamma, he laid her gently back upon the pillows, parted her rich brown curls nicely from her brow, gazed fondly into her loving eyes, then left the room.

Not forgetting his promise, Paul hastened to a large emporium for children's ready made clothing, and there, with perfect taste, selected a beautiful wardrobe of every necessary article that a child of her age would require, together with dolls, and dolls' appointments, he ordered them sent immediately to Dr. Hartley's, 24 —— Square, then passed on, to attend to the duties of the day.

CHAPTER XXXI.

THE MIDNIGHT FUNERAL.

"Rattle her bones
Over the stones;
'Tis only a pauper,
Whom nobody owns."

IT was night! starry night!

Over the city of London a beautiful full moon was hanging, while star after star, constellation after constellation, had taken its place in the sky, until a perfect myriad of twinkling orbs were floating in the broad expanse above.

Hushed and silent were the streets, for two o'clock had long since sounded, and all was folded in their deepest sleep. Now and then, to be sure, some drunken bacchanalian was to be seen, reeling homeward, or the watchmen's rattle told their presence, and their nightly task, but all else seemed wrapped in slumber, and in night's dusky wing.

At this still hour, slowly and solemnly a hearse was wending its way, followed by a single empty carriage.

Down this deserted street, and up another, these dim precursors of death rolled on, never pausing, never halting, until they stood before a church, whose rich, but unpretending front seemed even more sombre and massive, when looked upon amid the darkness and the gloom.

Here the two vehicles paused, while the men descending tied their horses, and silently passing around to a side door, they gently knocked. But a moment elapsed before the door opened, and both men stepped within, and joined two others who were standing near the altar.

There, dimly seen by the single lighted burner, reposing upon two benches in the middle aisle, was a neat, but plain coffin, beneath whose still open lid might be seen all that remained of Costanza, the dead gipsy.

Standing by the side of Mr. Russell, the three scarcely stirred, while Dr. Hartley, in deep but slow tones, read the burial service of the dead.

The dim glimmering light, the midnight hour, the holy hush, and the silent corpse, all tended to fill the bosom of each person there, with awe and solemnity.

The last word was spoken, the last prayer was said, then gently covering the face and screwing down the lid, the two men raised the coffin, and slowly bore it to the door, followed by Russell and the clergyman. Silently the corpse was placed in the hearse and the driver drove away, followed by the carriage containing the reverend gentleman and his friend.

So they moved along, slowly, solemnly through the dark and gloomy streets, on! on!

An hour passed, yet still they had not halted, until just as the time approached half-past three, the driver turned the horses' heads towards what seemed the high walls of a cemetery. Springing to the ground, one of the men applied a massive key to the large lock, thus opening the huge gates; when the funeral train passed through, and once more the double gate was closed and fastened.

Again the driver resumed his seat, and through winding

paths, nodding trees, and tall white tombs, the little cortege wended its way.

In a far corner, where the mounds were few, and the trees thick, the hearse stopped beside an open grave, and all alighting, the last words of the service were uttered, the body was lowered, dust was given to dust, and poor Costanza lay in her long resting-place under the branches of a drooping willow, where the singing birds would come, and the wild grasses would wave, until the last trump shall sound, and the morning of the resurrection shall cause the graves to open, and the sea to give up its dead. "*Implora pace.*"

CHAPTER XXXII.

LETTERS.

"In the dim recess of thy spirit's cnamber
Is there some hidden grief thou may'st not tell?
Let not thy heart forsake thee ; but remember,
His pitying eye, who sees and knows it well.
God knows it all!"

IN the afternoon following that midnight march to the tomb, Russell sat in his private study, which communicated with his bed-chamber. He had occupied the last half hour by playing on the splendid parlor organ, that stood in a large recess, upon one side the handsomely furnished room, to Liza's great delight. The little girl had quite recovered from her illness, and dressed in some of the rich clothing, bought so kindly by her benefactor, she stood with flushed cheek, and sparkling eyes, singing, by his side.

"Shall I sing the song papa loved,—next, Cousin Paul?" asked she, raising her eyes to his, as she spoke, with perfect love and confidence in the gaze.

"Yes, darling! let me hear that!" returned Paul; eager curiosity beaming in his looks.

Crossing her hands upon her bosom, Liza began, but her voice trembled, and her eyes filled with tears, as she proceeded. The words were Italian, and the air was strangely thrilling and beautiful!

A gush of tears followed the song, while the little one laid her head upon Paul's shoulder, and sobbed in silent agony.

"Why do you weep thus, Liza? Tell Cousin Paul," asked the young man soothingly, passing his arm around her, and gently stroking her sunny hair.

"Papa was going away, and he asked me to sing my pretty song before he left. I stood by his side, just as I stand by yours, and crossing my hands just so, I sang those words. Then he took me in his arms and kissed me, and after kissing mamma, he rode away in a carriage, but said he would be back again in two or three days. Cousin Paul, I never saw my papa again! for before he came, I was far away in the big, dark woods, the child of the gipsy mother."

A long pause ensued, broken only by the sobs of the weeping Liza. Paul allowed her to give vent to her tears unchecked; he felt that it would relieve her troubled heart, and indeed he had no words to offer that could alleviate such sorrow. He knew that all he could do now, was patiently to wait the leadings of Providence, and to God he committed her cause. He felt assured that He would guide him in this case of deepest mystery. That morning he had dispatched letters to Florence, addressed to Signora Fabretti, and also to several gentlemen whose friendship he had formed while sojourning there with Moreland, and felt sure that they would make instant inquiries around, and thus discover whether any woman and child had disappeared from that region, four years before. Now, he could only wait their reply.

But notwithstanding these letters, and the diligent search for information which these persons kindly instituted, no clue could be obtained in regard to the matter, and thus weeks and months of disappointed hope followed every effort, to ferret out the mystery.

Paul finally, wishing to leave nothing untried, bade Liza a fond farewell, and consigning her to Mrs. Hartley's motherly care, went himself to Florence, where, by advertising, and personal investigation, he hoped to hear from the unknown parents. But all was in vain; owing to the removal, two years before, of Signor Pompelli from that region, no tidings could be obtained, and weary and sad, Paul was obliged to return without the mother, for whom poor Liza mourned.

"Mr. Russell, here is a letter for yees, sure," said Rose one day, about six months after Liza's entrance into the family, as he sat in his room. Approaching through the open door, she handed him a neatly folded epistle, directed, evidently, by a lady.

Paul found it to be from his favorite Bessie Brown. It was written at Cedar Lawn, just after her return from New York, and was dated February 2nd, 1864.

The letter was long and interesting, giving an account of herself and her father,—of Minnie Morton's (how Russell started at the name!) visit to their quiet home, and of the pleasant time they had spent together. Then she described her visit to New York; how she had thoughtlessly given her rash promise to Minnie, to mingle *once* in each of her amusements, in order to judge for herself as to their propriety, without allowing herself to be biased by the opinion of others. Thus then she frankly confessed that she had allowed herself to be drawn into a whirl of excitement and dissipation, until her conscience had upbraided her, and she had torn herself from the snare, and while her gay companion mingled in each festivity, she was happy in the society of a lovely young widow, sister of Mr. Morton. Then came a description, full of girlish enthusiasm, of Mrs. Douglass; her rare beauty, her cultivation, her deep seclusion, and last, though not least, her ardent fervent piety.

"I wish you knew her, Cousin Paul," wrote the artless girl; "I wish you could hear her speak of Jesus, of the precious things He has done for her soul. I wish you could see the holy spiritual look that leaps over her face, when she speaks of her sins as having been all forgiven, *only* for the sake of her adorable Saviour, whose precious blood was shed," she would say, " even for sin-sick Rebecca Douglass." Then she would enter into all my feelings so sympathizingly, realizing herself, the sinfulness often met in fashionable life, and shunning gaiety in every form, she could point out to me the evil of such dissipations, and fully approve of my declining all persuasions to join the charmed circle of fashion and frivolity. Oh the pleasant hours I often spent in the apartments of this charming lady, I cannot describe! but I fear for her health, she seems so frail and so sorrowful. One day, I was speaking to her of you, of your similar taste for music, when she suddenly became so ill, I feared for a moment the result. But she told me she was subject to fainting, and I must not be alarmed, therefore I have scarcely reason to be so fearful. I know not why I have written this glowing description to you, of a stranger; why I take up your time portraying beauty and piety, which the broad waters of the Atlantic shield from your knowledge and observation. Why, but that I ever seem to link your names together in my thoughts, ever dream how much you are alike in your tastes and religious characters. But I must close my long letter, by asking of yourself, why you linger so long away from your friends? what induces you to stay? are you not lonely, or have you forgotten us? Write to me soon—very soon! Tell me every little item that might be of interest, so long as it is connected with one so highly esteemed, and so fondly remembered. Write thus, often, and freely, to your faithful

BESSIE BROWN."

There was a nervous twitching around the corners of Russell's mouth, a strange mournfulness in his large black eyes, as with trembling hands he folded the letter, murmuring, "Yes! she was beautiful, beautiful, beautiful,—and now with her changed heart, and love for Jesus, she must be superb! Oh Bessie, Bessie, why have you done this? why have you reopened that cruel wound?"

Burying his face in his hands, poor Paul remained, motionless and sad, lost in thought for a weary while. Rising at length, as if resolved to shake off his trouble, he approached his writing desk, and taking therefrom pen, ink, and paper, he commenced a letter in reply.

"Yes, I am lonely," he wrote; after giving a long account of his adventures, feelings, and pastimes, also the history of his interviews with the gipsy woman, and the sad story of little Liza, the stolen child, "lonely indeed! but the gratitude and love of this desolate one, is very dear to me, her beautiful voice, her pretty songs, whisper comfort to my lonely spirit, and I am glad to have had her with me, even these short six months, as she has been a sunbeam in my path, dear little Liza! Would, however, that I could find the father and mother, for whom she so unceasingly mourns; would that I might be instrumental in shedding peace upon her suffering, gentle heart. Sweet

Bessie, will you not join me at the mercy seat, and there pray that this poor weary bird may soon repose in her own mother-nest, happy, contented, and glad. To-day I feel a strange yearning to see my native land, my *never forgotten* friends once more; your letter, with its frank confidence, its interesting intelligence of yourself and companions, its pure loving words, has opened deep in my soul, the earnest cry for home. Yet little Bessie,—for I cannot picture you as other than that fair golden haired child, that sat upon my knee in days gone by,—yet, little Bessie, I may not, cannot yield to the wish. Duty bids me stay on these far off shores still another year, if not more. But I do promise myself, as soon as these tasks that now occupy my attention are completed, I do think and dream of coming home. Home! yes, home to my country, to your father's cheerful roof—to you, as I have no nearer ties on earth, no better friends. Adieu, now, gentle Bessie, my letter is already too long,—I fear I have wearied you! Remember ever with affection and with prayer, your deeply attached, though far away,

PAUL RUSSELL."

CHAPTER XXXIII.

RE-UNION.

> "I see thee still, * * * *
> Thou comest in the morning light,
> Thou'rt with me through the gloomy night;
> In dreams I meet thee as of old;
> Then thy soft arms my neck unfold,
> And thy sweet voice is in my ear;
> In every scene to memory dear
> I see thee still."
>
> CHARLES SPRAGUE.

WE will not linger to describe the daily events that transpired in the home where Liza was the pet and darling, but will merely state in passing, that the sweet amiability, the affectionate gratitude she displayed, together with her natural talents, won every heart in that household, each feeling for the little child a pure and fervent love. But to Paul she was indeed, as he had said in his letter to Bessie, a sunbeam. To him, the little one gave her fondest affection, by his side she was ever contented and happy. When the hour came for him to hasten to the Seminary, her eyes would fill with tears, while her arms would cling to him, as though she could not bear the parting; then, when his step again was heard, with joy pictured upon her face, and a smile upon her lips, she would rush to meet him, and almost overwhelm him with caresses and delight. So time had flown since her rescue, and while no word came to satisfy the hope of finding her relatives, yet she seemed contented and even happy, diverted, as she was, from her sorrow, by her warm affection for Cousin Paul, the music lessons he daily gave her upon the piano, and the books and toys he constantly purchased for her amusement and instruction.

One morning, Paul was preparing to leave his study, rather earlier than usual, thinking to walk awhile, before commencing the mental tasks of the day, when Rose knocked lightly at the door. Opening it, the girl informed him that a gentleman wished to see him in the parlor.

Waiting but to restore some pamphlets he had been glancing over, to the bookcase, and to receive little Liza's parting kiss, as he told her he should leave as soon as the person who had called departed, he sought the waiting visitor.

As he entered the parlor, a fine-looking stranger, apparently about thirty-eight years of age, advanced to meet him.

"This is Mr. Paul Russell, I believe;" he remarked.

"It is!" returned Paul, politely bowing in return.

"My name is Landon, and being from America, and a neighbor of your friend Mr. Brown, I have taken the liberty of calling upon you, bringing with me, at the same time, a letter of introduction from that gentleman."

The speaker seemed quite agitated as he proceeded, but pausing, he offered the letter mentioned to Paul, who, shaking hands with him, expressed himself happy at the meeting, and urged him to be seated.

"I will sir, but my deep anxiety to make known my business, must excuse my haste in plunging into it. God grant that my hopes may not be disappointed!" added the gentleman, a quiver playing around his lips as he spoke, and deep feeling expressing itself upon every feature.

Surprised exceedingly, at the agitation of the person

before him, Paul assured him, he would be happy to serve him in any manner possible.

" Miss Brown, Mr. Russell," returned Mr. Landon excitedly, seizing his hand, "received a letter from you, the day before I sailed, containing the account of your rescuing a little girl from the gipsies, evidently stolen in Italy. Mr. Russell, I lost a darling daughter, very mysteriously, four years ago, near Florence! Tell me, can it be, is it, my precious Liza?"

Delight, surprise, and deep thankfulness, spread over Paul's features, as wringing the stranger's hand, he exclaimed, "God be praised! I am sure the poor child is yours! Her name is Liza, she was stolen at that place, and certainly she greatly resembles yourself. But where, sir, is your wife, the dear mamma for whom she mourns? Is she living? Is she with you?" asked Paul, hardly knowing what he said, in his excitement.

" She is; she is waiting for me in a carriage in front of your door. Mr. Russell, she is nearly a heart broken woman since her loss. I dared not tell her one word of my hopes concerning this child, fearing there might be some mistake. Bessie sent for me immediately, allowed me to read your letter, and wild with joy I determined to sail in a steamer I knew was to leave next day. I hurried home, announced my intention of starting for London, on important business, and insisted upon her accompanying me, for the benefit of her health. But sir, let me see my darling, let me hear all the evidences, let me be certain it is really true, before I raise a single hope, that could not be fully realized. Her mind was clouded for a long while, and we feared her reason would never return. But by care and devotion, she is now restored, but of course we avoid every excitement."

Russell immediately saw that great caution must be exercised in her case, then relating in a brief manner all the incidents in regard to his finding the child, and exhibiting the box of clothing which Mr. Landon immediately recognized, (the chain and armlets having been a birthday gift from himself,) he suddenly asked, "but sir, was any other person missed at the same time?"

"Oh yes! the nurse-girl that took the child to walk, never returned. Her body was found in the Arno, having evidently been murdered, as three dreadful stabs were seen upon her person."

"The same! the very same! Sir, without a shadow of doubt, this is your daughter! She told me how Alfonso, the gipsy, stabbed poor Belle," cried Paul.

"Belle? yes! that was the girl's name. Dear Mr. Russell, please let me embrace my darling."

"I will, but promise me you will be calm; and Mr. Landon, there is no possibility of mistake! persuade your wife to enter, and together, you shall see and rejoice over your little one! Allow me to call Dr. and Mrs. Hartley, who shall first be introduced to you, then explain to Mrs. Landon, that you wish her to become acquainted with the family, and also persuade her to remove her bonnet, to see if Liza will recognize her. I will then bring in the little girl, and together you can meet her."

Mr. Landon consenting, Paul rang the bell, and when Rose appeared in answer, requested her to summon Dr. and Mrs. Hartley.

When they entered, Paul hastily introduced Mr. Landon, explaining, to their delight, that he was the father of their protégée, and that they wished to induce his wife to enter, in order to see if Liza, when brought forward, would recognize her.

After their congratulations had been received, and their wonder had a little subsided at this marvellous interposition of Providence, Mr. Landon stepped to the carriage, and after a little persuasion, returned with a delicate, but very handsome woman, leaning upon his arm, whom he introduced as his wife.

"I am so glad to meet persons from my distant home, and friends of Mr. Brown and his sweet Bessie, that I could not allow you to drive away without an introduction, and longer chat. I have so much to say, so many inquiries to make, that you must consent to passing a few hours with us," remarked Paul, as he warmly welcomed her.

"Yes indeed, Mrs. Landon," interposed good Mrs. Hartley, "I would feel greatly delighted if you would remove your bonnet and pass the day with us. Do please gratify us," urged she, as she saw the lady hesitate. "Mr. Landon has already half consented, therefore pray dismiss your carriage and grant us this pleasure."

Thus urged, Mrs. Landon could not refuse, and while her husband spoke to the coachman, she removed her bonnet and cloak, and was soon engaged in an interesting conversation with Mrs. Hartley, not noticing the whispered words that Paul had uttered to Rose, for whom he had again quietly rang.

Thus conversing, the soft, mellow light of the room, just glancing upon her lovely face, lighting up the full dark eyes, and falling gently upon the finely shaped head, Mrs. Landon sat near a window, while her husband stood a short distance behind her chair, close to her, yet so shielded that she could not see his face. Paul had placed his chair opposite hers, near Dr. and Mrs. Hartley, who rested upon the sofa.

Softly the door opened, and a child's voice spcke low, the words,

"Cousin Paul, shall I come in?"

"Yes darling, come!" was the reply, and Liza glided to his side, and stood encircled by his arm, leaning upon his knee, a perfect picture of innocence and beauty.

"Whose dear little girl is that, Mr. Russell?" asked Mrs. Landon; then, without waiting a reply, she added, "Come here, love, and speak to me, will you not?"

As Liza turned to advance to her side, Mrs. Landon started forward, and fixing her eyes upon her face, the same wild, agonized look floated over her countenance, that Bessie and Minnie had seen when she stood gazing at the portrait of her darling.

Liza passed nearly to her side, her large brown eyes never turning from the lovely face upon which they were riveted, then pausing, midway, between Paul and the one whom she so intently regarded, she pressed one tiny hand close to her bosom, and exclaimed, in a voice distinctly audible, yet scarce above a whisper.

"Cousin Paul, dear Cousin Paul, the lady looks so like my own mamma!"

"Does she, darling?" whispered Paul; "well, sing your little song for the lady, the one papa loved."

Crossing her hands upon her bosom, with her eyes still fixed upon Mrs. Landon, who remained motionless, gazing on her upturned face, with speechless emotion, Liza began, in tones bird-like, yet tremulous, the plaintive Italian melody she had sung before for her benefactor.

As she proceeded, a piercing cry escaped the pale lips of Mrs. Landon, who sprang forward exclaiming,

"Liza! Liza! my lily bud—my darling," and with this

cry sank senseless into the arms of Dr. Hartley, who stepped to her assistance.

It was but a momentary faintness, and in the brief spell while the Doctor and his lady were striving to restore her, Mr. Landon had caught his child to his bosom, saying, amid the kisses he lavished upon her,

"Yes! it is mamma, and this is papa, my own, precious daughter!"

Clinging to his neck, as he held her in his arms, the overjoyed child cried,

"Oh darling papa, never go away from Liza again! How I did cry for you and mamma!"

"Yes, poor little pet! and we almost died with sorrow, when we could not find our Liza. But see, mamma is better; you may speak to her in one moment, darling."

"Where am I?" murmured Mrs. Landon. "Husband, I had such a sweet dream! I thought I saw our Liza, alive, safe, and happy!"

"Mamma!" uttered a low sweet voice in her ear, while a pair of soft child arms wound around her neck, "it was no dream! it *is* your lily-bud—your darling!"

"Great God, I thank thee!" exclaimed the enraptured mother, folding her new found treasure in a passionate embrace. "Liza! my own! my own! Oh, husband, is it indeed true? has God restored our child?"

"Yes, Beatrice! Thanks to Him, and to Mr. Russell, she is saved from the gipsy band who had stolen her, and murdered Belle."

Then, with the child clasped closely, fondly, to her throbbing heart, Mrs. Landon listened to the thrilling story of Costanza, and with tears flowing freely at thoughts of the sufferings of her darling, she thanked Paul, together with Dr. and Mrs. Hartley, over and over again, for the care and affection with which they had watched and defended her dear one.

"But the gipsy band, where are they now?" asked she, shuddering, as she spoke their name.

"They disappeared very mysteriously, the second day after the death of Costanza. A party of police were delegated to search for them, but while they found where the camping-fires had been, the guilty Alfonso had evidently become alarmed by the disappearance of Costanza and the child, and so had fled."

"Can he never be brought to justice?" asked Mrs. Landon, indignantly.

"I fear not! their lurking-places are so little known. However, the police are on the lookout, and he may yet be captured."

After a little conversation, it was decided, through the urgent request of Mrs. Hartley, that Mr. Landon and wife should remain at their house until the following week, when they proposed returning to their distant home with their recovered treasure.

Paul heard with unfeigned regret, that he was so soon to part with the affectionate child; but on witnessing the joy of the re-united ones, he felt that all selfish feelings would be sinful, indeed.

The day for parting came, and after the farewells had all been uttered, the soft, clinging arms unclasped for the last time from his neck, the sweet pressure of those rosy lips had all passed away, a strange moisture gathered in Paul's eyes, a strange sinking fell upon his heart, and once more came the yearning cry to his bosom, for home—home!

CHAPTER XXXIV.

LEAVES FROM THE JOURNAL OF REBECCA DOUGLASS.

"We know not what's before us,
What trials are to come!
But each day passing o'er us,
Brings us still nearer home."

JULY 1st, 1865.—I can scarcely realize that nine months have passed away, since I bade farewell to my brother's house, and sailed for this distant land. Little did I think I should ever emerge from the seclusion to which I had so long been accustomed,—to mingle with the jostling world again! but such is life—one constant scene of change, change!

How well that we cannot read the future; and how true, that God alone marks out our pathway!

After relating the sad history of my life to Minnie, my young and lovely niece, I had the pleasure of seeing a marked and decided change in her every movement. She no longer seemed to pine for excitement and gaiety, but became thoughtful and much more domestic, and while her naturally buoyant disposition remained, her heart seemed to seek only enjoyment in the devoted love she cherished for the chosen one, to whom she had plighted her pure young affections. Gladly, I observed that the statement of my sinful career had proved a solemn warning to her soul, and that now she scorned trifling, and fashionable coquetry, as fully as I could wish.

No cloud therefore arose to dim her happiness, no jealousy to mar her prospects, and on the 28th of September, she was united to Charles Percy. The ceremony was performed in St. —— Church, sweet Bessie Brown being the first of her three bridesmaids. After the solemn vows had been exchanged, the bridal party returned to my brother's residence, and passed several hours receiving their friends.

All seemed charmed with the beauty of the bride, and manliness of the groom, and all passed off happily and well. I could not but notice the radiant countenances of Mr. and Mrs. Landon, who, with their lately recovered daughter, were present. When I thought of the years of agony those three hearts had endured, in that dreadful separation, I could not wonder at their perfect happiness. The dear little child is exquisitely beautiful, and certainly is strangely gifted in song. I conversed with her again to-day, after I had congratulated the bride, but her thoughts and words teem with affection for her dear Cousin Paul. I had no need to ask who that individual might be, as I had listened to the story of her rescue from the lips of Charles, and knew full well that it was the Russell of my former acquaintance. With all his faults, he has certainly been generous and noble in this case.

Ah, well! why should I listen to his praises? Why feel so interested in this child? Surely it is not because she is a protégée of his? No! no! It is only on account of her spiritual beauty, and rare intelligence!

Nothing more! I do declare, it is nothing more!

My health had been very delicate for an entire year, and at the time of this wedding, my friends were particularly anxious on my account. They could scarcely tell what disease was destroying me; my physician, however, assured us it was a general debility, and insisted that a change of air was absolutely necessary for my restoration; therefore, following his advice, and the earnest solicitations of all my relatives, I consented to accompany my new nephew, and my niece, on their wedding tour to Europe.

Thus, then, together have we wandered around many of the countries of the Old World, so often visited by travellers and described with enthusiasm and delight. Together have we visited England, but in passing through London, Percy insisted upon calling to see Paul Russell, "the gentleman to whom," as he said, "his sister was so deeply indebted." Fortunately for my peace of mind, when he returned to the hotel where he had left us, it was to announce that he was absent from the city. Thus did Providence avert from me a trial I had anticipated with the deepest pain!

After tarrying a few days in each city of note in England, we journeyed through Scotland, Ireland, France and Spain; leisurely and delightedly examining each, to our perfect satisfaction. Switzerland next came in for a share of our admiration, and with unbounded pleasure we lingered among her sublime, grand and noble scenery, always so enchanting, always so beautiful. We passed several weeks at the Hotel Byron, on the shores of Lake Leman, at Geneva, within sight of the castle immortalized by the poem of "The Prisoner of Chillon." The lake is fifty-five miles long, and in some places nine and a quarter wide, and is inclosed on all sides by mountains, studded by beautiful vineyards, charming villages, and luxurious residences, which causes it to assume the appearance of an earthly paradise. Poets and painters have caused this magical spot to be immortalized by both picture and song, and we lingered both days and weeks, amid its varied beauties, with breathless enjoyment.

Finally, tearing ourselves away from these matchless scenes, we climbed the noble peaks of that wonderful mountain chain, the Alps, and held our breath in awe at the grandeur of Mont Blanc, while we also admired with deepest enthusiasm the wonders of the Apennines. Weeks more, we tarried among the justly celebrated beauties of Italy; we roamed among the curiosities of Rome; we glided gladly over the enchanting waters of the Bay of Naples, or, seated in a gay gondola, we sailed among the buildings of far-famed Venice, listening to the songs of the gondoliers, or gazing into the bright eyes of the fair Italian maidens.

Weary at length with our wanderings, we again find ourselves in bonnie France, where we shall tarry at a cousin's charming residence, quite near, yet not exactly, in the city of Paris. We arrived this morning, and I gladly seat myself, to pen a few lines in my long neglected journal, before retiring for the night. My apartment is large and well appointed, opening upon a lovely garden, and as the window is raised, the perfume of the blooming flowers, the rose, and the mignonette, are wafted in, to charm me with their delicious fragrance. But however grateful the odors, however bright the stars in the clear canopy above, my senses can no longer enjoy them, for my weary frame and drooping eyelids whisper for rest.

July 10th.—A strange exciting day has this proved to be! My God! why am I so weak? why is my poor heart to be again thus lacerated?

This afternoon my nephew, niece, and Mrs. St Clair, with myself, left home, and drove directly to the palace of the Louvre, that grand museum of ancient and modern art. This palace having been united to the palace of the Tuileries, covers about sixty acres in the very heart of the city, and is visited by crowds of old and young, artists and travellers, every one, in short, that can admire statuary, paintings, medals and curiosities of ancient or recent date. The paintings alone, were a marvellous study. One, the "long gallery," as it is called, contains eighteen hundred paintings, of the old Italian, Spanish, and German schools, while other galleries are devoted to living artists, to relics or memorials of every sovereign of Europe, and again of naval architecture, Chinese art, &c. &c.

Thus, then, had we passed along, examining each curiosity that came in our route, until we entered the "long gallery," where we hung in rapture over the rare and celebrated works of art there exposed to view.

As I stood lost in thought before a painting of exquisite beauty, I was attracted by these words, spoken in English, by a gentleman near by, although his tones were low, and guarded, not wishing to be heard.

"Russell, do you see that splendid woman? I think I never saw a more beautiful face! I mean the one to your right, dressed in half mourning, with the black grenadine shawl, and dainty crape hat. See! she is looking this way!"

Unconscious that I was the person described, I had turned my eyes towards the speaker, and from him to his friend, and in an instant the blood seemed curdling around my heart, for I met a longing, mournful gaze from Paul Russell.

Never can I portray the agony that rushed over me, as my eyes caught sight of that man. All the horror of our parting hour seemed acting over, all the anguish of my long years of remorse and sorrow, were again brought up, and with a trembling hand and darkening vision, I grasped the arm of Minnie, whispering,

"Take me home!"

The pallid cheeks and strange accents of my voice alarmed her, so gently speaking to the remainder of the party, they turned to my assistance, but with a violent effort of will, I succeeded in becoming more calm, else had I fainted. As it was, I accepted the arm of Percy and turned to leave a place now so void of charm for me.

As I passed the two gentlemen, I distinctly heard the whisper of the former speaker, as he remarked,

"How singular that was! She seems to be ill; who can she be?"

Then the voice I knew so well, replied, "excuse me, Robert, I must leave you!" and as I passed out, I was conscious that he, also, was leaving the room.

We entered the carriage and drove homeward, and the grateful breeze revived me, while Minnie joyfully exclaimed:

"You look better now, dear Auntie! how strange that you should have been seized so suddenly!"

As the carriage turned into Mr. St. Clair's elegant grounds, I raised my eyes, and once more did my heart almost stand still, as I perceived a gentleman ride past, and in the graceful form, and splendid rider, I recognized the only one who had the power to cause such deep emotion.

Gladly, on entering the house, did I accept their urgent petitions to retire to my own room, and lie down; but with my first step into that chamber, I fell upon my knees, and implored my Heavenly Father to have pity upon me, and forgive my weakness.

I never thought that *seeing him*, could overcome me thus!

Frail heart! how must I ever battle with thee!

CHAPTER XXXV.

THE SERENADES.

"Bless thee, God bless thee, all the day long,
Softly I whisper in praise, and in prayer;
If thou couldst but strengthen, oh, I should be strong,
And light be my burdens, if thou couldst but share."

CLEMENTINE.

JULY 12*th*.—I never saw a brighter moon than the one that shone upon the garden, beneath my window, last evening.

Eleven had long since been pointed out by my watch, yet still I sat gazing through the partly closed blinds, into the winding paths, watching the moonbeams as they glanced through the parting tree-boughs, making everything perfectly visible below—then, darting long mellow rays up into the otherwise dark room where I sat.

With my head leaning upon my hand, and my eyes fixed, now upon the starry sky, now upon the graveled walk and blooming flower beds, my thoughts went backward to my early days, and my prayers ascended for forgiveness and peace.

Suddenly, my heart beat quickly, as beneath my window, fully revealed in the moonlight, appeared the form I had seen the day before in the palace of the Louvre. My breath came quick and fast, and once more I summoned all my strength to keep from fainting.

He stood leaning against a tree in a most dejected attitude, with his face turned towards my window. I sat so in the shadow, I hoped he could not see me, but I was not sure, and I dared not stir.

He stood thus motionless some moments, then raising his arm, I noticed that he had an instrument of music in his hand, and was about giving me a serenade.

Softly rose a sweet, low strain upon the midnight air—then, oh heart be still! those full, rich tones, that deep, yet powerful voice, that no other I ever knew could imitate, fell upon my ear, and held me breathlessly entranced.

Oh Russell! did you so long remember my passion for music? Did your soul dream that I could be so bewildered with that sad, mournful song? How those words sank into my soul as they issued from his lips! I could not breathe, and not until a gush of tears came to my relief, could I recover my composure, and self command. As I did control my tears, these words were vibrating in the air, and while the name "Rebecca," was still echoing around, he glided noiselessly away.

Give, oh give, some little token
That my love is not in vain!
Speak one word of hope to cheer me,
Dearest, when we meet again,
Oh Rebecca! Sweet Rebecca!
Do not keep my heart in pain.

When I was sure that he was nowhere to be seen, I arose, closed the blinds, and disrobing, threw myself upon my bed, but not to sleep! No! it was but to weep and pray, until morning came, and bade me rise and join the family below. As I did so, I felt the color mount to my brow, so fearful was I, that my serenade of the night before had been listened to by other ears than mine. As nothing was said, I concluded it had not been noticed, as their rooms were on the other side of the house, all but the one occupied by Percy and his wife.

Once, at the breakfast table, I caught the eye of Minnie looking peculiarly at me, but as she instantly turned away, I deemed it but imaginary, and so it made little impression on my mind.

July 14*th.*—Again yesterday, in an afternoon drive, did Paul Russell pass us on horseback. As my eyes encountered his, he gave me a pleading look, accompanied by a low bow, which, in my confusion, I did not return.

"Who is that splendid looking gentleman, Mr. Percy?" asked Mrs. St. Clair, as he passed away.

"I do not know, madam! Probably he mistook us for acquaintances.

"I wish I knew his name, I seem to meet him so often lately!" again remarked Mrs. St. Clair.

I said not a word! A sly glance from Minnie had startled me—but I held my own counsel. Could Minnie have guessed that the handsome stranger was the Leslie of my story? I felt uncomfortable at the very surmise, and my confusion was so evident that my tongue was mute, and my heart strangely excited.

I retired early that night; I did not allow myself my favorite enjoyment of sitting to admire the beauties of a summer night, but closing the blinds I sought my pillow. Eleven had again sounded, and my eyelids were just drooping into a sweet sleep, when the strings of a guitar were softly touched beneath my window, and again was the voice of Russell pouring his bewitching songs of fondest love into my ear.

Poor Russell! his love for me has been faithful and true! Would that he could bestow his affection now upon some other person who would return his devotion, and speak peace to his troubled heart!

July 20*th.*—I have not resumed my pen for some days, my mind has been in such continual excitement, constantly encountering, as I do, my former lover. He never attempts to speak to me, but each time we met I notice his dejection, while his songs beneath my window have been almost a nightly occurrence. Once, when the blinds were a little open, a rare bouquet fell into the room. I knew whose hand had thrown it there, but I could not raise it; some voice seemed to whisper, "touch not those flowers—they are only another temptation of the adversary!"

So they lay and withered, but I could not close my eyes to their beauty, nor could their fragrance be disputed.

The blinds were ever after carefully closed, notwithstanding the heat, and the wild craving of my heart for the moonlight, and evening breezes.

Last night, he stood longer than usual, leaning against the willow, before commencing his song, and from a concealed spot, I watched him. Once or twice I thought a tear glistened on his cheek in the moonlight, then, when he commenced to sing, his voice faltered, his tones were tremulous, and the words breathed a last farewell. He stood with his hand pressed upon his brow, as he ceased the song, then extending his arms towards my window, as if he would give a parting embrace, he moved down the walk, and disappeared, I well knew, to come again no more.

August 13*th.*—To-morrow we sail for our native land in

the same vessel that brought us hither. In order to be ready for its departure, we bade Mrs. St. Clair's family adieu, and returning to England took rooms in this hotel in Liverpool, where we will remain until going on board.

This morning I again strangely encountered Paul Russell.

We were going to drive around the city for the last time, as we go to the vessel early in the morning, and as we descended the hotel stairs, Minnie discovered that she had left her watch in her room, and returning to find it, I stepped into the public parlor to wait for her. As I entered, I suddenly started back in astonishment, for before me, upon a sofa, lay Mr. Russell.

He turned pale as myself, as our eyes met, and with his own native politeness, sought to rise, but sank back apparently, faint and ill.

In an instant everything was forgotten, save the one thought, that he was sick and alone, and going to him I exclaimed,

"Mr. Russell, I am sorry to see you an invalid! You seem to have been very ill!"

I extended my hand as I spoke, which he eagerly seized and carried to his lips, pressing upon it a long, passionate kiss.

"I have indeed been very sick, Rebecca, but I am almost well now. I am daily recovering. God bless you, my dear friend! Farewell!" he added, as I turned hurriedly to leave him, for Minnie's step was heard approaching, and I could not linger.

I was very silent during the drive, Minnie said, and I knew it; yet I could not overcome my excitement, or command my feelings. The pale, handsome face of Russell was ever before me; his kiss was even yet thrilling my hand. Unconsciously, I laid my other hand caressingly over the spot which those lips had pressed, to shield it from every other touch; it seemed so delightful to have had that pressure *there* once more, then—I drew back, astonished at myself.

Could it be possible that those old infatuated feelings were still in my bosom? Oh Rebecca Douglass! can you indeed be still interested in that man?

I was overcome with shame and confusion at the discovery, and I bit my lips in vexation, that I had spoken to him, while with my handkerchief I rubbed the offending spot, and drew on my gloves, resolving to wear them more constantly than ever, after that unlooked for weakness.

CHAPTER XXXVI.

ON THE OCEAN.

"Rocked in the cradle of the deep,
I lay me down in peace to sleep;
Secure I rest upon the wave
For Thou, O Lord, hast power to save,
I know Thou wilt not slight the call,
For Thou dost mark the sparrow's fall,
Then calm and peaceful be my sleep,
Rocked in the cradle of the deep."

AUGUST 15th.—At Sea. We left Liverpool yesterday morning. All seem happy in the thought, that we are homeward bound. I am quite comfortably situated, have a nice state-room, and am so entirely restored to health that I can scarcely believe I am the same poor, debilitated creature, that stood upon this vessel ten months since.

I imagine there is a sick person in the state-room next mine, as I often see the steward go there, with little dishes for invalids, while the inquiry, "How do you feel to-day, sir?" falls upon my ear, but the answer is so low, I cannot distinguish a word.

Poor man! he has my sympathy, whoever he may be, as pain is a poor companion while travelling!

I was interrupted in my writing a few moments since, by an unlooked for occurrence. Minnie came into my state-room to see me awhile, and I mentioned the circumstance of my sick neighbor.

"Yes, dear aunt!" returned she, "I saw him come on board. He was so feeble, that he had to be assisted to his state-room. He is gaining rapidly now, I think, for he walked alone on deck to-day, and I heard him say to the Captain, 'that every breath of ocean air he drew, benefited him!' I think I never sawso handsome a man, and his voice is music itself. Poor fellow! how sadly he used to sing under your window, dear auntie. I could almost weep at those despairing words and tones, while Percy slept so soundly, he never once heard him."

"Minnie!" exclaimed I, in a voice tremulous with anxiety, "what do you mean?"

"Forgive me, Aunt Rebecca, if I listened to those songs, and guessed the serenader to be Mr. Leslie, or, as I have since learned, Paul Russell. Charles is delighted to have him on board, and homeward bound, and I could not resist telling you my discovery."

"Dear girl! you have done nothing that needs forgiveness;" exclaimed I, but my tears stopped my words, and leaning my head upon her affectionate shoulder, I wept freely.

"Do not weep, dear aunt, but let me plead one little word for him. Think how faithful he has been to you, how devotedly he must love you, and who can wonder, for you are still young, only thirty-three, and if I do flatter, are a very beautiful woman. Aunt Rebecca, suppose you treat him a little more cordially, no one would blame you."

"Child!" exclaimed I vehemently, "you know not what you say! The injured blood of my husband presses too closely upon my heart, and Lucy's laugh rings too wretchedly in my ears. Never! Minnie, never! the thought alone, causes me to shudder!"

She said no more, but kissing away my tears, left me to my own reflections.

August 19th.—Still, still out upon the boundless deep! how rapidly we skim along over the waters. I thought to write, but the beauty of the scene calls me to the deck.

Later.—How terribly my poor heart flutters! I had stepped to the deck after so abruptly leaving these unfinished lines, and stood alone, near the side of the vessel, for Charles had a severe headache, and Minnie, like a true, devoted wife, sat beside him.

The scene was a charming one, and I watched the dancing waters, and the dashing spray, as the steamer sped between them, with the utmost delight.

'I never feel the presence of God so sensibly, Mrs. Douglass, as when I stand upon a vessel and gaze upon the wonders of the sea," said a rich, familiar voice by my side; without noticing my confusion, he continued, "I feel, then, that without His protecting care, how powerless are we, how soon a wreck, and in eternity. I was just looking at that little cloud. I have been so much upon the ocean that I am quite a weather prophet, and I think it promises a storm. Would you fear a storm at sea, Rebecca?"

"I should be somewhat frightened, I think; but, as our passage out was calm and delightful, we can scarcely test our courage, until tried! However, God can protect us, and with Him for our friend, we need fear no evil. But I will inquire after your health, and then retire to my stateroom?" added I, for I was anxious to end the interview.

"Nay! do not let me drive you from the deck, Mrs. Douglass. Forgive the presumption of which I was guilty in Paris, and extend to me the privilege of your friendship. I assure you, I will never wound your sensitiveness by word or look again, if you will suffer a pure friendly intercourse. Think not my presence here an intrusion; I never dreamed that you were a passenger on this vessel, when I embarked. But as God has ordered that we should be companions in this voyage, let us at least be friendly. Believe me, Mrs. Douglass, I am not the gay and worldly man you once knew; hopelessness of earthly happiness, has caused me to "set my affections on things above," and I now "look for another inheritance, one that fadeth not away." He raised his eyes as he spoke, for a moment upward, and the breeze throwing the jet black curls from his brow revealed yet more fully the spiritual look upon his noble features, while the soft smile that played upon his finely chiseled lips, was inexpressibly attractive.

Strange, how perverse a heart is mine! while he spoke so calmly, asking my friendship, and assuring me that he would wound no more by his *love*, for such I understood to be the import of his words, my heart sank, and a rebellious feeling caused a sigh to escape my lips. Can it be that the love of Paul Russell is of the least importance to me? Oh God! forgive me if such is the case, and help me to tear all such interest from my heart, forever.

"You asked after my health," continued he, as he turned his thoughtful eyes to mine, once more, "I am quite strong again, this ocean air has been a rare physician! Come, will you not walk awhile on deck?" and taking my hand respectfully, he drew it under his arm, and we paced up and down the vessel, while the intellectual conversation of my companion charmed, even while he sought to amuse me.

9 *o'clock*—A violent storm is raging! Russell was in-

deed a true prophet! Hark! how wildly the wind rattles around, and how heavily the waves beat against the vessel! I cannot write, so will secure these pages, with some other valuables, around my person, for no one but God can tell what may befall us in another hour?

CHAPTER XXXVII.

STORM AT SEA.

"The life-boat! the life-boat! how bravely she rides
The darkened and stormy, and treacherous main,
The wild moaning tempest, the fierce rolling tide,
Unite their dark powers to o'erwhelm her in vain;
The mariner sees her, and hope fills his breast,
The lamp from her bow gleams bright o'er the sea,
It shines as a star on the billow's fierce breast,
And mounts o'er the waters, so nobly and free."

NEW YORK, Sept. 9th, 1865.—Once more safely at home, but what dangers have we passed through, and how kindly have we been watched over, and protected. When I last wrote in the pages of my Journal, a violent storm was raging, so wild, that terror was depicted on every countenance. I had collected together my valuables, and bound them closely about my person, and throwing a sea-mantle around me, I awaited the result of the frightful storm, with Minnie clinging to me, when her husband was on deck, or, wildly rushing to him, when by her side, so nervous, and excited had the poor child become. We had all gathered together in the cabin, feeling lonely in our state-rooms, and there clinging to the stationary furniture, we stood, or sat, pale, and terrified.

Suddenly, a calm voice broke the silence ; a voice I well knew, and that filled me with awe.

"We are surrounded, my friends, by untold dangers, but our Heavenly Father is above, and around us, and His ear is ever open to the prayer of Faith. Shall we not invoke His presence, and His aid?"

Such a prayer as the lips of Paul Russell offered then, I never listened to before; so trusting, yet so pleading, so child-like and yet so beautiful,—all seemed soothed instantly, and all looked with gratitude towards him, as he concluded.

"Oh Thou!" he prayed, "who in the flesh didst by thy word calm the sea, and allay the stormy wind, we are in Thy hands, and we throw ourselves upon thy mercy! For Thy blessed name's sake, heed our unworthy, but earnest prayer.

"If it can be possible, now, speak that word that shall deliver us from our peril! By whatever means that seemeth good to Thee, bring us speedy relief. Show us Thy glory in Thy goodness, that shall remove from us the prospect of speedy death. Have mercy, oh Thou that canst show mercy!"

"But Lord, we desire not to dictate to Thee. We pray Thee subdue our every heart to feel submissive to Thy wise decisions. Let faith that links closely to Thine everlasting faithfulness, and rest calmly thereon, take possession of our hearts, and what seemeth good to Thee, do. We commit us to Thy wisdom and goodness; and whether we are soon to be rescued from danger and death, or to go to Thy presence, prepare us for it. We know Thee that thou art good, and doest good. Forgive us our every sin. Wash us white in that blood that cleanseth us from all sin, and make this solemn hour, an hour of grace and blessing, and eternal life, and then, under Thy Spirit's guidance, we shall in life, in death, and in eternity, praise Thy Holy name, for ever and ever, through Jesus Christ, Thy Son and our Lord. Amen."

Oh how I thanked him for those words! As he prayed he seemed invested with a new charm—the charm of *Faith.* I could scarcely believe that holy, spiritual man, the gay worldling, that had caused so much sorrow and misery, and I blessed God from my inmost soul, at the deeply apparent change.

On rode the storm; to and fro dashed the panting stream—but suddenly all the gentlemen were summoned to aid in saving the vessel by pumping, as she had sprung a leak.

Once more the frightened females clung to each other in those dreadful moments of suspense! but once did a sound approach, and then the voice of Russell was heard saying,

"The violence of the storm is abating; for this let us be thankful; but the vessel is in a bad condition! keep calm, and put your trust in Jesus."

Then came the booming of the gun, and the tolling of the bell, to signify distress, and still the work of the pumps went on. Men rushing hurriedly over the deck, evidently getting the life-boats in order, was the next thing heard, while courage and alacrity prevailed, but the wind was decreasing, and the violent motion of the vessel had ceased! This was in our favor, for no boat could have lived in the tumultuous sea of the morning,—for day had broken long before the violence of the storm had at all abated, and now another night would soon be upon us.

Silent and pale we clustered together when the order came for the women and children to be placed in the small boats, as nothing could save the Star of the Sea; the water was gaining so rapidly, she must soon go down.

There was a rush and confusion at the command, frantic

mothers clasped their children and struggled on deck; brothers sought their sisters and assisted them on; husbands attended to the safety of their wives, but I alone seemed to have no one upon whom to lean, in that terrific hour. Minnie was nearly helpless with fright, and bidding me follow, Charles hurried away with her; I started after, but others jostled between, and in the excitement and confusion I caught my foot in some unseen impediment and fell, spraining my arm, and so injuring me that I lay stunned and helpless, forgotten and alone.

All were seated in the boats, I was afterwards told, when Russell leaned over to Charles and exclaimed, "I do not see Mrs. Douglass—where can she be?"

"Oh Aunt Rebecca!" screamed Minnie. "Where is she? she will be lost, for she is not here!"

"Be calm Mrs. Percy! remain with your wife, Mr. Percy, I will seek her. Rest assured I will do my utmost!"

"This boat is too full now," exclaimed the Captain; "take to the other, Mr. Russell, if you find her; two seamen shall go with you!"

"All right!" returned the young man, and while the well filled boats pushed off, the other was fitted up with food, water and blankets, and in a moment Russell appeared bearing my senseless form in his arms, and we were soon out upon the ocean in our frail bark. Not one moment too soon, however, as the fast sinking vessel testified! Fifteen minutes passed, and then the waters closed over the beautiful Star of the Sea, and we were alone in a small boat, on the broad Atlantic, with the other boats in sight, but alas! no vessel of relief to be seen.

CHAPTER XXXVIII.

SAVED.

"He maketh the storm a calm, so that the waves thereof are still."
"Then are they glad because they be quiet; so he bringeth them unto their desired haven."—PSALMS, CVII. 29, 30.

WHEN I recovered my consciousness, Russell was supporting me, as I lay on the bottom of the boat; his breast was my pillow, while he was assiduously bathing my brow, and seeking to restore me. As I opened my eyes I met *his*, fixed with the utmost anxiety upon me.

"Thank God! you are better! But you seem to be in pain!" he cried, as an involuntary groan escaped me, a quick movement on his part, having sent a thrill of anguish through my frame.

"It is my arm! I fear I have dislocated my wrist in falling!"

A deep sigh escaped him as I spoke, and with much distress depicted upon his countenance, he exclaimed,

"Oh Rebecca! how dreadful that you should suffer, and no physician at hand. Perhaps I could replace it; I once commenced the study of surgery, but abandoned it, as I could not bear to witness the anguish of the afflicted. I know well that it must be replaced immediately, but the operation will be painful, and that will grieve me."

"I will bear it!" cried I, for I longed for relief. "If

you can replace it, do not once think of me—but go on, and do as you think best."

Without a word more, he took my poor hand in his, and as skilfully as any surgeon could have done, replaced the dislocated joint, and binding it with my handkerchief, he formed a sling with his own, and carefully laid my hand within it. The operation *was* a painful one, so much so, that I could scarcely keep from crying out; but it was too much in my weak state—my head swam—and once more was I unconscious. Another effort on the part of Russell fully restored me, and I soon raised myself from his supporting arm and looked around. Then, for the first time, I realized our sad condition. Out on the boundless deep, were we riding in a frail boat, while the sea was still rough and angry. Night was fast closing around us, and even then, we could see but a hand's breadth from our little boat. Before us sat two sturdy sailors, with the oars in their hands; Russell, by my side, seemed only anxious for my welfare, while ever and anon, he spoke soothing words of encouragement, and faith in God's protecting power.

"We can do nothing now, my friend, but pray, and leave God to dispose of us. He knows our sad condition, and can yet save us!"

Then, as night folded its dark mantle over our boat, he carefully drew around me a protecting blanket, and as we tossed upon the waves, and I constantly clung to the side of the boat, with my one uninjured hand, he gently passed his arm around me, and implored a brother's privilege of supporting me. How could I refuse so kind and necessary an offer—for I was much overcome with pain, and fear—and allowing him to draw me towards him, I leaned my weary head against his shoulder, and as he bade me, closed my eyes and sought to sleep.

But sleep came not to my relief! I could but listen to the pulsations of the generous heart against which I leaned; I could but think how strangely we had been thrown together, and how desolate a condition we were in. Then I longed to know, where was the boat containing Minnie and Percy; I feared that we should be widely separated before the morning light, and so my mind roved around, although my eyes were closed, and courted slumber in vain.

Russell did not once sleep during that long night. I knew it well by his careful manner of supporting my form, and adjusting the blanket, and I could ever feel his warm breath upon my cheek, as my face leaned against his shoulder. Once or twice I spoke and asked if he would not change his position, for I knew he must be weary, but he would not suffer me to move, assuring me he was happy—so happy in being useful to me.

So that long night wore on! Slowly and silently, scarce a word spoken, yet all wakeful, and on the watch. The midnight sky had cleared all clouds, and bright, beautiful stars were shining down upon us.

I could see the Pleiades with their silvery group, and Orion's starry belt; while Cassiopeia and a myriad of brilliant constellations shone upon the scene. Then the moon arose, and added her rays to the picture, but all seemed strange and mournful to me. At last Russell whispered, for he knew I was awake,

"See, the morning breaks, and soon, Rebecca, we can look for our friends. God has shielded us thus far, and our grateful thanks must be his alone."

With the morning light, we all eagerly looked around, while none could for a long time discover the other boats but finally the practised eyes of the seamen discerned some mere specks in the distance, which they assured us were those we sought.

After partaking of the biscuits and water we had been carefully provided with, the sailors exerted themselves to draw near our companions in peril, and so they labored hour after hour, while Russell and I watched the ocean for a coming sail.

So the day wore on, and all that had been accomplished, was to be able to speak to our friends. Charles assured us that Minnie was more calm than when we parted, and Russell bade them believe that he would devote himself to my welfare.

So that day passed, and again night hovered over us, and again did the protecting arm of Russell prove my support, and his shoulder serve for a pillow. But this night I slept; several hours of forgetfulness were granted me, and Russell watched over my slumbers.

Kind, devoted, Russell! I do not believe he allowed himself *once* to close his eyes in his carefulness of me!

The next morning, when the sun was about an hour high, one of the seamen suddenly snatched off his hat, and gave a shout of joy as he pointed to a sail, and truly our deliverance was near! they saw us and were fast coming to our rescue.

I will not linger to describe our joy when safely landed on the deck of the "Ocean Bride," we joyfully congratulated each other upon our wonderful escape. Minnie almost overwhelmed me with kisses, while Charles and Russell cordially shook hands.

Our homeward passage proved exceedingly prosperous, after this, nothing occurring to mar our progress. Russell I saw very little, for the exposure had given him a severe cold, and he was obliged to remain in the state-room, the

Captain had kindly assigned to him, most of the time; but whenever I did see him, he seemed happy, and exhibited a grateful pleasure that our friendship remained unchanged. Soon our vessel reached its destined port, and as I placed my hand in Russell's at parting, he bent partly over it, as if to press his lips upon its surface, then drew back, but not before I saw that his eyes were full of tears, while his lips quivered, as he murmured,

"Farewell, my dear Mrs. Douglass; that God may ever bless you, shall be the constant prayer of your friend! Farewell!"

I saw him no more! he had gone, but the painful beating of my heart, the loneliness that stole over my spirit, assured me that he was more dear to my soul, than I had imagined.

We arrived at my brother's in safety, and were joyfully welcomed by every member of the family, not excepting Dinah and Phillis, Pomp, and Sambo, the latter of whom exclaimed, as we each shook his ebony hand,

"Bress de Lord, Marse Percy, and you too, Missis Douglass and Missis Percy, fur his great condescension. Nebber was nobody so glad to see white folks as dis chile is to see your purty faces dis day. Laws now, hope you goin fur to stay hum a spell, fur you'd better blieve its bin dretful lonesum wid no young folks around to shine up de place somehow, as dey allers shua to do. It am a fact, Marsa! nothing like de light ob young faces to make de hearts sunshine. No sah! I knos dat from sperience, and you jes member what I say. Nothing like it, on dis lower globe! No sah, not one single ting. Tank de Lord!"

Since our return from that perilous voyage both Minnie and her husband have experienced a change of heart, and have become devoted followers of Jesus; thus have we cause to "extol thee, oh God, and to bless thy name for ever and ever."

I shall lay aside my pen now, for a while. Duties, home duties, as well as Church duties, are pressing around me, and in their full performance I shall have no time to write, even in my journal. It is well! Nothing but constant occupation can sever from my heart this fatal attachment, which has become so deeply rooted, and so difficult to overcome.

How thankful am I, that I have the wish and disposition to work in the "Master's vineyard," searching for, and assisting his poor and needy ones, when by thus obeying his command, the constant labor diverts my mind from trouble, and brings a blessing on my otherwise lonely pathway.

CHAPTER XXXIX.

CEDAR LAWN.

ONCE more we leave Rebecca, and enter the cozy library at Cedar Lawn, the residence of Mr. Brown. It is quite late in the evening, and Bessie sits in a small sewing chair by the centre-table, busily plying the needle, and at the same time watching for her father's return. Mr. Brown had been absent since dinner, and as this was quite an unusual circumstance, Bessie felt greatly concerned at the delay.

Wearily she waited, each moment growing more and more uneasy, until finally she heard his step approaching, and with a glad cry flew to meet him.

"Oh papa, I have been so lonely!" said she, as she received his affectionate kiss, and led him to his favorite seat beside her sewing chair.

"I feared so, daughter, but I could not return sooner. A very unlooked for circumstance, and one which I hope will result in much improvement to yourself, detained me."

"To me, papa," exclaimed Bessie with surprise; "how can that be?"

"You know, my darling," returned Mr. Brown, "how

much I have regretted that our residing in so secluded a place, should render it impossible for me to secure a competent teacher, one capable of advancing you in that art for which you have ever exhibited so decided a taste; I refer to your love for drawing and painting. But I am glad to tell you, that now your advancement is certain, and I hope you will find yourself happy with the teacher Providence has so kindly provided for you."

"Oh papa, this is indeed delightful news. Do inform me how it was accomplished?" asked the daughter.

"In a purely providential way, I assure you. After I left home this afternoon, I strolled towards the village for a walk. As I passed carelessly along, I heard my name pronounced by some person behind me, and turning quickly, I was delighted to see our old friend Mr. Moulton, who sailed for Europe after the death of his wife, you remember, and who has just returned, having been absent four years."

"Why papa," interrupted Bessie, her eyes sparkling with pleasure, "you do surprise me! Has he indeed returned, and did he bring sweet little Marion with him?"

"He did, my child. She is much altered, having grown exceedingly since last you met."

"You have seen her then? How I long to have the same pleasure. She must be fourteen years old, now?"

"Yes! fourteen next month she told me. But to return to my story: Mr. Moulton insisted upon my going to his house, and when there, urged me exceedingly to stay to tea. I enjoyed my visit with this intellectual, excellent man, vastly, and lingered with delight over the curiosities and magnificent paintings he brought with him from abroad.

"I am sure they must be truly splendid, if he, with his superior taste, selected them," returned Bessie.

"They are indeed; two in particular I hung over in perfect delight; one was a view upon the Rhine, and the other a charming scene in Switzerland. Mr. Moulton seemed to enjoy my pleasure, and took great pains to explain every little point of interest in those two paintings particularly."

"Does my young friend Bessie still retain her taste for drawing and painting?" he asked, as we were lingering over these pictures.

"She does indeed, Mr. Moulton," returned I, "but I regret that I have never been able to cultivate it, as there has never been a person capable of giving instruction in our village, since we made the place a residence."

"What a pity," replied my friend; "hers, I once thought a rare talent, and when such a talent is possessed it should by all means be improved. Does she not paint at all?"

"Yes," was my reply, "she has designed and painted many really beautiful Illuminated Texts, but they were of course done in water colors. She has never attempted painting in oil."

Mr. Moulton seemed to muse several moments after this; then he remarked:

"Mr. Brown, I have a proposition to make, which I hope will prove agreeable to you. It is this: I am about giving instruction to Marion in the art to which she also is partial, and I greatly desire that your daughter should enjoy the same advantage. Why not allow Bessie to come here every morning at ten o'clock, and spend a couple of hours in the study that I know she so much loves? I think Marion would be stimulated to greater perseverance with a companion, and might thus be aroused from the apathy into which she seems to have been drawn since the recent sudden and afflicting death of her grandmother."

I was delighted with the proposal, and expressed my pleasure and gratitude, but the question would present itself—

"Where will you find a suitable teacher, Mr. Moulton? Surely there is no artist in our village, or I certainly should have heard of him."

"You are mistaken, Mr. Brown. The artist whose works you have so ardently admired to-night, I mean the scene on the Rhine, and also the one taken from Switzerland, resides not far distant.

"Is it possible?" I exclaimed, "why, who, and where can he be, my dear sir."

"His name is Henry Moulton, and he stands before you!"

"You amaze me." I replied, with undisguised surprise, "I know in former days you made great use of the pencil and brush, for a diversion, but that you had become a proficient in the art, I never dreamed."

"You were ignorant also, probably, of the superior advantages that have been mine, during the last four years. I have studied with the first masters in Italy, I have spared no expense, which fortunately my ample means has fully allowed, and by close application and constant practice I have accomplished what you see. I needed some such diversion from my troubles, my friend!" continued he, sighing as he spoke. "But now, allow me to show you my studio."

Leading the way to a tasteful, cheerful room in another part of the house, he exhibited the beautiful arrangement of light and accommodation, gathered there, to aid him in the pursuit of this delightful accomplishment. The studio was, I assure you, a perfect gem of a retreat, handsomely furnished, and every way adapted for the use t which he has consecrated it.

"Here," said the generous man, "it will be my delight to instruct your daughter and mine, in this glorious art, and next week I should rejoice to commence. With your permission, Marion (who is very anxious to see her fondly loved Bessie) and myself, will call at Cedar Lawn to-morrow, and personally invite her to the Studio."

"Oh papa, I cannot tell you the joy this has afforded me," said Bessie; "the choice wish of my heart, is now obtained, and gladly will I improve the opportunity. Then I shall be so delighted to see that sweet child once more! Would that to-morrow were here, I am so impatient to clasp her in my arms."

"I think golden dreams will be mine to-night, dearest papa!" whispered the sweet girl, as after their evening devotions, she received the good night kiss of her happy parent, and sought her own apartment, there to think and rejoice over the advantages thus spread before her.

The next day, at quite an early hour, Mr. Moulton and Marion were announced, and with an eager delight, Bessie welcomed them home. Sweet little Marion, she found indeed altered, and exceedingly improved by travel and advantages, while Mr. Moulton seemed the same valued friend, only Bessie's quick eye detected a more thoughtful expression upon his handsome face, while she also noticed the sprinkling of grey hairs amid his hitherto dark locks.

The delightful hour of their stay soon glided past, and after extending the invitation already mentioned, which was accepted with many expressions of grateful pleasure, Monday was the day selected for the commencement of their lessons, and ten o'clock the hour agreed upon, to gather in the Studio.

With a warm kiss upon Marion's cheek, and a kind pressure from Mr. Moulton's hand, Bessie allowed her friends to depárt, and returned to her books and work, while her thoughts followed the sweet child and her father homeward.

CHAPTER XI.

MR. MOULTON.

IN a beautiful portion of the village of Spotsdale, stood the charming residence owned by Henry Moulton, the richest man by far in the place.

It was a spot which cultivation and an exquisite taste had rendered beautiful in the extreme. The house was large, with a wing upon each side, and vines and hanging roses were trained around the pillars that supported the front entrance, the balconies, and bay windows, filling the rooms within, in June, the rose month, with most delicious perfume.

The grounds around were extensive, and abounded in noble trees, winding walks, and vine-covered summer-houses that made it indeed a sweet retreat from the noise and dust of village life.

Never did flowers seem more rich and beautiful, than those blooming in the garden belonging to these domains; never were colors more brightly painted than rested upon the rose, the cardinal flower and the noble dahlia. While an extensive green-house was filled with exotics of the rarest elegance and beauty, and marble fountains here and there sent up sparkling jets of water heavenward, that seemed, as the sun glanced upon the crystal drops, like sprays of rarest diamonds.

Here then, surrounded by all the luxuries that wealth could gather, resided Henry Moulton, his wife, and little daughter, and with them, his wife's mother, Mrs. Vinton, a wealthy widow about fifty years of age, found a home.

Mr. Moulton was a most excellent person; pious, affable, and highly intelligent, besides being exceedingly benevolent; consequently he was greatly esteemed by the villagers and persons among whom he was associated. It would seem that such an abode, where wealth and excellence were so closely combined, might be exempt from the troubles of life—but not so. Death, that remorseless foe of mankind, entered those walls, and the wife and mother was summoned to pass that "bourne from which no traveller returns." Sad indeed, was that loving, but broken circle now, and desolate seemed the apartments that had before resounded with mirthful tones and happy laughter. Feeling deeply the shadows that had fallen around the hearts of his loved ones, Mr. Moulton closed his house and sailed for Europe, hoping by travel to restore calmness to his wounded affections. Little Marion he placed in a Parisian school, celebrated for superiority After a few months' pilgrimage around the most celebrated points of interest, and with Mrs. Vinton to take the charge of his home, he again commenced housekeeping, but this time, in a foreign land. Marion, a very interesting child, of quick perceptions, remarkably affectionate disposition, and withal very fond of study, improved rapidly, and seemed to have become quite happy and contented in her new home, and amid such a variety of new scenes, while Mr. Moulton applied himself to the pencil for recreation and diversion. No advantage that unbounded wealth could procure was denied, in order to perfect himself in an art, which with him had become the master passion of his soul. Having a decided genius for the study, he made rare progress, and his paintings were admired and lauded, far and near. So absorbed did he become in this, to him, delightful pastime, that three years glided away unnoticed, and almost unheeded, when suddenly a new affliction aroused his slumbering energies, and spread another pall of sorrow over his home. Mrs. Vinton, while in the daily performance of her duties, without a warning, suddenly dropped upon the floor a corpse, caused by unsuspected heart-disease. Poor Marion, who was devotedly attached to her fond grandmother, became almost beside herself with grief at this sudden calamity, and, much to the concern of her father, sank under the violence of her sorrow. Immediately following the advice of skillful physicians, Mr. Moulton withdrew her from the institution where she had made such rapid progress, and with her for a companion left his late residence, and started to make an extended tour throughout Europe.

So nine months flew by, amid changing scenes, and varying landscapes, and then the thoughts of both seemed to centre upon their native land, and once loved home. After three months of artistical improvement in Italy, under the first masters that could be found in that classical land, Mr. Moulton embarked for his distant home, and after a safe passage, once more entered the village from which he had so long absented himself, and received with pleasure the warm welcome that there met him on all sides, from former dear companions. Among those he met with the most unaffected joy, was Mr. Brown. This excellent man had ever been to him a disinterested and warm friend, while Bessie, a child of thirteen years when he left, had been an especial favorite, not only with himself, but with his departed wife, while their little girl had always seemed to place *her* next to her parents, in her affectionate love.

He was greatly surprised, then, when, upon calling at Cedar Lawn, Bessie made her appearance a young lady, where he had expected, strangely enough, to meet a child. It served to remind him of the rapid flight of time, and caused him to think how old he must appear in her sight. He was exceedingly pleased with the warmth of her greeting, and the sprightly cheerfulness and animation of her conversation and countenance.

"What a perfect sunbeam that sweet golden-haired girl is, in Mr. Brown's home!" thought he, as he drove homeward. "It is no wonder he never thinks of a second marriage, when her glad young face smiles so lovingly upon him."

A sigh followed this thought, and for some moments the two rode on in silence; then Marion remarked, as she raised her dark eyes to his,

"Papa, I think Miss Bessie one of the sweetest young ladies I ever met, don't you?"

A startled expression floated over the father's face as he replied, laughingly,

"Really, Marion, I hardly dare go to quite that length in expressing myself, but certainly, I found Miss Bessie a very delightful companion, and I have no doubt but that the time passed every morning in her society will be very profitable, as well as agreeable to you."

"Yes, indeed, papa. I long for Monday to come."

CHAPTER XLI.

THE STUDIO.

"Thought, strength and energy are tried
Upon the oar of manly strife;
But woman's hand alone may guide
The bark of Love, and make it glide
In safety down the stream of life."

THE Studio was indeed a quietly beautiful room, and when Bessie and Marion entered it the following Monday, Mr. Moulton smiled as this thought presented itself:

"Ah, friend Brown, I shall by this means obtain the glory of thy sunbeam, to cheer my lonely home for some hours each passing day. Surely it is a good thing to have even borrowed sunlight a little while!"

So Mr. Moulton gladly welcomed his young friend, and as he gave them their first lesson in mixing paints, thus preparing for further progress, he watched her sparkling looks, and pleased expression, with unbounded delight.

Bessie felt timid upon her first introduction to the Studio. A slight tremor passsed over her as she thought how simple and ignorant she must seem, before so finished an artist and scholar; but the kind cordiality of his manner, the gentle interest that beamed upon his handsome face, soon dispelled all nervous fears, and placed her at ease.

Mr. Moulton was truly a fine specimen of manly beauty and worth. He was fully forty years of age, and his dark chestnut hair was quite sprinkled with grey, while his ample beard also had silvery lines plentifully mingled with the original color. His eyes, however, still retained the fine expression of youth, while his teeth were remarkably even, firm and white. His form was noble and commanding, his smile winning and attractive, and Bessie thought she had seldom seen a more perfect gentleman.

"You see Miss Bessie," said the kind man, "there is much to be learned before we can commence using the brush; the skillful blending and mixing of paint, is a great and important part of an artist's work. Not an attractive feature, but necessary and useful."

"So in the employments of every-day life, Mr. Moulton," returned Bessie, reflectively, "we find unattractive duties necessary, and by no means to be despised, or dispensed with."

"Just so," replied Mr. Moulton, "but how apt a person is to neglect those homely duties and pass on to the pleasing and delightful."

"Papa," interposed Marion, "if the useful and plain parts of the duties of life were ever neglected, the beautiful would become few and marred, would they not?"

"Certainly, my child, for in many instances there is often so close a connection between the two, that both would be injured, were either neglected. How many of our beautiful flowers think you would come to maturity and perfection without the daily and tedious labor bestowed upon them by the gardener, of preparing the earth around them, planting, trimming and watering?"

"Not many, papa, but I had never before given it a thought."

"Then again, how many of our beautiful garments would be gathered around us, for our comfort and pleasure, without the laborious process having first been accomplished, of spinning, weaving, cutting and construction?"

"Very few, I know," replied the little girl.

"Then, without the cutting of stones, and the making of bricks, mixing of mortar, with all the other ugly, yet absolutely necessary employments of the different laboring classes, we should be without handsome houses, and gay parlors, and bedrooms, in which to dwell."

"Thus then, Marion," demurely interposed Bessie, "after all the ugly part of paint mixing and learning are accomplished, we may expect so see a magnificent landscape, or perfect picture of some bright object, as the result of our well deserved labor."

"Exactly! I see you are as quick at jumping to conclusions, as you are expeditious in learning how to mix paints!" laughingly returned Mr. Moulton.

So the two girls and their instructor chatted and worked on, quite delighted with their efforts and advancement in this, their first meeting in the Studio. The two hours thus passed away rapidly, and when the time came for Bessie to return home, it was with the bright prospect of another lesson on the morrow to encourage her heart.

"Well, daughter," said Mr. Brown, as the sweet girl had stolen softly behind him, and placing her white hand over his eyes, had planted a loving kiss upon his lips, "how comes on the painting?"

"Nicely, papa; I enjoyed the two hours in the Studio vastly. Mr. Moulton is not at all stiff nor stern, but is one of those who understand making persons feel comfortable, and upon good terms with themselves and those around them immediately. It is a rare faculty, not practised by half the inhabitants of this world."

"I am glad you were pleased, darling," returned Mr. Brown, affectionately patting her rosy cheek.

The next day again found Mr. Moulton in the Studio, with his pupils beside him, and again the good man secretly congratulated himself upon his borrowed sunbeam, as Bessie leaned over an easel and took a first lesson in the use of the pencil. He watched her varied color with delight, her beaming blue eyes as they now and then were turned to his, while receiving a direction, her golden hair that seemed to shed such a glory around her, and as her soft white hand often came in contact with his, he felt a new and unlooked for interest in his pupil.

So the days sped on! so sweet Bessie Brown brought cheerfulness and joy into that house, that otherwise would have been sad and gloomy, so, daily the interest of Mr. Moulton in the young girl deepened unperceived, while she as unconsciously thought of him, as a superior and exceedingly attractive man.

Ah! beware, Mr. Moulton! Beware, Bessie Brown! There is danger lurking near! Heard you ever of the little god Cupid, with his bow and arrows, hiding in unsuspected places, and shooting random shots at unguarded heart-citadels?

Beware! The small arch rogue may linger around that easel; may peep from beneath yon palette and brush, and unawares, *you* may be a victim.

The painting lessons thrived vigorously the next few weeks. Bessie was a quick scholar, and made rapid progress under such an instructor, and Marion also pleased her fond father by her interest and application.

"Miss Bessie," said Mr. Moulton one day, as they busied themselves with their tasks, "did you ever see any of the paintings owned by Mr. Landon of our village, or are you not acquainted with him and his family?"

"Oh, yes! I am not only well acquainted with them, but with the pictures to which you refer. I have spent many an hour in his picture gallery. Do you not think his collection a fine one, Mr. Moulton?"

"I do, indeed! I found several perfect gems upon those walls. They are a very interesting family."

"They are to me;" replied Bessie. "You have heard I suppose the romantic story of the loss of their daughter and her recent restoration?"

"I never heard it until last week," was the reply, "when your father related it to me. Yesterday, when I called in to see Mr. Landon, little Liza entered the room, and I was almost bewildered with her surpassing beauty."

"Did you hear her sing?" inquired Bessie, with animation.

"Yes! I never heard such remarkable compass and expression in a child! The melody of her voice is perfect, and the power and harmony complete. The parents seem perfectly happy in their daughter, but Miss Bessie, I fear their joy will be a short-lived one!"

"Why so, Mr. Moulton?" exclaimed the startled girl; "you do not think Alfonso will ever find her here?"

"Oh, no!" quickly returned Mr. Moulton, "by no means! But she seems very fragile to me. The hardship she endured in that gipsy camp, have made a sad impression upon her constitution. Miss Bessie, there is a transparency about her skin, that seems to me unnatural! the white and rose are far too delicately blended."

"You really alarm me, Mr. Moulton," exclaimed Bessie,

tears filling her eyes at the fears that rushed to her heart for her favorite; "the second loss of that child would certainly kill her mother."

"It is an old quaint saying, my dear girl, that 'God tempers the wind to the shorn lamb.' Losing a darling child by violence, might kill, but to see her dear one gently fall asleep in Jesus, while it would grieve, would not destroy a Christian mother. Little Liza seems fast ripening for heaven; her father told me many instances of her devoted child-like faith in the Saviour, of whose loving kindness, and suffering death for sinful men, women and children, she first was told by the pious gentleman who rescued her from her fearful condition."

"Oh, yes! Cousin Paul took great delight in telling her of heavenly things. He found her ignorant even of the existence of God."

"You are acquainted with Mr. Russell, I see," remarked her friend.

"He has been a friend of papa's for years, and being often at our house, I cannot remember when I did not know him. Did Liza mention him to you?"

"She did, and her brown eyes fairly danced with delight, while speaking of a recent visit he made them. Paul Russell must be a splendid man to have won so many hearts."

"He *is* an uncommon man. You will find him, if you ever chance to meet—one of God's noblemen. You would find delight in his companionship. I wish he had staid a few days longer—he only left our house the day before you arrived."

"Indeed! Was his visit so recent?"

"Yes; it was delightful to meet him again, after so many years' separation, but owing to some business engagement, his stay was but three days. He will visit us again this autumn, when we hope for a longer enjoyment of his company."

"I trust I shall then make his acquaintance—I have heard so much of him recently, I quite desire his friendship," replied Mr. Moulton.

The entrance of Marion, who had been called away to receive a visit from a young companion, here ended the conversation, and the painting upon which Bessie was at work, made great progress during the next hour.

As the time approached for Bessie to leave, she gathered up her implements, putting them carefully away, then placing her becoming round hat upon her golden hair, she bade her companions good morning, and passing down the winding paths, emerged upon the street, and thoughtfully turned her steps homeward.

She was obliged to pass Mr. Landon's on the route, and as she did so, the words of Mr. Moulton came vividly to remembrance.

"Alas! what a dreadful sorrow seems to hang over that poor mother! God grant that the fears expressed by Mr. Moulton may be groundless!"

As she passed on with these thoughts in her mind, a man arose suddenly from the ground, where he seemed to have been sitting or lying,—near, but not in sight of the garden gate, and without heeding her presence, stretched himself up to look over the row of hedge that surrounded the grounds. He was a desperate looking villain, and a malicious expression lurked around his mouth, as Bessie had a full view of his countenance. She shuddered as she saw the wretch, her first thought being of the descriptions she had often heard given by Liza, of the gipsy Alfonso.

"What can that dreadful looking creature want, peering

thus, into Mr. Landon's premises. I trust Liza is within the house!"

Suddenly a sweet song burst upon the ear, and little Liza was seen singing in an open window, upon the second story.

The man crouched down again, out of sight, as the words floated upon the morning air, but not before Bessie had a view of a triumphant leer that spread over his features. Picking up a small parcel containing old umbrellas and a case of tinker's tools, the man passed up the road when he saw that he was observed, and Bessie also resumed her usual rapid walking gait. But the face of that man, his fiendish expression, and strange, peering ways, haunted her thoughts all the remaining portion of the day, and indeed far into the night.

Her father listened to her account of the strange individual she had encountered, listlessly, and told her probably it was some itinerant tinker, watching for an employer, while Mr. Moulton, when told the next day, listened with interest, and said "a watch should be set about the village," but added, "Really, Miss Bessie, I think it impossible to have been Alfonso, as the ocean rolls between this, and that gipsy camp. How could he have tracked the little one so far?"

"It does seem improbable, I confess," returned Bessie, "but the movements of that mysterious tribe are ever strange and uncertain. I cannot help trembling with an unknown fear whenever I think of that hideous person."

"Strive to banish him from remembrance, then, dear Miss Bessie," returned the gentleman, giving her a tender and impassioned look, that called a blush to the bright face, and made the blue eyes fall in evident confusion. "It would sadden my heart to see you unhappy; promise me you will not brood over it, nor borrow any trouble on his account. Anxiety will be a poor companion for light hearted Bessie Brown."

There was a tenderness in the tones, that caused a thrill of pleasure to enter the bosom of our gentle friend, and with a happy smile she gave the wished-for promise, and once more applied herself to the occupation of which she was so enthusiastically fond.

Her walk home that morning was unattended with incident; no strange man startled her by his appearance, and with the tender glance of Mr. Moulton still distinct within her memory, she tripped on, unchecked by a doubt, a fear, or an untoward circumstance.

CHAPTER XLII.

THE MISUNDERSTANDING.

"Our cross and trial do but press,
The heavier for our bitterness."

THE next morning arose bright and beautiful! Not a cloud obscured the horizon, not a shadow seemed to fall upon the glad heart of Bessie, as she wended her way to the stately residence, where so many hours had passed pleasantly, and where she knew a warm welcome would surely await her. She smiled unconsciously, as she walked along; the very breath of the morning air, as it played around her cheek, seemed joyful to her spirit, and the rippling of a tiny waterbrook, which she passed before she came to the village, together with the chorus of voices that burst from the feathered race, as they flitted among the treeboughs, seemed to fill her with unwonted joy. It was the last of September, and the air was soft and balmy, and was laden with the sweet perfume of monthly roses, mignonette, burgamot, and other flowers, from the still gay gardens in the village, while tiny wild flowers and beautiful grasses peeped from beneath her feet, when she glided over an uncultivated spot.

She seemed to live in a new atmosphere lately; her heart was all glowing with a sweet delight, and her spirit seemed to awaken anew to the love of her great Redeemer, and Heavenly Father. She knew not what had caused the light heartedness that was hers; she did not pause to analyze the feeling; but her soul rejoiced in perfect peace, and she was indeed happy.

Sweet Bessie Brown, had love—that great refiner of the human heart—anything to do with this quiet joy? Had the memory of one tender glance from certain eyes she had dreamed of, aught to whisper to her girlish heart of hope, or future happiness?

She had not thought of these questions; the feeling, *if it existed*, was new-born, and as yet was unconsciously fostered. So, with the secret peace softly nestling in her heart, she walked along until she approached the residence of Mr. Landon.

Suddenly she started back a step, with a thrill of terror in her bosom, while the color left her lips, and her eyes dilated with fear; for before her, leaning against a tree on the opposite side of the road, yet in full view of Mr. Landon's grounds, stood the hideous individual she had encountered two days before, near the same spot.

"Good morning, miss," said the fellow impudently, as she sought to pass on, while a grin swept over his features; "could you tell a poor man where he could find a job of work, mending umbrellas, or tins, in this village, to save himself from starvation?"

"You can find employment probably further on, where the houses are thicker," replied Bessie, trembling as she spoke.

She walked directly to the gate after making this reply, determining in her own mind to place Mrs. Landon on her guard. As she opened it to enter, the man gave her a fiendish look, blending both surprise and hatred, then taking up his box of tools he hurried away.

Mrs. Landon was home, and in a few words she told her of the suspicious character she had twice seen hovering around the premises, and charged her on no account to allow Liza to go out alone. She might be fostering fears, she added, " but some secret dread kept whispering that it was Alfonso."

The mother turned deadly pale at the very mention of the name, and with trembling voice thanked Bessie for the caution, which she told her should be strictly observed.

That morning as Bessie sat in the studio, the conversation turned upon the marriage of one of the villagers, a widow and friend of both, to a gentleman living in a neighboring State.

" I was extremely surprised to hear that Mrs. Orne had married the person she did," said Mr. Moulton, " as, before I went abroad, I thought your father would seek her for a wife."

" My father!" exclaimed Bessie in surprise. " You are joking."

"No, I am not, Miss Bessie! I, as well as others, often wondered if it would not be the case."

" Mr. Moulton, I do not think my father ever thought, or would allow himself to think of a second marriage. His love for my precious mother was too holy, too deep an affection to be lightly thrown aside."

A shadow of the deepest pain floated over Mr. Moulton's brow as Bessie uttered these words. She was bending over her easel, thinking only of her work, therefore did not notice the effect they had produced upon her companion, for some time; then, when his gravity became apparent, she had entirely forgotten them.

" I wonder why Mr. Moulton appeared so different today," thought she, as she left the house. "I never saw him so sad and thoughtful. Can it be that he has heard any distressing news? He certainly was very depressed in spirits for some cause."

Bessie was right; Mr. Moulton was depressed in spirits. The remark she had made about the second marriage of her father, seemed a knell to the fond hopes he had unconsciously nourished from the day his borrowed sunbeam had entered his studio as a pupil. He thought in that remark he could read a decided opposition to second marriages; he fancied that she had taken that quiet mode of informing him of this, her opinion, and his heart sank within him at the bare idea! He leaned his head upon his hand after the girls had left him, and sadly pondered his forlorn condition. He found that he loved devotedly! He had not acknowledged it before, but now the fact was too palpable to be mistaken. He loved,—and he felt after that remark, that his love was hopeless! Bessie probably regarded him as a good friend, old, and wedded very properly to the memory of his wife. She looked upon his second marriage with the same eyes that she regarded the marriage of her father, as a wrong and sacrilegious proceeding; then she could not of course love him, and he saw that he had been foolish in supposing a young girl of eighteen could love a man nearly forty years of age.

Yet the blow was a severe one, his love was too deep not to feel keenly the sentiments a few hours had revealed to him.

He strove to cast off the anguish that held his heart with an iron clasp, to arouse himself from the wretchedness that enveloped him, to no purpose; the hopelessness of his love was ever presenting itself, and Bessie seemed floating off, far from his reach, whenever he sought to think of her gentleness and youth.

"Oh, Bessie! sweet golden-haired Bessie, this has been a bitter blow to me! How can I give you up in all your innocence and purity, my love, my darling?"

The strong man seemed all unnerved by the violence of his emotion; his frame trembled, and his eyes wore a sad and wretched expression, quite foreign to their usual sparkling intelligence. Suddenly he arose, and pacing the floor, exclaimed,

"But why do I thus despair? Did a faint heart ever yet win a fair lady? Perhaps time may change her opinion; perhaps devotion may yet inspire love! I will not give up thus hopelessly, but will strive yet to win her affections. God grant that I may succeed, for failure would bring bitterness indeed. Life without that sunbeam to smile upon my path would be cheerless, desolate, and sad."

Still, with the determined resolution of once more seeking to win her love, he could not shake off the foreboding that had spread such a depression over his spirit, and his countenance day after day continued grave and sad, while Bessie noted the change, and silently wondered as to its cause. While pondering over the gravity of her teacher, Bessie was led to examine her own heart more closely, and with the scrutiny came the knowledge of the true state of her affections. The tender solicitude of Mr. Moulton's manner towards her, led her to feel that the sentiment was reciprocated, although his strange reserve and melancholy was unaccountable.

"Why has this thing been allowed?" questioned she of her own heart, within the solitude of her chamber. "Why have I permitted myself to love a man so much my senior? Am I right in thus fostering the feeling—and were he to seek my hand, would it be well for me to accept him? Would that I had some suitable adviser!

Would that dear Mrs. Douglass were only here, with her good judgment, and excellent principles. I will write to her, claiming the visit she promised me long ago. I will tell her that I need counsel upon an important subject; then she cannot refuse to pass a few weeks at Cedar Lawn I know I shall feel calmed by her presence and advice!"

After asking permission from her father, to solicit a visit from her much loved friend, which was immediately granted, Bessie dashed off a few lines, and then eagerly waited a reply.

It came in a few days, and to her great joy the invitation was accepted, the second day of October being appointed for her arrival.

CHAPTER XLIII.

CONFIDENTIAL TALK.

"The most delicate, the most sensible of all pleasure, consists in promoting the pleasures of others."

BRUYERE.

BESSIE counted the days before the presence of her much loved friend should give her joy, and gladly she hailed its near approach.

"Dear Mrs. Douglass, how I long to press her loving lips once more, and to meet the affectionate glances of those splendid hazel eyes!" thought she. "What a strange thought will come into my mind since the reception of her letter. Suppose papa should fancy her, and ask her to be his wife! Mr. Moulton spoke several weeks since, of his second marriage. If he only would marry her, I think I would be quite contented, although she is much too young for him, and besides, I doubt if she will ever wed again. Yet she certainly has changed somewhat since I first met her; then, she never left the seclusion of her room, save to attend church, or on some errand of pure benevolence; now she visits her friends in a quiet way, and seems more cheerful, it is said, since her return from Europe. I think if such a marriage could be brought about, it would be an excellent thing for dear papa, and indeed for me also, she is so beautiful and good."

Wednesday was ushered in with a gush of sunshine, while the very birds seemed to sing a song of welcome to the new comer.

Bessie received her friend with open arms and wild expressions of delight, while Mr. Brown rejoiced in the happiness of his child, and strove to entertain his fair guest to the best of his ability.

Rebecca was much pleased in thus meeting again her favorite, as she had not seen her since her return from Europe, some weeks before, and so much had she to relate, that it was time to retire, before either realized that the evening had passed away.

The next morning found our young friend and her guest seated in Bessie's pleasant room, engaged in an earnest conversation. The accustomed visit to the studio was to be omitted during the period that Mrs. Douglass remained, in order that Bessie might devote her whole mornings and indeed her whole time, to the entertainment of her friend.

This morning they were occupied with their needlework, while at the same time their tongues were working as busily as though their hands were not thus actively engaged.

"You wrote me, my dear girl, that you needed advice upon a very important subject; will it not be a good opportunity now, when we are alone, to discuss the matter, and settle the difficulty that seems to be yours?"

"It will, Mrs. Douglass; but now that I have you here, I am quite at a loss how to inform you of my feelings!" returned the young girl, a burning blush diffusing her cheeks, and deepening even around her graceful throat.

"That blush tells the story for you, darling!" said the observing lady; "if I mistake not it is some heart history that is to be communicated. Do not fear to tell me, Bessie, you know it is woman's lot to love?"

"Yes! Mrs. Douglass, you are right; it is of the affections I would speak, as I greatly need the counsel of some womanly experience. You know I have no mother's bosom to confide in? No mother's lips to speak to me a word of advice and sympathy."

"My poor child," returned Rebecca, kindly, "you must indeed miss that loving guidance! If I can assist you in any way, I assure you I will cheerfully do so; therefore, keep back nothing, for of course your confidence shall be held perfectly sacred."

After a slight pause, during which the crimson spot upon Bessie's cheek grew brighter and brighter, she spoke again these timid words:

"Then, Mrs. Douglass, tell me what you think would be the consequences of a reciprocated affection being indulged, between a young girl of eighteen, and a gentleman of forty?"

"In some cases, as with a diversity of sentiment, a want of congeniality, a cold disposition on one side, and warm enthusiasm on the other, I should judge it must be most disastrous," was the reply.

"But with a different state of disposition, with congeniality, and love, do you think a marriage under such circumstances would result in happiness?"

"Stay! let us understand each other more fully. For instance, let a warm hearted, affectionate, pure minded girl, like yourself, become attached to a gentleman of similar warm-heartedness, one most congenial in tastes and disposition, you ask whether a marriage with this great disparity of years between them would naturally bring happiness? Is that it, darling?"

"It is!" was the timid response.

"My answer is, then, Bessie, that I do not see why it could not. Of course it would be far better to have love inspired where the ages are more suitable; but in case the affections of both are fully enlisted—mind, I say *the affections*, not the worldliness of both, or either, but the pure deep affections of the heart are engaged, surely happiness must, and will follow."

"The worldliness, dear Mrs. Douglass; what do you mean by that?" inquired Bessie, thoughtfully.

"I mean the frequent marriages for position or wealth, so common among young people in the present age." A sigh followed these words of Rebecca's, for a picture glided before her of a worldly marriage and a thoughtless bride, where her husband's heart was the sacrifice laid upon the altar, and her home had been laid waste under the blighting breath of her own folly.

Another pause followed, during which both ladies seemed to be plunged in deep reflection.

"A close examination of your own heart is requisite, my dear Bessie," continued Rebecca, at length breaking the silence, "in order to ascertain clearly, in your case, whether mercenary motives have aught to do with the preference you may feel for your friend. I know not what person has lately entered the thoughts of Bessie Brown—whether he be rich or poor; but I implore her, as she values her future happiness, to weigh the matter well, to be certain that a mutual love exists, and to be equally sure of congeniality of thought and disposition, before any vows of a binding nature take place."

"Thank you, dear Mrs. Douglass, for your kind advice; I shall certainly follow it. Nothing may ever result from the attachment I feel for the person to whom I refer, but I can assure you solemnly, no thought of worldliness has ever been mine during the acquaintance, nor has one longing wish for the wealth he certainly does possess, ever once influenced my heart. No! were he a poor man, earning his bread by his daily labor, I should still prefer him to all others, still regard him as the most excellent of men."

"With such devotion then, Bessie, I should not hesitate one moment to accept his offer of marriage, if the affair ever comes to such a point."

Here the subject of conversation was changed, other matters coming up for discussion—scenes that had happened in the lives of each since they had last met, being related with animation and interest.

"Oh, Bessie," said Mrs. Douglass after a while, "how are the Landon family? Dear little Liza I suppose you see often!"

"Yes, and each time I converse with her, I find her growing more and more interesting. But Mrs. Douglass, I must tell you of a dreadful creature in the form of a man who has been prowling round our village, especially around Mr. Landon's premises, within the last few days, and who ever fills me with untold dread."

"Who is he, darling?" asked Mrs. Douglass with surprise.

"No one seems to know. His occupation seems to be that of an umbrella-mender, but his movements to me seem very suspicious. The thought constantly presents itself, that it must be Alfonso. Do you think such a thing could be possible?"

"Hardly, I imagine. How could he have traced her across the Atlantic? Have you seen him very lately?"

"No, not since I one morning entered the house, and informed Mrs. Landon of his presence; that is now about ten days since. As he saw me enter the gate, he seemed surprised, then giving me a look of bitter hatred, he gathered up his box of working implements from the ground, and hurried away."

"It may be that he has left the place, and perhaps it was some straggling vagabond, who will never return."

"I sincerely hope so! But you must see the family soon. They will call on you probably to-day, then you can take an early opportunity to return the visit."

The Landons, with little Liza, did call upon Mrs. Douglass that morning, and after a long and pleasant chat, they obtained a promise that they should within a day or so receive her at their home, and have the privilege of entertaining herself and Bessie an entire day.

CHAPTER XLIV.

ANOTHER FRIGHT.

"The way to heaven is by Weeping Cross."

AT the time appointed, Bessie and Mrs. Douglass early presented themselves at Mr. Landon's, where a warm reception met them, and where joy and peace seemed to fill the bosom of each member of the family.

Bessie could not but contrast the playfulness and animation of Mrs. Landon with her former appearance on a day she well remembered to have passed with Minnie, now Mrs. Charles Percy, in those same apartments.

Both Mr. and Mrs. Landon expressed, several times, the wish that Charley and Minnie were only present to complete the group, and to add to their pleasure.

"You left them well, I presume, Mrs. Douglass?" inquired Mrs. Landon.

"Quite so: but both are exceedingly taken up with the preparations for housekeeping which they are making. Charles intends purchasing a place near the city, yet in some quiet village, where he can enjoy the pleasures of rural life at the same time that he transacts his business in the great emporium of trade. If, for instance, he is so fortunate as to secure a suitable place in Connecticut or New Jersey, convenient to the railroad, a few hours will land him at his store, while the pure air will revive him upon his arrival home in the evening."

"Do you think Minnie will like so quiet a life, after having been brought up amid so much gaiety?" asked Mrs. Landon.

"Minnie is greatly changed since her return from Europe, and our narrow escape from death upon the ocean. She is not the wild and thoughtless girl of former days, but the gentle loving, Christian woman," returned Rebecca.

"I am delighted to hear it, I assure you, dear Mrs. Douglass. Religion is surely a necessary requisite to the formation of a happy fireside. My brother also I believe rejoices in the glorious hope of salvation," said Mrs. Landon.

"He does indeed. They are perfectly united in affection and religious principles. Theirs will prove, I confidently trust, a truly happy marriage. But Bessie, do you remember the comical negro my brother had in his employ during your visit to New York?"

"Oh, yes! who could forget Sambo Johnson, with his aristocratic airs and genuine darkey talk?" replied Bessie.

"Then if you recollect him so well, I will tell you what happened one morning last week. Mrs. Morton and myself were busily sewing in the family sitting-room, when Sambo made his appearance, and after innumerable bows and flourishes, said,

"'Missis, sorry to 'sturb you, but I hab a perquest I would like to spread afore your sideration.'

"'What is that Sambo? What can I do for you this morning?' returned Mrs. Morton, kindly.

"'Well now, you obsarve, Missis, that I lubs good Marsa and you, to 'straction; but pears like I can't stand dat Pomp, and all dem debilish niggers down in dat kitchen no how you can fix it, and I don't blieve dere is a spectibul collured pusson in dis yere confisticated world, what can. Now Missis, dems my sentiments, privately expressed, you know. Well as I was about to obsarve, dat young Marse Percy berry nice individual, and Missis Percy, she perticular splendid in my pinion, and I tinks I knos a ting or two bout dem kind of tings, and now what I'se gwine for to say, was, if you has no special 'jections I would lub to change Marsas. Not dat I'se got prejudiced agin Marse Morton, tank de Lord, taint dat; but the fact is, I specially fond ob dat chile Miss Minnie, and I jist want to take good care of her, long as de bref ob life lasts, and when we all goes to de land ob Canaan, I jist wants to be sartin dat all obstructions am lifted out ob her way. Dat's de pint ob de hul bizness. Missis, it am a fact now, true's my name's Sambo Johnson, at your particular service.'

"'Well, but Sambo, how will you clear away obstructions from Mrs. Percy's path to heaven?' I asked, quite bent upon hearing him explain himself.

"'Laws a massy! Missis, it's mighty easy fur dem dat knows how, to accomplish dat matter, I assure you. Now when I gets up yonder, de door keeper he'll say, 'Who's dar? and de obstructions will be, dat de mighty doors be all shut agin dark folks, so I'll hide behind missis, and say softly, like as if 'twas her own blessed mouf speaking, 'It am Missis Percy,' so de obstruction fly open in one flash, and we both rush rite in, shoutin, Hallelujah, Amen! Tanks be to God, Amen!'

"'Well, Sambo, I will speak to Mr. Morton and Mr. Percy about the change you desire, and will let you know their decision,' returned my sister-in-law, much to the joy of the humble petitioner.

"Charley and Minnie were delighted with the proposal, for Sambo is a faithful and excellent servant; therefore he was duly informed that they had consented to the plan.

"The negro received the intelligence with a real darkey laugh, and ran down stairs, two at a time, exclaiming at the top of his voice,

"'Glory grachus! aint dis yere chile a lucky dog dis day? Bress de Lord! Spect now to get to hebbin mighty quick, as it's all a strait road dar now, wid no debilish niggers to pull back one's coat tails wid dere nonsensical talk. Golly! aint Sambo made up now? Ki! yi!'"

Bessie and Mrs. Landon laughed heartily at this relation of the peculiarities of Sambo, and after a little more conversation, all repaired to the dining-room, at a summons from the dinner-bell, where they did ample justice to a delicious, and well gotten up repast.

After dinner while Mrs. Landon attended to a person who called, upon some little business matter, Mrs. Douglass and Bessie accompanied Liza into the garden, and green-house, where they were delighted with the beautiful display of autumnal flowers, there growing in the greatest perfection.

"Mrs. Douglass, there is a charming echo behind the green-house that usually delights strangers; would you not like to listen to it?" asked Liza, as the ladies turned to leave the garden.

"Yes, very much!" returned Rebecca. "Bessie spoke of it the other day, as being remarkably fine."

Turning into one of the winding paths, the ladies followed the interesting child to the place designated, and were indeed delighted with the distinct and beautiful sounds that reverberated here and there, at but the raising of the voice.

"Sing that lovely Echo Song of Jenny Lind's, now darling. Its wild notes echoing around, are so thrillingly grand," said Bessie, passing her arm fondly around the little one as she spoke, thus affectionately encouraging the gifted child of song.

Standing in a certain position, where her voice would be sure to catch the Echo, Liza commenced singing, and as the words left her lips, the Echo repeated them, now here, now there, with an effect remarkably beautiful.

"Birdling! why sing in the forest wide? Say why? Say why?
Call'd thou the Bridegroom, or the Bride? And why? And why?
I call no Bridegroom, call no Bride,
Although I sing in forest wide,
Nor know, nor know, nor know why I am singing
La—la—la—la—la—la—la—la.
Nor know why I am singing.

"Birdling! why is thy heart so blest? Oh say? Oh say?
Music o'erflowing from thy breast? Oh say? Oh say?
My heart is full and yet is light,
My heart is glad in day or night,
Nor know, nor know, nor know I why I'm singing,
La—la—la—la—la—la—la—la,
Nor know I why I'm singing.

"Birdling! why sing you all the day? Oh tell! Oh tell!
Do any listen to thy lay? Oh tell! Oh tell!
I care not what my song may be,
Now this, now that. I warble free,
Nor know, nor know, nor know, yet must be singing,
La—la—la—la—la—la—la—la.
Nor know yet must be singing."

"Charming! exquisite!" exclaimed Rebecca, catching the little minstrel in her arms from pure delight, and kissing, over and again, the lips from which such melody had just issued. "Dear little girl, please sing again the last verse, it is so wildly sweet."

Once more, for the gratification of the enthusiastic lady,

did Liza sing, prolonging the notes where the Echo answered so distinctly, until her hearers fairly trembled with delight.

"Ha! ha! ha!" uttered a voice at their side, just as the last lines were dying away, which filled the ladies with the utmost alarm.

Raising her eyes to the hedge near which they stood, Rebecca caught sight of the fiendish face of a man, just as it disappeared behind the green.

"Oh take me home! Please take me home to mamma!" whispered the frightened child, as, pale and faint, she clung to the dress of Mrs. Douglass.

Passing her arm around her, the lady, with Bessie's assistance, half carried, half supported, the drooping form towards the house. Not a word was spoken until within its welcome shelter, they placed their now unconscious burden upon a sofa, and tenderly sought to revive her.

"Has he gone? Tell me quick, dear Bessie, has he gone?" exclaimed she, when the power of articulation returned, while she clung, as she spoke, to her frightened mother, terror filling her beautiful brown eyes, and causing her whole frame to tremble.

"Who, darling? What frightened my lily-bud so dreadfully?" asked Mrs. Landon.

"Oh mamma, it was Alfonso! I heard him laugh, and then I saw his dreadful eyes staring over the hedge. He has found me now, mamma! He will get me again I know! Oh mamma, mamma, what shall I do? where shall I go, for Alfonso has found me?"

"Do not be so terrified, dear child; Alfonso shall not harm you! Papa will have the country searched, and he shall be placed where he can do no harm. Fear not, my lily-bud, my darling!"

It was long before the little one could be calmed, so perfectly paralyzed had she become with fear, and when finally she did lie quiet in her mother's arms, a sudden closing of a door would cause her to start, while any quick or unusual sound would dilate her eyes with extremest terror and alarm.

Mrs. Douglass and Bessie remained with the poor nervous mother and child, until Mr. Landon returned from a drive he had been obliged to take after dinner was over, in order to transact a matter of business that needed immediate attention. They also lingered until he had entered a complaint with the authorities of the place, and had thus set in motion a diligent search for the villain who had so disturbed the comfort of his family. It would have been a relief to all the villagers could he have been caught, as Liza, with her remarkable talents, and extraordinary beauty, had become the darling of the place; but, notwithstanding the most faithful search had been made in every portion of the town, as well as in the country around, no clue to the strange man could be found, and although ten days elapsed during which the watch was continued, no trace of him could be discovered, and they were obliged to give the matter up at last, all seeming to arrive at one conclusion, that the creature, becoming alarmed at his own imprudence in thus discovering himself to Liza, had precipitately fled.

For some time the family lived in constant fear and anxiety, scarcely daring to leave the house, so great a terror had the appearance of the gipsy in the neighborhood sent through their hearts; but as days passed on, and no further annoyance was experienced, the feeling gradually wore away, and once more, but always attended by some faithful friend, the little girl was allowed to take open air exercise, which was deemed absolutely necessary by the physician, and which did seem to revive her drooping frame, although she continued exceedingly fragile, and indeed was anything but well.

CHAPTER XLV.

A RESCUE.

"For courage mounteth with occasion."

KING JOHN.

"IT is a bright and pleasant morning, Mrs. Douglass," said Bessie, some time after the incident mentioned in the last chapter, as she entered her friend's apartment, arrayed for a walk—"will you not accompany me to the village, as I have an errand to do, and long for companionship?"

"With pleasure, Bessie; I think a walk will do me good, as I have a slight headache this morning."

Rising and laying aside her embroidery, the fair widow was soon equipped, and the two passed out of the grounds into the road beyond.

"How charming everything looks in this bright morning sunlight, Bessie! See! the dew hangs still upon those blades of grass, sparkling like diamonds of the purest water. Then the trees appear so beautiful in the changing, many-colored hues of October, while the air is mild and balmy, it is really to me a most delightful season of the year."

"Do you ever think," continued Rebecca after a pause, "how much there is to admire in the works of creation, how much that should serve to draw our hearts closer to Him who fashioned each leaf and flower, for our benefit and pleasure? I think the true Christian sees more of the beautiful, when, with his heart full of thankfulness to God, he views each tiny shrub, each clinging vine, and each tinted flower, as fresh from the hand of the Almighty, than does the cold child of the world."

"How true your remarks are, Mrs. Douglass," returned Bessie. "I remember before I became a Christian I never saw half the beauties that are so thickly spread upon the lap of nature, and the reason was, I think, because I did not see God in them all. But now, how different! I never pluck a flower, and examine closely its delicate colors, with the graceful shape of its petals and its calyx, its tiny stamens and pistils, but I think of Him who fashioned such rare perfection, and formed what no man can ever imitate. How strange it is that, with all these beauties, spread so thickly around us, so many of the human race remain in ignorance of God."

"I sometimes think it a willful ignorance," replied Rebecca, "and how can it be other wisethan willful, when there are on every side, so many voices in nature and revelation, constantly shouting the name of Jehovah? The blazing firmament proclaims 'God is, and is light, and in Him is no darkness at all.' The stars, like lights in the windows of Heaven, twinkle forth, 'God the High and lofty One, inhabiteth eternity!' The Mountain in imperial dignity stands up and declares 'God is on a throne high and lifted up.' The Cataract thunders forth, 'God doeth wonders.' The Streamlet murmurs out, 'God giveth grace to the humble.' The Pines of the earth wave out the cry, 'God giveth gifts to men.' The Bible says 'God is in Christ, reconciling the world unto Himself, not imputing their trespasses unto them.' The heralds of salvation, with feet upon the mountain of honor, in the house of God, stand like signal fires, dotting the land, warning men of good tidings of good, that 'God reigneth.'"

"I believe you are right, dear Mrs. Douglass! It must be truly a willful ignorance that ignores the existence of a great and wise God."

"Your village is beautifully situated, Bessie," again remarked Mrs. Douglass as they walked slowly along. "This view, as we approach it, is particularly grand! See how tastefully the residences are arranged, while the thick growth of trees that wave over the house-tops, makes it almost deserve the name of Forest City. Then this graceful little stream, winding here and there through the streets, with these rustic yet beautiful bridges, and rippling, sparkling waters, is a great improvement and addition to the beauty of the place. The poet was right when he wrote,

"There's beauty all around our path, if but our watchful eyes,
Can trace it mid familiar scenes, and through their lowly guise."

"He was indeed, but here we are at Mr. Landon's, Mrs. Douglass; suppose we drop in a moment, and ask Liza to accompany us in our walk? The poor child has been so closely confined of late, I think a stroll would be a great pleasure, and with both of us to accompany her, there can be no danger, as all the villagers agree in the opinion that Alfonso has left the place."

"Very well thought of, dear! I should love to hear the prattle of the interesting and beautiful child as we wander on."

So the two kind-hearted ladies entered the pleasant,

peaceful home of their little favorite, and soon made known the object of their visit to the fond mother, and the delighted child. It did not take long for the little one to prepare herself, and promising to bring her back in a very short time, the three were soon walking along, enjoying every sound, and admiring every point of interest that came in their way.

"Whose magnificent grounds are these?" asked Rebecca of Bessie, for this was the first time she had been so far, as they neared the residence of Mr. Moulton. "Really this reminds me of some of the elegant palaces of Europe, with all these accompanying splendors of fountains, shrubbery and flowers!"

"It is the abode of Mr. Moulton, a gentleman who has but recently returned from abroad, and who is giving me lessons in painting."

A tell-tale blush mounted to the brow of the artless girl, as she uttered these words, and that blush being quietly observed by her friend, told more than poor little Bessie dreamed could be possible.

So they rambled on, Bessie's errand being long before accomplished, until the village lay quietly behind them, while a beautiful country scene was spread around.

"Here is a charming spot in which to rest," observed Rebecca, "before we turn homeward. This beautiful coppice, with its graceful elms and oaks close by the roadside, its inviting shade, and yonder pleasant seat, bids us welcome; then that huge rock, covered with moss and ivy, really is quite romantic."

Turning into the grove the ladies sat some time refreshing themselves under the shadows, chatting every moment with animation and pleasure.

"Sing something, Liza dear, while we rest; we both love

music and would delight to hear your voice again," said Bessie.

"Oh, yes! darling, sing some little couplet before we return," exclaimed Rebecca.

"Shall I sing a little song I learned the other day, called "Speak to me kindly?" asked Liza, fixing her beautiful brown eyes inquiringly upon the eager faces of her older companions. Being answered in the affirmative, the little girl folded her hands and commenced to sing—

SPEAK TO ME KINDLY.

Speak to me kindly! I never could bear
The unfeeling word or the harsh angry tone!
Kindness may win me, but harshness may wear
The gall on its brow, which will poison alone.
Speak to me kindly.

Speak to me calmly! when breathing the tale,
Wrought with the heart's blood and coming to chill,
Broken unwisely my spirit would fail,
Leaving the young heart all bleeding and still.
Calmly, speak calmly.

Speak to me gently! from childhood's young day
I have loved not the rough jest, the loud laugh of glee.
Gently as fades the last sunbeam away,
Softly as leaves fall, oh, thus speak to me.
Gently, speak gently.

Speak to me fondly! my young spirit grieves,
For the pet names of love, and affection's low tone,
I pine for the gladness a loving word leaves,
As music at nightfall is craved by the lone.
Speak to me fondly.

The words were exceedingly touching to Rebecca, who had never heard the song before, while the voice of Liza seemed almost spiritual in its pure beauty and harmony, and held both her hearers spell-bound, as the delicious sounds floated around. As Rebecca listened intently, her eyes happened to wander towards the rock she had noticed upon entering the grove, and there to her horror she saw a man's head just rising above it, while the same look of fiendish triumph that she had seen upon a former occasion, was printed upon his horrible features.

Trembling with alarm, Mrs. Douglass arose, and clasping the child's hand in hers, she turned with a faint cry to leave the spot.

Quicker than thought, as the wretch saw the movement, he leaped from the rock, and with one spring gained her side, and wrenching Liza from her clasp, he exclaimed, heedless of the shrieks that burst from both child and ladies:

"Ah! fools! did you think I would give up my game so easily? Did you think I would not yet benefit by that voice? Yes! by heaven, she is mine, and no power on earth shall drag her from me!"

Dashing a furious blow at Rebecca, who had again seized the child, now lying perfectly unconscious in his arms, the gipsy shook off her clasp, and rushed away, bearing poor Liza's inanimate form, as easily as he would the merest trifle. On he went at the utmost speed, followed by both Rebecca and Bessie, as fast as possible, while screams for help issued at every step from their livid lips.

Over bush and brake of that lonely country road, ran pursuers and pursued; for the grove where they had rested lay beyond the village, and Alfonso had started off towards the open country, and now seemed making for a dense wood that lay about quarter of a mile beyond. Nothing daunted, the ladies rushed after, determined not to lose sight of the wretch until help should come.

Faster and faster flew Alfonso, who now was far ahead, while his malignant laugh was borne to their ears by the wind, and they knew the forest would, if gained, effectually hide him from their view.

"Will no one come?" they shrieked. "Help! help! will no one come?"

Hark! surely the tramp of a horse's hoofs are sounding in their ears. Yes! a horseman dashes to the spot, attracted by their screams.

"God be praised! she may yet be saved!" exclaimed Rebecca and Bessie in one breath.

"Halt, there! stop, if you don't wish to be shot!" shouted Mr. Moulton, for it was he, but only the same "Ha! ha!" was sent back in answer, as the wretch still dashed on, and both ladies saw that the threat to shoot was a vain one, as Mr. Moulton had no sign of a weapon upon his person.

Alfonso had, however, they soon found to their horror, for wheeling around for one instant, he raised his arm, and taking deliberate aim at Mr. Moulton's head, he fired, while at the sight a fearful scream burst from Bessie's pale and trembling lips.

A harmless shot it proved to be! The ball missed its mark, and Mr. Moulton was unhurt.

On dashed the horseman, and on went the gipsy, but just as they neared the wood, where the brush was so thick that a horse could not have followed, Alfonso caught his foot in some unseen impediment, and fell headlong to the ground, while the groan and fearful oath he uttered as he dropped his burden, told that he was severely hurt.

Dashing to the spot and vaulting from the saddle, Mr. Moulton grappled with the fiend, who was vainly seeking to rise, and with a powerful grasp held him down, until Rebecca and Bessie came panting to the spot.

While Rebecca drew the body of the insensible child away from the writhing man, to a safer distance, Bessie rushed to the side of Mr. Moulton, exclaiming, "How can I assist you? what shall I do?"

"Hand me that pistol, please, that lies on the ground. Yes! all right; I see it has one barrel yet undischarged. Now can you think of anything with which I can tie this fellow's hands? His ankle I think is sprained, from the manner in which it was doubled under him. If I could tie his hands, we might stop these struggles!"

"The halter!" exclaimed Bessie. "No, that is too stiff! Stay! I have it." Taking a shawl from her shoulders, she ruthlessly tore it in strips, then tying the parts together, it formed a long, stout, cord, which answered admirably for the purpose.

"Give me the pistol now!" said Rebecca, coming to his side. "I can fire it off, if he resists. I will hold it to his head while you bind him tightly, and his life pays the forfeit if he stirs! I understand the process of shooting well, and I shall not flinch."

Standing guard thus by the fallen gipsy, her beautiful face full of unshrinking determination, her eyes fixed firmly upon his, the noble woman kept the trembling wretch at bay, while Mr. Moulton securely tied his arms in such a manner as to leave him powerless.

Then taking the pistol from Rebecca, he stood over the prostrate, swearing man, while the two ladies sought to restore animation to poor little Liza. With all their efforts, however, their tender words, their gentle tones, they could not bring her back to consciousness, and with pale faces, and looks of agony, they again consulted what had next best be done.

"Let me go for assistance!" exclaimed Bessie; "I will use the utmost speed."

"No, darling!" said Rebecca, "you support the fainting child, while I mount that horse and ride to the village."

"The horse *is* a gentle one!" said Mr. Moulton. "If you can manage to keep on a gentleman's saddle, it would be best."

"I can do it! I could ride the wildest horse bare-back, on an occasion where life is at stake."

Leading the animal to a stump close by, the fearless woman sprang from it to the saddle, and in a moment was flying towards the village. Fortunately, before she reached the grove, she saw a carriage coming towards her. Hastily approaching its side, she explained the situation in which her friends were placed, and thus obtained the ready assistance of the man who drove, and the gentleman seated within. Returning rapidly to the spot, the inanimate child and the two ladies were placed upon the cushions of the carriage, and while the strange gentleman staid beside Mr. Moulton and the prostrate, groaning gipsy, the driver was instructed to take them to the residence of Mr. Landon, and then obtain the services of the constable, and return immediately for the prisoner.

Another hour found Alfonso safely secured within the county jail, where, under the strongest locks, he was to await his trial for the murder of poor Belle, and for his other many crimes, and in dismissing him from our pages we will only add, that upon that trial, which took place immediately, he was found guilty of murder in the first degree, and in four weeks from that day, his crime-burdened soul took its flight from the gallows, upon which he suffered the just penalty of his transgressions. While in prison, previous to his execution, the wretched man was informed of the death of Costanza, and of the place of her burial, but, as was expected, he exhibited little or no emotion, at the affecting recital. After much questioning and many persuasions the gipsy made a full confession of his guilt, and gave an account of the accidental manner in which he had discovered Liza's far-off home. He was carelessly wandering upon the wharf at the time of the embarcation of Mr. Landon with his wife and child, and was first attracted by seeing the name of Landon upon some trunks, that were being taken on board. Knowing well the name of Liza's parents, he watched every face that passed to the vessel, from a secure hiding-place, and thus saw them as they bade adieu to Paul Russell, and took their departure for America. It was some time before he could follow them across the ocean, and when he did so, some months passed away before he could find their residence; but all had finally been accomplished, and could he have gained the wood with Liza, where Bob, who had accompanied him, was secreted, he could easily have escaped with the prize, and should have immediately returned to Europe, where he hoped to have realized a handsome sum, by the aid of her exquisite voice. The wretch died in a hardened, unmoved manner, and although a diligent search was made for Bob, he was never captured. The cave in which both had been secreted so long, the existence of which had never before been known, was discovered, but the guilty companion of Alfonso had precipitately fled, and was never more heard of in the country. A general opinion prevailed among the villagers that he had returned to Europe, and was once more following the wandering fortunes of his race.

CHAPTER XLVI.

PASSING AWAY.

We missed thee from our side one day, when at the house of prayer
We saw thy seat was vacant, thy sweet face was not there!
And when the hymn ascended, thy thrilling voice was gone;
We missed thee then, and even yet we miss our child of song.
But ah! that voice that charmed us long we may not hear again,
It chants a heavenly anthem now, a wilder, sweeter strain.

DEAR little Liza never recovered from that dreadful shock, although the fondest care that affection could devise was bestowed upon her. She recovered, indeed, so far as to be able to move around the house, but the physician saw plainly that an affection of the heart would soon summon her to the better land.

The remainder of Rebecca's visit was unmarked by incident, or adventure, and one week after the arrest of Alfonso she called at Mr. Landon's, to bid Liza and the family adieu.

"Farewell, dear Mrs. Douglass!" sighed the beautiful child, as with one arm wound around her neck, she laid her pale cheek against her shoulder. "You will not see me, when you come again, for I am going to live with Jesus, up in the beautiful blue sky."

"Why does my darling think so, when she is so much better than she was?" asked Rebecca mournfully, for she could not hide the truth from her own heart, as she gazed upon that pale, young face.

"Yes! I know that I am better now, but this improvement will last but a short time; just to reconcile my dear papa and mamma; then the angels will come and Liza will follow them to heaven. Good bye, until we meet in that holy, happy place, where we shall never part again."

Kissing passionately the beautiful lips of the child, Rebecca withdrew to hide the tears which she could not repress.

"You weep, Mrs. Douglass!" said the anxious mother, as she followed her from the room, having noticed her tears, although she had lost the whispered words. "Tell me, did Liza speak to you of dying?" Tears trembled on the eyelashes of Mrs. Landon as she asked the question.

After a moment's hesitation, Rebecca took the hand of the sorrowful woman, and without concealment related the words uttered by her darling.

"It may be a mere foreboding of our little pet's, caused by nervous fears, but it would be well, my dear friend, to consider how easily death might separate you from that precious child, and thus prepare yourself for any event. Those pale cheeks and sudden turns of faintness are often sad forerunners of fatal disease."

"I know it, Mrs. Douglass; I know it well, and I will strive to say, the will of God be done, whatever may happen! But oh, she has been so precious to me, that it will be like tearing out my heart to see her die! But better far, a peaceful summons to the 'shining shore,' than to have had her fallen a living prey once more to that fearful Alfonso, and his gipsy followers. Yes, I will strive to see God in all that may befall my child, and then——Oh Mrs. Douglass," she added, a burst of tears coming to the relief of her full heart, "pray for me: unceasingly, pray for your poor sorrow-stricken friend!"

"Mamma! has he come?"

These words were uttered by the silvery, yet feeble voice of a dying child, just as the sun was sinking behind the hills, filling the village with a flood of splendor, before it was exchanged for the sombre shades of night.

"Has Cousin Paul come?"

"Not yet, darling! Try to rest awhile will you not? I trust he will soon be here." The mother spoke almost in a whisper as she clasped the hand of her suffering little one in hers, and strove to soothe her, although her own eyes were full of anguish, and her own lips were pale with woe.

"Mamma!" again murmured the child, "I shall soon be gone, then you will have no Liza to love, no daughter to comfort you. But you will not fret, mamma, since it is God that calls me away. You will let papa console you and strive to be cheerful for his sake, will you not, dear precious mother?"

"Yes! darling; yes!" gushed from the quivering lips of Mrs. Landon.

"Heaven is not far off, mamma, and life will be very short, at the longest; you will join me dear papa—sweet mamma, in the beautiful land above!"

As the child spoke, she motioned for her father, who, with Bessie and Mr. Brown, stood near the foot of the bed.

Mr. Landon bent over her, and pressed his lips upon hers, with a yearning kiss of unutterable agony.

"Papa, you will not weep for Liza when she is going to the arms of her precious Redeemer;" she whispered, as a hot tear from the father's eyes fell upon her upturned face. "You will give me up without a murmur, when Jesus calls me home, will you not?"

"Yes, darling, God helping me I will."

"Thank you, dear papa! Hark! did a carriage stop? Has Cousin Paul come?" again questioned the fast expiring child.

"No, darling, not yet."

A sigh escaped the heaving bosom of the sufferer, as she whisperod,

"Oh! I have prayed so fervently to see him once, just once before I leave this world, but God has not thought it best. Mamma, tell him when he comes, that—hush! surely I hear his step. Papa, God is merciful to Liza, Cousin Paul *has* come!"

With a glad cry as she said these words, she turned upon her pillow, and the next moment was clasped to the bosom of Paul Russell.

"My precious one," exclaimed the young man, as he fondly kissed the lips, cheek, and brow of his dying pet.

"Cousin Paul, you are just in time to take my last farewell. I love you, dear Cousin Paul, for to you I am indebted for the first knowledge of my Saviour, and for my rescue from the deepest woe. I have prayed that I might see you, to thank you once again for restoring me to my pleasant home and to the arms of my loving parents. But I am going now to a fairer home than even this, and the arms of Jesus are open now to receive me. Farewell dear papa and darling mother. Farewell Cousin Paul, and Bessie and you too, kind Mr. Brown; there will be no sorrow there, nor tears, nor night. It is growing dark; I cannot see! Mamma, where are you? Surely this is death. Pray."

Kneeling by the bedside, with one hand clasped by the angelic child, while she lay upon her mother's bosom, Paul sent forth his prayer to God, that he would pour the balm of peace into the wounded hearts of that stricken group, and that he would also bless the dying little one in her heavenward flight.

As the words ceased, before Paul and the kneeling, sobbing friends could rise from their knees, the voice of Liza floated through the room in wild and thrilling melody, that filled her hearers with awe and wonder. It seemed a farewell song that she was attempting to sing; her last farewell! but before it was quite finished, the words became inarticulate, then grew fainter, and fainter, her eyes closed, and all of that stricken group held their breath as the soul of little Liza drifted towards heaven.

"Oh husband, has she gone? My only precious child!' sobbed the mourning mother, bending over the just breathing form, while the utmost agony wailed in the cry "Liza, Liza! my lily-bud, my darling, speak once more to your mother. Let me hear your voice once again before it is hushed for ever. Oh, Liza!"

Opening her dying eyes at the call, while a faint smile played around the exquisite mouth, she murmured "Mamma! dear mamma!" then with a long drawn sigh, her eyelids drooped, and her spirit passed to the bosom of her Saviour and her God.

"Dear child!" said Cousin Paul, as he lifted her from her mother's arms, and gently laid her back upon the bed, at the same time kissing the cold dead lips of his fondly loved pet—"dear child, her voice is hushed forever on earth, but she now sings the triumphant song of praises to the Lamb."

"The Lord gave, and the Lord hath taken away," sighed the weeping father, "Blessed be His holy name, for ever."

"Amen!" burst from the lips of the mother, as with bowed head and trembling frame, she allowed her husband to draw her away, from what was now but the cold corpse of her precious, peerless Liza.

CHAPTER XLVII.

BESSIE'S LOVER.

IT was in a clear, yet cold morning in December, just two weeks after the funeral of Little Liza, that Bessie once more bent over her easel in Mr. Moulton's studio, while that gentleman silently took his place by her side.

"Where is Marion?" asked the young girl, finding that her little companion did not make her appearance.

"She is quite unwell this morning, having had a violent sick headache all night—an affliction to which she is quite subject."

"I am sorry to hear that she is suffering;" replied Bessie, "Can nothing be done for her relief?"

"Oh yes! she is already relieved, but will not be able to join us this morning! You look quite yourself again, Miss Bessie; I feared that grieving for that dear little girl was making sad inroads upon your health, so pale and sad have you been recently."

Bessie sighed, while tears rushed to her eyes as she heard her lost favorite thus spoken of; but quickly rallying, she remarked,

"I did grieve for our Liza sadly, but I saw Mrs. Landon yesterday, and her sweet resignation, with her firm reliance upon the goodness of God, even in her affliction, quite cheered me. Both Mr. and Mrs. Landon are devoted Christians, and bear their loss with a meek and gentle spirit, unusual and pleasant to behold. Liza was their joy and pride, yet they could resign her, at the Master's call, without murmuring, or complaining."

"I rejoice to hear it Bessie; do you remembermy telling you that such would be the case, when I first saw the seeds of disease upon her countenance?"

"Yes! and you proved a most true prophet!" returned Bessie.

A silence followed, and for some time the landscape upon which Bessie labored, advanced rapidly. It was a beautiful scene, and very tastefully was she touching it, blending its colors with great beauty and skill, under the direction of her kind instructor; but as she gently applied the brush she could not fail to observe the unwonted restlessness of her companion.

"Have you heard from your friend Mrs. Douglass lately?" at length asked Mr. Moulton, thus breaking the silenc

"Not very! but I am expecting a letter daily. Do you know, Mr. Moulton, I was silly enough to wish to detain her always at our home, I was so happy in her society?"

"Indeed, and she would not remain?"

"Not at least in the capacity I secretly hoped for."

"What capacity was that?" asked Mr. Moulton, interestedly.

"I fear you will ridicule my foolishness, Mr. Moulton, but she is the only woman I ever saw, that I think would exactly suit my father But strange to relate, they neither of them seemed to have the same opinion, therefore my secret hope died for want of nourishment."

"Miss Bessie," exclaimed Mr. Moulton, "is it possible I hear you aright. I was under the impression that you utterly opposed second marriages."

"You were entirely mistaken and misinformed then, Mr. Moulton. I see no reason—where real love is inspired in the heart of a person once bereaved, I see no reason why a second marriage should not take place."

"What a load those words have lifted from my heart dear Bessie!" said her companion, delight beaming in the tender glance he fixed upon her bright young face. "Throw aside that palette and brush for a while, and listen to me a moment, darling."

Gently taking the implements from the hand of the blushing girl, Mr. Moulton drew her to the sofa, and seating himself beside her, with her hand fondly clasped in his, he told her the story of his love—the sadness her misunderstood words, uttered weeks before, had caused him, and finally ended by asking her to become his wife.

The fond caress that followed, together with the happiness that sparkled in the eyes of both, whispered that the answer he received was highly satisfactory, and the enthusiastic lover felt that now, since he could claim that lovely sunbeam as his own, he should be blessed forever.

When Mr. Brown was waited upon by Mr. Moulton the next day, craving his consent to the union of himself and Bessie, he was greatly overcome by the surprise occasioned by the unsuspected state of affairs; but when assured by his daughter that her heart was deeply interested in his giving a favorable answer, he laid her hand in that of his friend, and with tearful eyes and choking voice implored the blessing of God upon their union.

The marriage it was decided should take place early in the spring, and after much persuasion Mr. Brown promised to rent his furnished house to a neighbor known to be in want of such a domicile, and then find a home with them, as Bessie strenuously objected to a separation.

So preparations for the wedding commenced briskly at Cedar Lawn, while all the villagers rejoiced that their favorite, Bessie Brown, was so soon to become the wife of an excellent and conscientious man, while at the same time, she would continue to reside in their midst.

CHAPTER XLVIII.

LEAVES FROM REBECCA'S DIARY.—THE NEW PASTOR.

" Jesus is our Shepherd, guided by his arm,
Though the wolves may raven, none can do us harm;
When we tread death's valley, dark with fearful gloom,
We will fear no evil, victors o'er the tomb."

CONNECTICUT, April 9th, 1866.—A long time has elapsed since I penned the last lines in the pages of my long neglected journal! Come out from thy retreat, now, old friend, while I am in the mood, and we will once more indulge in a confidential interview. But before I proceed with the narrative of my daily life, let me explain, that Percy has succeeded in purchasing a charming place in Connecticut, about thirty miles from New York city, and having become quite domesticated in their new home, they have insisted upon my leaving the city and spending the summer with them. This will account for my being in the State, where I date these pages, as I have accepted their kind invitation, and now find myself happily situated in their delightful home, surrounded by magnificent scenery, and indulging in the loved society of my favorite niece, and her excellent husband. There is another also, to claim my love and caresses; a sweet baby-boy just two months old, lies sleeping in a cradle, in its mother's cozy room.

Dear Minnie makes a devoted wife and mother, and Percy may well be proud of his beautiful, loving, and domestic companion. They have a tasteful residence, handsomely furnished, and now that little Frank has been added to their number, they seem as happy as mortals well can be.

Sambo Johnson accompanied them to their new home, and that "respectible cullered pusson," is flourishing around the establishment in the grandest possible manner.

"Now, Missis Douglass," said he, as he welcomed me to the place, "it is just the nicest place for you to step your purty foot in, dat ever was. Golly! but Marse Percy am a happy man, wid dat blessed wife and baby. Cutest little image, dat young Marse Frank is, you ebber see. Dem eyes ob his'n, oh laws now, but dey am just like buttons, and his hands, gosh! dey jest no hands at all; dey ain't much bigger than a tree cent piece. But you run up stairs and see for yourself, and if you don't find the beautifulest little face in dat ar cradle, you ebber clapped eyes on, den dis chile don't know beans from a bull's foot—Dat's all!"

I agreed with Sambo perfectly, for it certainly was a handsome baby that opened its great black eyes, and gazed so innocently at me from the ruffled pillow-cases and soft rose blankets that nestled around him. As I burst forth in several warm expressions of delight, a true darkey chuckle came from the hall, and there, peering through the half open door, was the laughing face of honest Sambo, who had been interestedly listening for the praises he was so sure would come.

"Dar, now missis, didn't I tell you so? Dar nebber was such a baby growed, as dat ar blessed little Frank Percy. Fact now!"

April 10th.—One beautiful afternoon, a few days after

my arrival, Minnie said, as we were leaving the dinner table,

"Charles invites us to drive at three can you be ready? I cannot promise the rich treasures of curiosities, a drive in the Old World so often exhibited, but we can show you a charming Connecticut village, with a splendid view of the Sound, and its surroundings."

I was glad to accept the invitation, for the day was very delightful, and I knew it would be a pleasant hour. Charles first proposed showing me the village, so street after street was entered and duly admired.

"This is our church, dear aunt! Is it not a fine structure, for a village of this size?"

"It is beautiful, but whose is that lovely residence next to it, Minnie? It is the very abode of taste and elegance!"

"That is the Rectory," answered Charles, before Minnie could reply. "Is it not almost a mistake, that so charming an abode boasts not a mistress? Our new rector is so unfashionable as to be a bachelor. He is very wealthy, and seems to take much pride in adorning his residence, but as yet withholds the greatest ornament of a home, a good, true wife."

"From your speaking of him as your new rector, I judge that he has but recently come among you. May not a wife yet be added, as a later, and most welcome appendage?"

"I confess the thing is not impossible."

I saw my two companions exchange a sly glance, and smile, but as I did not understand the cause of the communication, I remained silent, and as other subjects presented themselves, our drive was delightfully concluded.

Sabbath, April 12th.—A holy Sabbath day again dawned upon us, and with a heart fully alive to the solemnity of the hour, I passed to the house of God, with Minnie and her husband. Everything seemed unusually beautiful to me; the opening verdure of the early spring, the refreshing looks of the green grass, waving in the gardens; then, the stillness so different from the noise of a Sabbath in the city, seemed to attune all my spirit to devotion and praise, and I passed up the aisle to Percy's pew, with a sweet sense of enjoyment and peace. The anthem was still being sung, when from the vestry emerged the white robed pastor, and solemnly knelt beside the chancel.

I felt the hot blood rush to my brow! I felt my heart beating tumultuously, for something in the cluster of jetty curls that was pushed from his brow, something in the step and form, something in the graceful motion of the white hands to which his face was bowed, reminded me of Russell. I held my breath as he arose and commenced the solemn services of the morning.

There was no mistake! that inimitable voice, that was music even in reading, those large speaking black eyes belonged to no other than the lover of former days. Yes, Paul Russell stood before me, a clergyman of the Episcopal Church.

Once I looked towards Minnie, but my eyes were full of tears, and I could not see the look of sympathy which I felt was there. Yet still the holy services went on, that voice sounded in my ear, and I knew it was no illusion, no phantasy of the brain, but a true, glad reality.

Gradually I became more calm, and by the time he had taken his place in the pulpit, I was ready to listen to his sermon, with a heart full of thankfulness, and earnest attention.

His text was from John x. 11: "I am the good Shepherd." "Of all the images," he said, "which our Blessed Lord employs to shadow to men His peculiar mission, disposition, and relations, none can convey Him with sweeter charm than this. The most touching picture which the customs of Palestine presented was, and is still indeed, seen in pastoral life. It always presents the choicest green spots that the sunny side of mountain slopes, and valley plains, could afford, as the background of the picture. An essential feature also is the sparkling water brooks; the prominent figures are the flock, lying beside the 'still waters,' or, nibbling the green pastures, or indulging in innocent gambols, and the shepherd with staff in hand, exulting in their composure, or delighting in their playfulness, or watching intently to discover any interruption of their repose, any trace of discomfort—and especially any token of the approach of the beast of prey.

* * * * * * *

"Our Blessed Lord was familiar with this picture, and so also those to whom he spoke.

* * * * * * *

"When he said, 'I am the good Shepherd,' He singled himself out as *standing alone*, in such a relation. Shepherds there were many, but *the* 'good,' was but one, and he alone could exhibit in His ways, with those He called '*His sheep*,' those capacities, qualities and powers, which are set forth in revelations, statements and doctrines.

* * * * * * *

"Here the flock is pictured to us as scattered over the mountains, and in the valleys, through the wilderness, away from the fold, and the chosen pasture, and the Shepherd is scouring the country, and calling for the lost sheep and bringing them one by one, to the safe and pleasant inclosure, and the rich and nourishing feeding places. This indeed is just the counterpart of the natural state of Jesus' people. They are represented, as 'the children of God, that were scattered abroad.' They are spread throughout the many nations and tribes, and tongues that inhabit our earth.

* * * * * * *

"The Son of Man is come to seek and to save that which was lost. He searches them out, discovers them to themselves, and to others; by the appointed means of grace. He calls them through the ordinary instruments, and He brings them into His fold and his pasture, away from the dangers and darkness of the wilderness, by the power of His Spirit, when men heed the call thus made. The conversion of a soul to God is no accident, even though immediate circumstances may appear so isolated as to have no connexions leading to such an issue. The sheep was roaming in the wilds and among the dangers and exposures of nature. The Shepherd was on his track, following him from stage of life to stage of life, from influence to influence, nay, perhaps from country to country. All this while he was wild, thoughtless, indifferent. At last a very trivial circumstance, a word, a casual event, arrests him. He stops, he thinks, he finds himself wretched, miserable, helpless, because of his sins. He repents, he believes, he prays. He lays hold on Christ. He opens his eyes upon a new world. He feels the flow of n w desires, new impulses within him. He hopes, not feebly, not tremblingly, not with doubts, but perfectly for the grace that shall be brought unto him, at the revelation of Jesus Christ. This is the Shepherd finding him.

* * * * * * *

"But 'fat pastures' are spoken of. Are not these those *peculiar privileges of the Church,* which are indeed like sun-lit heights, rising out of the plains of ordinances? See we not here the sacraments, especially the Lord's Supper which is named *a feast*, and is indeed a feast of *fat things?* The food that crowns the board, is to Faith's eye the very life of Christ, the outgushing of His Great Heart. This is indeed the fat pasture of the Christian's heritage.

* * * * * * *

"And then, are there not 'still waters.' Are not 'the ways of wisdom,' 'ways of pleasantness?' Here are waters never ruffled by storms, never angry in aspect, and always speaking of the security which His unresisted dominion brings. Oh, what an attraction for the pining and weary soul! Here is food for the hungry! Here is rest for the weary! Hither come, seek admittance to the fat pastures, on the high mountains of Israel.

* * * * * * *

"But He goes with His sheep through death's dark vale. Says the Psalm'st, 'though I walk through the valley of the shadow of death, I will fear no evil; for Thou art with me! thy rod and thy staff they comfort me.' Between the 'green pastures,' and the 'still waters,' of privilege and promise, and that 'inheritance,' whose sunshine is the triumphant Redeemer's glory, lies a *narrow valley.* Who treads the verdant fields of Heavenly felicity, and walks beneath the shade of the tree of life, and basks beside the 'river of the water of life, clear as crystal,' has gone through that vale. It is deep, and dark, and cold! No rays of natural day find access there. The damps untempered rise, and fill the atmosphere with chill, and cold and shade combined, sending their influence to some distance this side the entrance, give it an aspect of gloom, the sight of which sends a shudder through the frame, and withal hideous spectres, ghastly, and uttering doleful sounds of sorrow and woe, flit always here and there, in the darkness. Oh! it is a fearful place to pass through alone!"

* * * * * * * *

"Yet through this terrible vale, with all these distressing accompaniments, all the living must go! For to this one passage all the ways of this life converge. This is death, that event that happeneth alike to all. Now, to the followers of Jesus, the terrors of this vale are but shadows in the dim distance. By his own death He hath in their behalf destroyed him that had the power of death, that is the Devil, and thus he hath taken out of death its substance, and with that, its sting, 'sin,' and now, to his redeemed it is only 'the shadow of death.' Now, only its lengthened shade, its dark, substanceless outlines, thrown by the rays of unrevealed divine precept, lies stretched across the way to the Heavenly paradise. As the traveller looks at it afar before him, it seems, as does the distant cloud covering the mountain-side, black and terrifying. But on the near approach, like that same cloud it is found to be but a passing vapor.

* * * * * * * *

"Even through this vale, in natural features so frightful, viewed at a distance, the 'Good Shepherd,' is still with them. On all the passage, He is at their side. His presence, as a pillar of light, casts away all gloom; His 'rod' of grace upholds the waning soul, and His 'staff' of promise, in the pilgrim's hand, mounted as it is with a gem of Divinity, sends into his heart the beams of glory, that shine from the Heaven before him. * * * Well may he say, 'I will fear no evil.'

* * * * * * * *

"My friends, some of you are without the fold, in the

thickets of neglect and the rocky barrens of disobedience, where grow only the rank weeds of dissoluteness, and the bitter, coarse, poisonous herbage of impiety. Take some idea of your condition, by reversing the picture we have drawn. Without the fold, is 'without Christ,' and that is 'aliens from the commonwealth of Israel.' But even yet, while you live in the midst of the ordinances, and holy influences, Jesus may be something to you. He is not yet a Judge. He is yet a Prince and Saviour, to give repentance to Israel, and remission of sins. You are sinners, and He came into the world to save sinners." * * * * *

"He calls. He says stop your wandering. Turn back from the ways of indifference, and thoughtlessness, and aimlessness, and neglect. 'Come unto me! take my yoke upon you, and learn of me, for I am meek and lowly in heart, and ye shall find rest unto your souls.' Remember what truth says of your condition, and your prospects, as immortal, accountable beings, with righteous judgment before you, and take the alarm."

Thoughtless sheep, without a guide,
Heed a warning voice to-day—
Satan lurks about thy side,
Fly! or thou wilt be his prey.
While the "Shepherd," loved of old
Beckons thee! oh! join His fold.

In that fold are "pastures green;"
There "still waters," gently roll;
While on Satan's plains are seen
Poisoned streams, that kill the soul.
Stop! poor sinner! hear my voice!
Pause this day and make thy choice.

Tell me, shall that choice be made,
Shall the Lord, thy Shepherd be?

Wandering Sheep,—be not afraid,
Even now he calls for thee,
Answer, ere you leave this spot,—
Wilt thou seek His fold, or not?

I will not pause to describe the effect of that thrilling sermon upon the crowded audience;—the breathless silence, the holy awe that clasped each heart, as those powerful words fell among them! To me they were indeed a feast of "fat things," rare pearls, dropped from a jewelled cluster—grapes, from a fruitful vine. I felt refreshed, gratified, strengthened.

I do not think he was aware that I was present, until the sermon was nearly over, and then I knew the moment of the discovery; for as his eyes met mine, he hesitated, turned a shade paler, but then recovering himself without the pause being apparent to any but a close observer, he went on, seemingly, as calm as before. When the services were concluded and we turned to leave, he was still kneeling! Was his prayer for strength to overcome his weakness? Was my name even then upon his lips?

Ah, me! why should I wish to know? God pity me! he is far above me now!

"Minnie dear, why did you not tell me your pastor's name, when you spoke of him yesterday?"

"Do not chide me, Aunt Rebecca! I could not resist surprising you. Had you any idea, when he was our fellow passenger upon that frightful voyage, that he had prepared for the ministry while abroad?"

"No, dear, I never thought of it! He told me he was an altered man, and intended ever to lead a holy life, but as he spoke little of himself, he told me no more."

We had reached home as I spoke, and I hastily retired to my room, to calm my disturbed spirits before again meeting the family.

CHAPTER XLIX.

CONCLUSION.

"She is thine! the word is spoken!
Hand to hand, and heart to heart,—
Though all other ties are broken,
Time these bonds can never part."

MONDAY, April 13th.—To-day, I was passing through the upper hall to my apartment, when in answer to the door-bell, and inquiry for the ladies, I heard the servant say, "Mrs. Percy is not at home, but Mrs. Douglass is; will you walk in, sir?" and the well known footstep of Russell entered the parlor.

I waited but to cool my burning cheeks with a dash of cold water, then hastily arranging a few stray curls, I descended.

He stood before the book-case as I entered, examining a volume which he had taken from the shelves, but instantly he laid it aside, and advanced to greet me, with extended hand. Mine trembled as it lay in his, but as he led me to a seat, saying, "I could not resist bidding you welcome to our village, Mrs. Douglass," I assured him I was happy to meet him, and soon recovered my self-possession.

In the conversation that ensued, he referred to our

nights of peril on the Ocean, and asked "where I had passed my time since we parted?"

I informed him of many little events that had transpired, and then spoke of my surprise in meeting him in this place, and especially in seeing him in the pulpit the day before, telling him I had no idea that he had studied for the ministry.

He smiled, one of his old, sad smiles, as he replied,

"You never seemed sufficiently interested in any of the affairs, or pursuits of Paul Russell, to warrant my speaking of my future path in life, Rebecca!"

I blushed painfully as he spoke, and seeing my confusion, he changed the subject of conversation.

He sat about an hour, chatting on different themes, and all the while my cheeks were hot, and my heart was strangely tremulous, while *he* seemed calm and self-possessed. When he arose to leave, I followed the promptings of my soul, and asked him to call again.

I was astonished at the look of delight he gave me, and I could not but think he had been fearful he would be unwelcome before he had ventured in.

Would he come *again* and *soon*, I wondered as I closed the door?

Would he ever care again to please Rebecca Douglass?

June 12*th.*—He *did come* again, the next night, and as the family were all together, we had a delightful hour of communion and intellectual conversation, and after this, often did he find his way into our parlor, and when the month of June opened upon us, that lovely month of roses, and singing birds, all embarrassment at thoughts of former scenes had died away. I looked upon him no longer in the light of previous short-comings; I saw now, only the pure, devoted servant of God.

I was sitting by the parlor window reading, this afternoon, when Russell entered; his eyes sparkled with pleasure as he saw me, for that day I had yielded to Minnie's earnest pleadings, and had thrown aside my black robes, and was now, for the first time, arrayed in colors. It had seemed almost a sacrilege for me to clasp around my form the pure tissue, with its delicate pink spot upon the white ground, but when I added the pink neck-ribbons and belt, my fingers trembled as though I was committing a wicked action.

"Now," said Russell, as a smile lighted his expressive eyes, "now, I see the Rebecca of former days, again! You need but this, Mrs. Douglass, to make the toilet complete!" then taking a beautiful moss-rose from a bouquet upon a table near by, he gently and skillfully fastened it in my hair.

How my heart thrilled beneath the touch of those fingers, now so dear to me! how the blood flowed into my cheeks, at meeting the impassioned glance that was fastened upon me, as, for an instant, his hand rested upon my hair. But a step approached, and turning again to the table, he seemed to be admiring the flowers, as Percy entered.

June 14*th.*—I am exquisitely happy to-night, for I am the promised bride of one dearer to my heart than words can tell. Oh Russell! how long, and how unconsciously has my whole heart been yours! Noble man! May God bless your path through life, and make us a blessing to each other!

I can scarcely tell how it all came about, but as these pages have listened to my secret misgivings and trials, so now shall they chronicle my joy.

"Your place should be called Rose Villa, Mr. Russell;"

said I, last evening, when, as I had stepped out for a summer stroll, after tea, I passed the Rectory, as he stood leaning against the gate that inclosed his elegant grounds.

"Why so?" asked he, as he smilingly returned my salutation.

"The roses are so fragrant and so numerous;" replied I, the color mounting to my brow again, at meeting his expressive eyes.

"Will you not come in, and see these floral pets of mine, Rebecca? Surely it is time you enter the Rectory!"

He took my hand as he spoke, and drew me into the garden walks.

I always loved flowers, but now I surely did admire those clustering and carefully trained roses, more than any I had ever seen!

Was it because they belonged to the noble man beside me?

We lingered among those garden treasures, until the evening shadows grew quite deep, and dark, then telling me he had lately received a beautiful present from a friend in Italy, of a rare piece of statuary, he led me to the house to examine it. As we entered the drawing-room I was astonished at the taste and elegance of every arrangement! The softly shaded light, that shed such an inviting air around; the tasty adjustment of the rich lace curtains, with their costly cornices, and the elegant paintings and statuary that were so thickly placed around.

"To think," said he as, after admiring the splendid specimen of art, to which he had referred, I had seated myself upon a cozy chair—"to think, that I should ever be so happy as to have Rebecca Douglass beneath my roof!"

He stood beside me as he spoke, but his eyes were bent

upon me with the look of other days, and I knew well what would follow.

"Darling, may I speak once more of my never dying love?"

Poor man! so fearful was he of another repulse, that he mistook my silent confusion, for contempt, and commenced pacing the room, in extreme agitation. I knew not what to say, I felt so utterly bewildered at his vehemence. At last he stopped his wild walk, and planting himself before me, he exclaimed,

"Rebecca, this cruel suspense must end! I cannot bear this state of things longer. I love you, I do believe, as no woman was ever loved before! Rebecca! for fifteen years you have been the one thought of my heart. When I offered you my hand, nine years ago, and you so coldly rejected me, it nearly drove my reason from me; for weeks I hovered between life and death! I lived, but I became a different man, dedicating myself to God and his holy work. But we met again, and once more my love for you burst forth, and carried me away with the current. Rebecca, you looked upon me then, with cold reproach. Oh God! I cried, will she never love me? Once more, we met; you were in danger, and I was your only protector. How I restrained my emotion, when I held you in my arms, those fearful nights, I know not: but this I know, I did refrain from taking the one kiss for which I panted, I did keep from troubling you with one word of love, when love was consuming my heart. But now, I will not be silent, even if you forever cast me off. Dear Rebecca, I do implore you, once again to love me! Darling! will you not come to my poor heart?"

He extended his arms as he spoke, and as I glided into their embrace, I felt to thank God for his devoted love, and as he kissed again and again, my willing lips, and whispered, "my own, darling Rebecca!" my heart knew a blessed peace, it had not known for years before.

Sept. 1st.—It is over! the marriage vows have all been spoken! the wedding ring is upon my finger, and I am again a happy wife! Russell's wife! My noble Russell's wife! I shall write no more in these pages! my heart is too happy to need words to portray its emotion. Calmly loving and beloved, shall our days pass on: my husband working in the holy calling to which he has devoted himself, and I constantly striving to make his home the one earthly spot to which his heart will ever turn for affection and rest.

Reader! would you know more? would you have one more view of Paul and Rebecca, before we close these pages? Come softly, then, and parting these clustering roses, trained so lovingly around this window, look within.

Hark! a gush of music, most exquisite, fills the air, the noble, soul-stirring sounds of an organ fall upon the delighted ear. Surely, but one person can produce such bewitching melody! It is Paul, playing an evening anthem, to please the beautiful woman, the admiring friend, the young bride, and the tender maiden of fourteen, who are his eager listeners. Rebecca, now his own dear wife, sits smilingly near by, her loving eyes turned fondly towards him, as he bends over the instrument; while Bessie, now Mrs. Moulton, her husband and Marion, who are there upon a visit, stand by his side.

Shall we enter, and thus disturb, by our presence, the harmony of the picture? No, did you say? then with that happy group daguerreotyped upon our hearts, with those rippling, mellow cadences, those exquisite solos floating through the evening air, softly, slowly, tenderly, let us whisper, Farewell

THE END.

Mrs. Mary J. Holmes' Works.

'LENA RIVERS.— . . . . A novel. 12mo. cloth, $1.50
DARKNESS AND DAYLIGHT.— . do. do. $1.50
TEMPEST AND SUNSHINE.— . do. do. $1.50
MARIAN GREY.— . . . do. do. $1.50
MEADOW BROOK.— . . . do. do. $1.50
ENGLISH ORPHANS.— . . do. do. $1.50
DORA DEANE.— . . . do. do. $1.50
COUSIN MAUDE.— . . . do. do. $1.50
HOMESTEAD ON THE HILLSIDE.— do. do. $1.50
HUGH WORTHINGTON.— . . do. do. $1.50
THE CAMERON PRIDE.—*Just Published.* do. $1.50

Artemus Ward.

HIS BOOK.—The first collection of humorous writings by A. Ward. Full of comic illustrations. 12mo. cloth, $1.50
HIS TRAVELS.—A comic volume of Indian and Mormon adventures. With laughable illustrations. 12mo. cloth, $1.50
IN LONDON.—A new book containing Ward's comic *Punch* letters, and other papers. Illustrated. 12mo. cloth, $1.50

Miss Augusta J. Evans.

BEULAH.—A novel of great power. . 12mo. cloth, $1.75
MACARIA.— do. do. . . do. $1.75
ST. ELMO.— do. do. *Just published.* do. $2.00

By the Author of "Rutledge."

RUTLEDGE.—A deeply interesting novel. 12mo. cloth, $1.75
THE SUTHERLANDS.— do. . . do. $1.75
FRANK WARRINGTON.— do. . . do. $1.75
ST. PHILIP'S.— do. . . do. $1.75
LOUIE'S LAST TERM AT ST. MARY'S.— . . do. $1.75
ROUNDHEARTS AND OTHER STORIES.—For children. do. $1.75
A ROSARY FOR LENT.—Devotional readings. do. $1.75

J. Cordy Jeaffreson.

A BOOK ABOUT LAWYERS.—Reprinted from the late English Edition. Intensely interesting. . 12mo. cloth, $2.00

Allan Grant.

LOVE IN LETTERS.—A fascinating book of love-letters from celebrated and notorious persons. . 12mo. cloth, $2.00

Algernon Charles Swinburne.

LAUS VENERIS—and other Poems and Ballads. 12mo. cloth, $1.75

Geo. W. Carleton.

OUR ARTIST IN CUBA.—A humorous volume of travel; with fifty comic illustrations by the author. 12mo. cloth, $1.50
OUR ARTIST IN PERU.— . do. do. $1.50

A. S. Roe's Works.

A LONG LOOK AHEAD.—	A novel.	12mo. cloth,	$1.50
TO LOVE AND TO BE LOVED.—	do. . .	do.	$1.50
TIME AND TIDE.—	do. . .	do.	$1.50
I'VE BEEN THINKING.—	do. . .	do.	$1.50
THE STAR AND THE CLOUD.—	do. . .	do.	$1.50
TRUE TO THE LAST.—	do. . .	do.	$1.50
HOW COULD HE HELP IT?—	do. . .	do.	$1.50
LIKE AND UNLIKE.—	do. . .	do.	$1.50
LOOKING AROUND.—	do. . .	do.	$1.50
WOMAN OUR ANGEL.—*Just published.*	.	do.	$1.50

Richard B. Kimball.

WAS HE SUCCESSFUL?—	A novel.	12mo. cloth,	$1.75
UNDERCURRENTS.—	do. . .	do.	$1.75
SAINT LEGER.—	do. . .	do.	$1.75
ROMANCE OF STUDENT LIFE.—	do. . .	do.	$1.75
IN THE TROPICS.—	do. . .	do.	$1.75
THE PRINCE OF KASHNA.—	do. . .	do.	$1.75
EMILIE.—A sequel to "St. Leger."	*In press.*	do.	$1.75

Orpheus C. Kerr.

THE ORPHEUS C. KERR PAPERS.—Comic letters and humorous military criticisms. Three series. 12mo. cloth, $1.50

AVERY GLIBUN.—A powerful new novel.— 8vo. cloth, $2.00

Thos. A. Davies.

HOW TO MAKE MONEY, and how to keep it.—A practical and valuable book that every one should have. 12mo. cl., $1.50

Comic Books—Illustrated.

JOSH BILLINGS.—His Book, of Proverbs, etc.	12mo. cl.,	$1.50
WIDOW SPRIGGINS.—By author "Widow Bedott."	do.	$1.75
CORRY O'LANUS.—His views and opinions. . .	do.	$1.50
VERDANT GREEN.—A racy English college story.	do.	$1.50
CONDENSED NOVELS, ETC.—By F. Bret Harte. .	do.	$1.50
THE SQUIBOB PAPERS.—By John Phœnix. .	do.	$1.50
MILES O'REILLY.—His Book of Adventures. .	do.	$1.50
do. Baked Meats, etc. .	do.	$1.75

"Brick" Pomeroy.

SENSE.—An illustrated vol. of fireside musings.	12mo. cl.,	$1.50
NONSENSE.— do. do. comic sketches.	do.	$1.50

Joseph Rodman Drake.

THE CULPRIT FAY.—A faery poem. . . 12mo. cloth, $1.25

THE CULPRIT FAY.—An illustrated edition. 100 exquisite illustrations. . . . 4to., beautifully printed and bound, $5.00

New American Novels.

TEMPLE HOUSE.—By Mrs. Elizabeth Stoddard.	12mo. cl.,	$1.75
THE BISHOP'S SON.—By Alice Cary. . .	do.	$1.75
BEAUSEINCOURT.—By Mrs. C. A. Warfield. .	do.	$1.75
HOUSEHOLD OF BOUVERIE. do. do. .	do.	$2.00
HELEN COURTENAY.—By author "Vernon Grove."	do.	$1.75
PECULIAR.—By Epes Sargent. . . .	do.	$1.75
VANQUISHED.—By Miss Agnes Leonard. .	do.	$1.75
FOUR OAKS.—By Kamba Thorpe. . . .	do.	$1.75
MALBROOK.—*In press.*	do.	$1.75

M. Michelet's Remarkable Works.

LOVE (L'AMOUR).—Translated from the French.	12mo. cl.,	$1.50
WOMAN (LA FEMME).— . do. . .	do.	$1.50

Ernest Renan.

THE LIFE OF JESUS.—Translated from the French.	12mo.cl.,	$1.75
THE APOSTLES.— . . do. . .	do.	$1.75

Popular Italian Novels.

DOCTOR ANTONIO.—A love story. By Ruffini.	12mo. cl.,	$1.75
BEATRICE CENCI.—By Guerrazzi, with portrait.	do.	$1.75

Rev. John Cumming, D.D., of London.

THE GREAT TRIBULATION.—Two series.	12mo. cloth,	$1.50
THE GREAT PREPARATION.— do. .	do.	$1.50
THE GREAT CONSUMMATION. do. .	do.	$1.50
THE LAST WARNING CRY.— . .	do.	$1.50

Mrs. Ritchie (Anna Cora Mowatt).

FAIRY FINGERS.—A capital new novel. .	12mo. cloth,	$1.75
THE MUTE SINGER.— do. .	do.	$1.75
THE CLERGYMAN'S WIFE—and other stories.	do.	$1.75

Mother Goose for Grown Folks.

HUMOROUS RHYMES for grown people. .	12mo. cloth,	1 .25

T. S. Arthur's New Works.

LIGHT ON SHADOWED PATHS.—A novel.	12mo. cloth,	$1.50
OUT IN THE WORLD.— . do. . .	do.	$1.50
NOTHING BUT MONEY.— . do. . .	do.	$1.50
WHAT CAME AFTERWARDS.— do. . .	do.	$1.50
OUR NEIGHBORS.— . do. . .	do.	$1.50

New English Novels.

WOMAN'S STRATEGY.—Beautifully illustrated.	12mo. cloth,	$1.50
BEYMINSTRE.—By a popular author. .	do.	$1.75
"RECOMMENDED TO MERCY."— do. . .	do.	$1.75
WYLDER'S HAND.—By Sheridan Le Fanu.	do.	$1.75
HOUSE BY THE CHURCHYARD.— do. .	do.	$1.75

www.ingramcontent.com/pod-product-compliance
Lightning Source LLC
LaVergne TN
LVHW020210110826
845151LV00003B/666

* 9 7 8 1 4 2 5 5 3 4 3 2 5 *